ULTIMATE TRUTH

MICHAEL WINSTEAD

ACKNOWLEDGMENTS

My gratitude to editor Joanne O'Sullivan, who helped shape the story to its rightful end.

Thanks also to Caroline Green Christopoulos, of Gold Leaf Literary, for helping me navigate the fast-changing world of book publishing.

Vally Sharpe of United Writers Press designed a great and intriguing book cover.

Finally, I thank my wife and children for their love, support and ideas.

Published by Michael Winstead Enterprises

Cover Design by V. Sharpe

PRAISE FOR WINSTEAD'S NOVELS

"A smart thriller that will keep you guessing until the end, *Ultimate Tribunal* brings readers into a shadowy world of secret tribunals and deadly secrets, where it turns out that taking the law into your own hands may deliver a fate you never could have imagined." – Joanne O'Sullivan, Author, *Between Two Skies*

"*Ultimate Tribunal* is an action-packed story that will be loved by people who enjoy suspense and legal thrillers. Laced with intrigue, yet thought-provoking, Michael Winstead's second novel successfully combines an excellent plot with a fascinating glimpse into courts and the criminal justice system. – Susan Keefe, TheColumbiaReview.com

"For lovers of crime novels and courtroom drama, *Ultimate Verdict* by Michael Winstead delivers an exciting story that moves along without getting stuck in legal humdrum, builds up suspense and intensity, and makes us think hard and feel deeply while we turn the pages. Highly recommended!" – TheColumbiaReview.com

"Winstead has created an engaging cast of secret society members who close loopholes in the legal system using their own brand of vigilante justice. After years on the 'right' side of the law, their compelling arguments for stepping over the line may cause you to struggle with some of your own doubts and demons, as you discover your Ultimate Verdict." – Blair H. Clark, Author, *Answers to What Ails You*

"Winstead excels at weaving philosophical questions of good and evil into realistic legal, professional and human conflicts. The cast of characters is well developed, alive and very human. The plot is rich with creative twists and blind turns, leading to a satisfying (and surprising) conclusion that ties up closely with the original crime and the initial injustice that propelled the judge and his team into action." – Avraham Azrieli, Author, *Deborah Rising*

This book is dedicated to all the innocent victims of violent crime, whose names and lives should never be forgotten.

A portion of the book proceeds will be donated to victim relief funds.

1

Abdul Alnoor lay on his bunk in a federal prison cell. His murder trial was scheduled to start in a few hours. He was accused of killing thirty-six people with a semi-automatic rifle at a Christmas party. The evidence against him was overwhelming. He had posted messages in an internet chat room just days before the massacre, threatening to shoot up a shopping mall or a school. The FBI found an AR-15 rifle buried in his back yard, with the barrel marred to prevent ballistics matching. It was his rifle. He could not deny it. He had purchased it at a gun show a few weeks before the shooting. The FBI also found a case of ammunition in his garage. Most damning, droplets of his blood and shreds of his skin were found at the crime scene. He had no alibi for that night. Not a single person could place him at home, or anywhere other than the country club, where all those people died.

He was just a teenager.

And he was innocent.

He could not sleep. He didn't know how anyone facing what he was facing could have slept. His hands shook. His legs trembled. Inside, every part of him seemed to vibrate.

His tan prison uniform was stained with sweat. It was the sweat of fear, the foul sweat of the condemned man. He hoped they would let him take a shower before he put on his court clothes. His attorneys had brought him two sets of clothes to wear for his trial. Two pairs of slacks—one khaki the other navy—hung with two blue oxford shirts in a metal locker inside the small shower room. He had a canvas belt, and a pair of slip-on shoes in dull, black leather. His underwear and socks were federal issue.

Inside his holding cell, there was no clock. He was not allowed to wear a watch, which could become a weapon in skilled hands. Without a way to measure time, he remained in an anxious state, never knowing if they would come to get him in a minute, or ten, or in hours. But soon enough he would be escorted to the elevator by two US Marshals and go up to the courtroom, an ornate room of polished wood, where he would face his jurors, twelve strangers who would undoubtedly convict him of murdering all those people.

Abdul rolled onto his left side with an old man's groan. A harsh light angled through the small window in the door to his cell. The light was always on. He stared at the video camera in a metal cage high up on the opposite wall, its red light blinking as somebody watched. Placing his back to the camera was the only privacy he could find.

He examined the block wall, painted the color of peanut butter. It was his reading material. He was not allowed books or magazines or a radio, and certainly not a television or anything with which he could access the internet. He ran an index finger over the blocks, feeling the smooth mortar between, the lines straight and solid in vertical increments sixteen inches apart, eight inches on the horizontal. Impenetrable bricks that subdued all thoughts of escape. Beneath the thin paint was the scrawl of a prisoner who preceded him. He could barely make out the words, yet they left him despondent. Abdul wondered if his predecessor had been convicted, if he had received the death penalty.

Other than his attorneys, with whom he met in a cramped room off the main courtroom, he'd had no visitors since jury selection began. It seemed even his parents had abandoned him. Alnoor rounded his shoulders, attempting to curl in on himself, and closed his eyes. He prayed, the words escaping his lips in a whisper. He prayed for the truth to emerge. He prayed for the real murderer to be caught. He prayed for a miracle. He prayed for deliverance.

That's when they came for him. The first man covered his mouth and grabbed his wrists. The second man, a huge man, flipped him onto his back and sat on his legs. As he struggled, Alnoor heard blood rushing in his ears. He tried to scream, but nothing came out. The large man took a syringe with a long needle, raised his arm, and plunged the needle into Alnoor's chest. The needle pierced his uniform and seemed to go straight through his torso. It was the second most painful thing Abdul had ever felt.

In a few seconds, his lungs stopped working. He gasped for air, but nothing happened. A bubble of air escaped his throat. He tried to reach for his asthma inhaler on the metal shelf beside his bed, but all of his muscles were frozen. He could move nothing but his eyelids. Then the blood rushing in his ears stopped. He felt his heart stop beating. The last thing he saw was that the red light on the camera in the corner of his cell was no longer blinking.

2

A doctor leaned over Abdul Alnoor and shouted at him. Alnoor did not respond. Following the protocol for confirming death, the doctor slapped Alnoor's left cheek, then grasped his jaw and shook it vigorously. Again, the prisoner failed to respond. Looking for a pain response, the doctor dug his fingernails into the sensitive flesh inside Alnoor's left elbow. This produced no reaction. Alnoor lay prone on his thin mattress, his body limp, a tinge of blue in his skin.

The doctor stacked his hands on Alnoor's chest and pumped his palms over the heart thirty times. Then the doctor stopped and placed two fingers against Alnoor's carotid artery. He could not find a pulse. He pulled up Alnoor's left eyelid and shone a penlight into his eye. He repeated this with the right eye. Both pupils were non-reactive and dilated. Finally, he searched for a pulse on the inside of Alnoor's left wrist.

The young doctor, on prison rotation for the week, did not want to be there. He knew this prisoner was going on trial in the morning, and he knew why. He did not want to be the one to announce it. He did not want to be the person responsible for declaring that one of the country's most notorious mass murderers—accused mass murderer—had died before his trial. The doctor straightened up and rubbed his own, red eyes. He took a deep breath to steel himself, then turned to Marcus Cunningham, the US Marshal who had called him. The doctor shook his head.

"He's dead?"

"Yes, he's gone, Marshal."

The doctor removed the stethoscope from his neck and stuffed it into his medical bag. He pulled his cell phone from his jacket pocket and tapped the recording icon. "Abdul Alnoor, prisoner. Time of death: 3:24 a.m. Place of death: federal courthouse in Asheville, North Carolina. Cause of death: asphyxiation."

Marshal Cunningham sidled through the cell door, his bulk almost filling the opening. The doctor followed him into the tiled hallway. As they walked toward the security desk, their steps echoed in the corridor.

Ignacio Perez, the other US Marshal charged with custody of Abdul Alnoor that night, stayed inside the holding cell. He glanced up at the camera on the wall and its blinking red light. He checked his watch. The doctor had been inside the prison cell less than three minutes.

In the hallway, the doctor said, "You said he had asthma?"

"Yes, sir," Cunningham said. "Earlier in the evening he was complaining of breathing problems. He has an inhaler. I saw him use it once or twice after dinner. I guess it ran out of medication. We didn't know it was empty."

"Makes sense," the doctor said. "Going on trial for mass murder is as stressful as it gets. That kind of stress could cause breathing problems in a healthy person. In an asthmatic . . . well . . . this time it was fatal."

"Yes, sir." Cunningham nodded.

The doctor's pager went off. He checked the message. "An emergency at the county jail." He sighed in exhaustion. "I've got to go."

"I need you to sign out," Cunningham said, handing a clipboard to the doctor.

The doctor checked his watch and scribbled the time and his initials on the last column of the visitor log.

In tandem, they moved to the steel security door separating the two holding cells from the rest of the federal courthouse. Out of habit, Cunningham glanced through the small plexiglass window, reinforced with steel mesh, then checked the video monitor to confirm the outside hallway was clear. He and Perez were the only US Marshals on duty that night. Cunningham pushed a button next to the steel desk, and the door swung open with a harsh buzz.

"I'll escort you down."

They rode the elevator to the first floor in silence and walked down the dark corridor, passing empty courtrooms. They stopped at the main entrance to the courthouse, where Cunningham pushed another button to unlock an exit door leading out onto the front portico.

"I'll fill out and sign the death certificate later today, or tomorrow," the doctor said, running his hand through his hair.

"Yes, sir. Thank you for coming."

Cunningham held the door open as the doctor hurried through, then re-locked it. He watched the doctor drive off, then pulled out his cell phone and tapped Judge Westlake's private number. "Sir, it's done," he said.

3

Judge Raleigh Westlake stood on his apartment balcony, gazing at the courthouse where he had presided for more than a decade. Its square columns and gray granite portrayed a certain stolidity about what went on inside, but he knew it wasn't true. What he'd just done defiled the oath he'd taken and every judicial tenet he'd ever vowed to obey.

He rode the elevator down and walked out onto an empty, darkened street. Rain glistened off the asphalt. He glanced around, as if expecting police cars to come screeching up to him, but the streets remained quiet.

He began to run. In two blocks he passed the courthouse. The building was dark, except for a dim light inside on the first floor. He ran through a stoplight and down toward the river.

The asphalt path along the river was shrouded in trees, the water an unseen presence on his left, flowing against him. Thick clouds covered the moon. He could barely see the trail. Several times he veered off the pavement, stumbling onto grass thick with dew.

As he wound his way through the darkness, the two wolves within him—one representing good, the other evil—began to snarl and wail. Six secret trials, six dead criminals, will do that to a man. The first was Henry Lawter, who had killed Hannah Sullivan with an icepick on the snow-covered slope of Mt. Pisgah. After a trial in which the jury found Lawter guilty and Westlake sentenced him to death, the court of appeals reversed the conviction on a technicality. Westlake had been forced to set Lawter free. That miscarriage of justice never left his mind. But Lawter's reprieve had been temporary. In an act of covert retribution—an endeavor Westlake thought of as serving justice despite the bounds of the law—Westlake and his men had tracked Lawter down in Florida and put him on trial in a secret courtroom. From a small, wooden table barely elevated above the accused, Judge Westlake had delivered a verdict from which there is no appeal. Lawter died on a beach, a heroin needle sticking from his arm. The local coroner ruled his death a suicide. It was the cabal's first execution.

The other five trials had followed the same pattern. Guilty men, and one woman, were secretly brought to his mobile courtroom and prosecuted for crimes for which they had escaped justice. All had confessed. In each case, Judge Westlake found them guilty and gave them the ultimate verdict.

He followed a curve the river had cut into the bank eons ago, when the land had been wild and his Cherokee ancestors had roamed there uninhibited. The wolves were howling now, an incessant cacophony that only he could hear. Their clamor stole his energy and overwhelmed him. He stopped and bent over, gripping his knees, breathing heavily. He straightened and slapped his right cheek, and then his left, feeling the sting on face and palms. "Stop it," he commanded them. "Stop it. It had to be done." His rebuke was swallowed by the fog.

When the howling abated he began to run again, placing his feet carefully in the dark, with nothing but feel and a silent river to guide him. Alone, this was the time to second-guess all of it. The first secret trial, through to the last, in which US Attorney Caroline Bannister had executed a man they now knew was innocent. She had been blinded by a relentless quest to find her sister's killer and bring him to justice, only to learn that it had been a terrible mistake. The truth had emerged too late. And now they were all in peril.

The night before, they had received the blackmailer's clear demand. They must either kill Alnoor, or be exposed. The blackmailer knew what they had done. He knew they had assassinated the Mayor of Charlotte and buried his corpse in a shallow drainage ditch along a country road. The blackmailer might not know why they had done it, or that the Mayor was not the first defendant they tried in secret, but it didn't matter. The blackmailer had photographs. Photographs of Westlake, Caroline and David Johnstone huddled outside the secret courtroom. Pictures of Cunningham and Perez carrying the Mayor's body. And photographs of the Mayor's slack face, with a mortal wound and dried blood on his forehead. It was damning evidence that would convict them all. And they had no idea who was blackmailing them.

Westlake almost ran into a stone pillar that marked the turnaround point, detecting the marker in the gloom just in time. Perhaps it was a glint off the water or a reflection from his soul, but he eased up, touched the column with his right hand, and turned around.

He pushed ahead, trying to reach that state where his muscles consumed all of the oxygen, and his brain would go quiet. He trudged up the last hill, his thighs burning, his head down, his arms propelling him forward until he reached the top. His breathing was ragged. He felt the runaway thump of his heart. He looked back at the federal courthouse, the gray granite lit by a peach-colored dawn.

The rattle of a cargo door shattered the silence. Food delivery trucks navigated the streets to service the restaurants and hotels that had sprung up everywhere. He entered his condo building with a key card, grabbed the Citizen-Times newspaper beneath his mailbox, and rode the elevator to his unit.

Caroline was up, her face puffy, dark half-moons beneath her eyes. "Morning," was all she could manage. The events of the past two days had left her woozy and sullen, as if she were at the end of a drunken weekend, though she'd remained sober through it all. Her forehead was creased with the knowledge that she had executed an innocent man. And in so doing, she'd opened the door to the blackmailer. Their collective peril was her creation.

Raleigh kissed Caroline's cheek in the ceremonious way of mourners united in common grief. In the breadth of two nights, his feelings for her had diminished to ambiguity. He had discovered things about her he didn't want to believe. Caroline had admitted altering the recording of the phone call in which the Mayor had allegedly confessed to killing her sister. It was the single piece of evidence that had convinced them all to put the Mayor on trial in secret. Before Westlake could issue a verdict, Caroline had pulled out a cattle gun, placed the muzzle against the Mayor's forehead, and ended his life.

Now, gazing through French doors at the hazy peak of Mt. Pisgah to the west, Westlake juxtaposed her deception against intimate moments they had once shared. How could these acts have come from the same woman? Was it all just a ruse? Had she simply been using him for vengeance?

"Did you sleep?" she asked, approaching him from behind.

"I went for a run. You?" he said without turning toward her.

She huffed out a breath of stale air at the apparent inanity of his question. "Not much." She took a sip of coffee from a mug emitting wisps of steam, the caffeine not yet working.

He finally turned toward her. "There will be no trial today. I don't think I need to say any more than that."

"Understood. You went for a run in the middle of the night?" Her voice was tinged with a longing for attachment.

He shrugged. "It's how I cope. It's worked for about forty-five years."

"Some things you can't run away from," she said, the caffeine eroding some of the fog from her voice.

"Not away from—into. I run straight into it. I have to shut them up. It's the only way I can think clearly."

"The wolves again?"

He nodded. "With this Alnoor situation, they're howling like they smell blood."

"Anything from David?"

As a member of their secret team, attorney David Johnstone defended their targets, criminals who had no true defense. It gave them a murky imprimatur of due process, even though the sentences were preordained. But Johnstone had been appointed by another judge to represent Alnoor in his murder trial, scheduled to take place in public, in the light of day. The outcome was not predetermined.

Westlake shook his head. "Nothing from David."

"Iggy, Marcus?"

"They're both soldiers. They did what was necessary. I'm sure they'll appear normal, with pressed jackets and spit-shined shoes, when Court convenes this morning."

"And you, Raleigh, how are you?"

He stared at her face for a moment, noting creases that had not been there a month ago, then locked onto her eyes. "I'll be ready."

"A better question: How are we?" she asked. Caroline fingered the locket at her neck, the engraved initials of her dead sister on the back.

He couldn't answer that question. Not now. He wasn't sure if there was still an "us." He turned away to get ready for Court.

4

As Judge Westlake ascended the bench in his federal courtroom, the spectators fell silent. He stood for a moment, scanning the gallery. The first few rows of wooden benches had been reserved for injured victims and families of those who had been killed in the massacre at the Eagle's Nest Country Club in Charlotte. Several victims in wheelchairs sat in the carpeted main aisle. They would never walk again. Members of the press occupied cramped rows of folding chairs pressed against the rear wall. The rest of the seats were filled by ordinary citizens. All had come to see the trial of the teenaged terrorist.

From his perch, Westlake nodded at Caroline and her co-counsel, John Nahurst. They sat at the counsel table next to the empty jury box. A few feet away, David Johnstone and death-penalty specialist Holly Humphries slumped in chairs behind the defense table. All of the lawyers had been briefed on Abdul Alnoor's death. Their pallid faces revealed the fight had been bled out of them.

Westlake slid into his high-backed chair and took a deep breath. "Bring in the jury," he said.

As the jury filed in, looking unrefreshed despite the weekend off, the courtroom was silent.

"Ladies and gentlemen," Westlake began even before the jury fully settled, "I regret to inform you that Mr. Alnoor has passed away. It happened early this morning. Out of respect for the privacy of the family, I am not at liberty to disclose any details. There will be no trial."

Gasps from the gallery grew to a raucous frustration. A heavily anticipated trial full of drama and intrigue had been abruptly cancelled from their lives. The accused terrorist was dead, and they'd been given no explanation.

Judge Westlake scowled and banged his gavel twice, quelling the disruption. He turned to the jury box. "Ladies and gentlemen of the jury, I thank you for your service. You are discharged as of this moment."

The jurors looked at each other, unsure what to do. Marshal Perez stepped to the end of the first row of the box and beckoned them toward the jury

9

room. The jurors rose and shuffled out of the courtroom.

Once the jury had exited, David Johnstone stood from his chair, his hands clasped in front of him. He waited until the courtroom quieted. "Your Honor, the defense moves to dismiss all charges against Mr. Alnoor." Johnstone sat down, convinced that nothing more needed to be said. His client was dead, and he didn't need to cite legal authority for the proposition that you can't try a dead man.

Caroline Bannister rose from her chair without invitation. Johnstone's motion had caught her off guard. In their deliberations about whether to acquiesce to the blackmailer's demand, this had not been discussed. She smoothed the front of her blouse, then gazed at a spot on the paneled wall a couple of feet to the left of Raleigh's head. "Your Honor, we'd like a little time to make a formal response. This is all so . . . sudden. We came here today with the intention of starting our trial, to seek justice for these victims." With a sweep of her arm, she turned to the side. "We are not prepared to fully address the defense motion at this time. The victims of this horrific crime may also want to intervene to file a response to the motion to dismiss." Caroline glanced at Johnstone. He refused to acknowledge her.

"How much time do you need, Ms. Bannister?" Westlake tried to keep the annoyance from his face. The legal precedent was clear. The indictment had to be dismissed. While there were some recent cases refusing to apply the abatement doctrine when a defendant died on appeal after conviction, there was no basis for allowing the charges to stand when the defendant died before trial.

"Seven days should be sufficient, Your Honor."

Westlake tapped a pen against his legal pad. "I'll expect the United States' response by Friday at 10:00 a.m. That gives you four days." He addressed the gallery. "Ladies and gentlemen, for those of you who are victims of the shooting at the Eagle's Nest Country Club in Charlotte, or who have family members who are victims, I understand that this announcement has been a great shock to you. I wish there was something I could do to relieve that shock. But such things are out of my hands. And while I am not prejudging anything you might wish to file with this Court, I can tell you that all of the legal precedent would require me to dismiss the charges against Mr. Alnoor. However, if you wish to submit something for my consideration, whether that is a formal response to the defense motion to dismiss, or something less formal, please do so within fourteen days. I'll issue a briefing order that we'll also post on the Court's website."

Westlake turned his attention back to the attorneys. "Is there anything else from the defense?"

Johnstone stood. "After we see the government's response, we may wish to file a reply brief, Your Honor. Although, as you noted, the legal precedent in this Circuit is clear—dismissal is mandated."

"Anything else from the prosecution?" the Judge asked.

"Nothing from the United States," Caroline said without standing.

The Judge paused for a moment, taking it all in, remembering that the victims, those in the courtroom and without, were the reason he had embarked down this path in the first place. He brought to mind the visage of Hannah Sullivan, who had been brutally murdered with an icepick by Henry Lawter. Her enlarged photograph was still propped in a chair in the study at his lake house. It came to him then, as if it had not been discernible in the chaos of the past few days, that what he had just done to the victims had deprived the very people he wanted to protect.

5

Viktor Volkov descended the granite steps in front of the federal courthouse, feeling relief when he reached the sidewalk. He tucked a flowered blouse into the waist band of a gray, pleated skirt that descended to mid-calf. He squinted through thick eyeglasses at the morning's light. In low-heeled black shoes, he shuffled from the building with the rest of the spectators, his eyes cast down.

Sitting on a wooden bench in the courtroom, he'd heard the Judge's announcement that Alnoor had died in the night. He was curious how the Judge had done it. Had Alnoor been found hanging from a bed sheet? Had he been suffocated with a pillow intended to mimic an asthma attack? Had they loaded his asthma inhaler with a fast-acting poison? Undoubtedly, the Judge and his cabal had been clever about it, leaving no trace of suspicious circumstance. He knew what they were capable of. He had the photographs to prove it.

Volkov paused on the sidewalk and removed the oversized glasses that made his face look wider. He dug into the small purse that held lipstick, rouge, tissues and other things. He pulled out a pair of dark sunglasses and slipped them on, then carefully placed the eyeglasses in a plastic case.

Crossing the street, he immersed himself in the babble of courtroom spectators voicing suspicions over Alnoor's death.

"How does a defendant in federal custody die the night before his trial?" one man said.

"Did he commit suicide?" asked the woman next to him.

"Don't they have cameras so they can watch prisoners?"

"Shouldn't he have been on suicide watch?"

"Maybe it wasn't a suicide," another man said.

Volkov didn't trust his voice to match his disguise, so he remained silent. At the parking deck, he separated from the crowd and veered left, crossed behind a bank and the newspaper office, still in view of the courthouse. He thought with irony that the system of justice chugging along imperfectly within that outdated building was indeed blind, for the perpetrator of the mass shooting and the mastermind of the Charlotte bombing had been inside, sitting a few rows behind some of his victims. He had settled in the courtroom only steps away from the Judge and the jury and the empty defendant's chair he rightfully should have occupied. He was not so much on the loose as taking a scripted stroll among them. And no one knew.

He traversed the perimeter of the courthouse with a short-strided sway befitting a woman of seventy, glancing only briefly at the spot by the parking lot wall where he had paused to aim his rifle at Abdul Alnoor on a stormy morning only a week earlier. That he had missed and, instead, struck a US Marshal in the neck, was no longer a blotch on his record, for Alnoor was dead. Not by his hand, but dead nevertheless.

Volkov found himself lingering as he re-created the rifle shot in his mind, picturing a bullet that had veered inches off line, possibly because of the wind, or a lurching head climbing the steps, or a heartbeat appearing within him at the wrong moment. His internal movie rolled frame by frame, and he turned, his gaze landing momentarily on a US Marshal standing at the side entrance to the courthouse. It was the same man he had photographed digging the Mayor's grave. Their eyes met briefly across the parking lot but did not lock. Volkov willed himself not to look again. Without speeding up, Volkov turned the corner of a brick building, his back to the federal courthouse now, an edifice he never intended to see again, whether from the inside or out.

He drove west in a rented van, away from his medical practice and the turmoil that still gripped Charlotte two days after the bombing. The mountain vista opened up to him, an irregular ridge that, in the light of mid-morning, appeared a dark verdant, shrouded in a blue, rising mist.

After putting a dozen miles between himself and the cabal he was blackmailing, he veered into a pullout on a paved road beneath arching trees. He waited for a few minutes, watching the side mirror to see if anyone had followed him. Satisfied he was safe, he crawled into the van's cargo area, pulled a duffle from the floor, and changed his clothes. He peeled off the remodeled nose and enhanced brow made from makeup putty, then wiped the residue of spirit gum from his face. With nail polish remover he erased the scar on his left cheek. The rest of the makeup came off easily. The gray wig and clothing went into a plastic bag, which he emptied piece by piece in trash cans along his route.

Free of the evidence of his disguise, he pulled the van into a restaurant that served country breakfasts and ordered three eggs, a biscuit with gravy, and a bowl of fruit. He ate less than half of it. Twice he checked the burner phone to see if he had missed a call or a text message. Only one person had the number, and that person had not called. He had done everything they asked of him, accomplished several missions without leaving any evidence that could be traced to him. He deserved to return home. They had promised him that.

With the death toll from the Charlotte bombing rising every hour, he almost expected to see police cars with flashing lights and blaring sirens chasing him down. Despite all the precautions he had taken, he found it highly improbable they would be fooled forever. As with the shooting at the country club, for which he had framed Abdul Alnoor with an impeccable trail of planted evidence, the FBI would discover faked evidence that would lead them to someone else. But no plan was perfect. Undoubtedly, he had left a loose end.

He followed a narrow, two-lane road into the Nantahala Gorge, tracing a river that meandered not far from the pavement, with water that sparkled between stands of river birch. It was moments like these, when gazing upon nature in its finest glory, that he could almost forget what he had done. Almost. When at first he tricked Abdul Alnoor into thinking terrorist thoughts and leaving a digital trail of terrorist markers, Volkov had experienced a tiny bit of remorse. After all, he was planning to frame a young man, a man who believed many of the same things as did he, for mass murder, using his former patient's own blood and skin tissue to cement the case.

This remorse had quickly retreated into a locked compartment in Volkov's brain. Over the years, Volkov had learned to view his actions with a veneer of justification. Justice could not attain without at least a modicum of injustice. Happiness could not exist without recognition of suffering. For good to triumph, it needed evil. People had to die and suffer. Anything less failed to capture anyone's sustained attention.

That Alnoor, who had been raised in America, had been willing to turn to terrorism so easily was not to be credited to Volkov's skills as an alchemist. Simmering hatred and vengeance were the ingredients of his concoction, and Volkov had been studying Alnoor for years, often conversing in quiet whispers at his hospital bedside while Alnoor emerged from the murky haze of anesthesia. It was there, while stroking the boy's forehead and admiring the grafts he had stitched onto the boy's cheek and jaw, that Volkov learned of Alnoor's insecurities and his deep hatred of the Americans for killing his mother in an air strike in Iraq. In these moments of brief revelation, with the incessant hissing and ticking of medical machinery in the background, Volkov had first planted the seeds of violence in his patient's young brain. When the time came, the maturing Alnoor was an easy convert. While Alnoor had not perpetrated the shooting at the country club, his simmering rage over the death of his mother had provided a plausible motive. Alnoor had posted messages in chat rooms threatening to shoot up a school or shopping mall. He had purchased a semi-automatic rifle for the occasion. In that way, Alnoor had begun to implicate himself.

Volkov stopped at a paved pullout along the river, checking again for signs of a surveillance car. He observed the traffic for a few minutes, cataloguing the infrequent passing vehicles, analyzing for redundancy. Concluding he was not being followed, he walked across the road and made his way through the birch trees to the water's edge. He stood on the rocky shore with hands on hips. The water flowed slow and clear, foaming around a few boulders, burbling through riffles. The wind fluttered yellow birch leaves onto the surface of the water, where they were carried away.

He scanned the river, the opposite bank, a house or two perched upon a distant hill. Not another soul in sight. He returned his attention to the river and saw, in a sunny pool behind a boulder, a trout sip an insect off the surface. He imagined the arc of a fly line, curling and uncurling, depositing an artificial fly inches upstream from the feeding trout, the trout taking the fly, and with a gentle tug he snared the trout in its top lip. He had never been fly-fishing. The scene came to him from a movie he had watched. He smiled at the illusion.

His cell phone buzzed in his jacket pocket. He pulled out the burner phone, but the screen was blank. Then he withdrew his personal cell phone and stared at it. It was the hospital. He swiped the screen, and a voice he did not recognize said he was needed. He must come to the hospital immediately. All medical personnel were being called in to treat the bombing victims. Only Viktor Volkov knew they were his victims.

6

When he arrived, Volkov saw the hospital had expanded outside of its normal confines into a dozen tents, set up on every open piece of ground. Temporary pavilions for triage, emergency surgery and treatment of non-life-threatening injuries had been erected on the lawn and in the parking lot to treat thousands of victims. Orange barricades bordered the perimeter. Uniformed officers manned the entrance, directing traffic, scanning with hand-held wands all medical personnel entering the grounds.

Less than two miles away, the sports arena still smoldered.

With his back straight and his chin up, Volkov walked through the throng, his medical ID hanging from a lanyard around his neck. There must be hundreds of doctors on the grounds, he thought. He made his way to a security kiosk, presented his ID and his credentials, and was directed to a surgical tent across the way.

He ducked through the heavy flaps of a canvas tent and stood, with arms raised, on a rubber mat. Two nurses sprayed him with an aerosol decontaminant. He entered a short passageway and turned left into a makeshift dressing room, where he stored his street clothes in a plastic bin and donned blue scrubs, a cap, sterile shoe covers, and a mask. At the next station, he washed his hands and forearms thoroughly with antimicrobial soap, dried them beneath a blast dryer powered by a long extension cord, then donned medical gloves. With hands raised, he backed through the swinging door.

Volkov had never been to war, but he imagined this is what it would look like. Medical personnel bustled about like frantic ants. Despite exhaust fans, the smell of blood and decaying tissue and death hovered in the heavy air of the tent. He was bombarded by a hundred voices at once. Urgent voices shouted orders. Patients, arrayed on canvas cots, screamed and moaned and cried, creating a disorienting din. Carnage and chaos were the two words that came to mind.

At the far end of the tent, bodies lay strewn on plastic tarps, next to a heap of body bags already zipped. He had been told to expect the worst nightmare of his life. Volkov didn't have nightmares. He closed his eyes for a moment, transformed himself into a caring and sympathetic doctor, the saver of lives, a man who could repair tattered and torn bodies.

A doctor whom he had passed on occasion in the hospital halls held a computer tablet in the center of the room. Volkov approached and announced himself. He was directed to a patient beneath a plastic sign with the letter A.

"What is the patient's name?" Volkov asked.

"No idea. A-12. STAT," the doctor said and turned away to tend to the next emergency.

Volkov moved toward the patient designated A-12, sidling between cots crammed together, dodging nurses and doctors half-running for equipment and supplies. At the patient's cot, he retrieved two pages of notes and scanned them quickly, noting the vital signs and blood type had been recorded. The last entry read: "Amputation of upper extremities at SHLDR. ASAP. NF."

The patient's arms were infected with flesh-eating bacteria. Her face was crisscrossed with slashes of red. Glints of glass peered from inside some of her wounds. Her right cheek was torn away. The white bone gleamed beneath.

The blast side.

He lifted the sheet, which was pocked and stained with blood. She was naked except for a paper gown. Her entire right side was littered with cuts and gashes. She had a deep, purple bruise on the exterior side of her right breast. Her right tibia had a compound fracture that had not yet been set. Her arms were swathed in bandages. If he didn't amputate her arms, the flesh-eating bacteria would move to the rest of her body. She would probably die.

I wonder where she was when the bomb went off?

He had interned in an ER decades earlier and remembered the basic protocol, though he'd never examined a bombing victim. He lifted each eyelid and flashed a penlight into her eyes. "Mydriasis of the right pupil," he whispered to himself. "The left pupil is normal and reactive. She may have increased intracranial pressure."

Her scalp had been shaved, revealing scattered cuts and contusions. He moved away and stared at this patient. She was young, perhaps 30. High cheek bones, a slender nose and generous lips revealed she had once been pretty. Before all of this. Before the shrapnel from his bomb had sliced into her body. She was athletic, with good muscle tone in her legs. On her lower abdomen she had an old, faded scar.

Volkov mentally prioritized her injuries. CT would determine if she had brain swelling or bleeding. Her tibia fracture needed to be set. The amputation sites would require extensive skin grafts. She would need an abundance of antibiotics to stave off infection. And then all the rest.

He nabbed a nurse racing by and asked if there was a portable CT available. She pointed to a doorway he had not noticed before. "In the truck—through there," she said in a voice full of hurry.

He could not transport the patient on the cot. "Gurney?"

The nurse eyed his hand on her wrist, conveying something beyond mere annoyance.

"Sorry," he said, and released her. He took a step back.

"No worries. None of this is normal. Get an orderly to help you, doctor. They're shuttling back and forth to the temporary morgue." She pointed in the direction of the tarps and body bags.

The transport to the CT station inside a shipping trailer was long and perilous, even though less than 150 feet of journey. The rows between cots, which had been set up in haste, were not wide enough in all places to accommodate a gurney and its attendant poles and bags and tubes. They were forced to nudge cots from the path, often creating a groan or a whimper from their occupants, until finally they arrived at the steel lift at the back of the CT trailer which, for the moment, was available.

The scan showed patient A-12, name still unknown, had ICP, which might be the cause of her blown right pupil. She needed surgery to release the intracranial pressure. Volkov and the attendant wheeled her back across the tent, where Volkov found the triage doctor. "This patient needs a ventriculostomy, STAT," Volkov reported.

The triage doctor, dark circles beneath his eyes, stared at Volkov as if he'd requested a time machine. "There's a waiting list," he said, consulting his tablet. "Looks like six to eight hours before an OR opens up. And then you have to find a brain surgeon. Or you could do it."

"I'm a plastic surgeon, not a brain surgeon," he responded. "It would be malpractice for me to open up her skull."

"That's the least of our concerns right now, doctor. Save every life you can. God knows we're losing them left and right."

Volkov did not comment, but headed to an equipment locker in search of a hand drill and supplies. When he returned to A-12, the orderly had departed and was nowhere in sight. Volkov folded the plastic pillow and propped the patient on it so her head was slightly elevated. He spotted a nurse wandering among the cots, a tablet in hand, making notes with a smart pen. "Nurse," he shouted, louder than he intended. "I need you."

She came over, adopting an uncertain posture.

"Are you sterile?" he asked.

She showed him her left hand, which was gloved.

"I need your help to drill a hole in this patient's head."

"I'm not an OR nurse," she said.

"And I'm not a neurosurgeon. This patient has ICP, probably has . . . since you know, they brought her in. And if we don't drain the fluid, she's going to experience severe brain damage, or worse. Do you have internet access on that tablet?"

The nurse nodded.

"Find a video on how to do a ventriculostomy."

The nurse typed in the search term and, after a few seconds, found a video of the procedure. She sidled next to Volkov, tilted the screen toward him, and tapped the play icon.

"Skip the ad," he said tersely.

Volkov watched the video of the procedure, which had no sound but included typed, overlaid instructions at each step. He first measured the skull of patient A-12 to find Kocher's point, marked it, and emptied a syringe of lidocaine beneath the spot. After making a small incision, he placed a self-retaining retractor. He was ready to make the burr hole. He steadied the drill perpendicular to the skull, then hesitated.

"What's your name?" he asked the nurse.

"Gretchen. Gretchen Fulmer."

"Have we ever worked together before, Gretchen?"

"I don't think so, doctor. As I said, I'm not an OR nurse."

"All right. My name's Viktor Volkov. I can't watch the video and the drill at the same time. I've got to be incredibly steady here. I'm going into this patient's brain. Tell me if I'm missing something."

He began to crank the drill with his right hand. It took little time to spin away seven millimeters of A-12's skull. When he reached the dura, he pulled the drill and made a sharp incision, then placed a retractor. Using a trocar, he tunneled a hole beneath the dura, then fished a ventricular catheter into the patient's brain. Cerebrospinal fluid began to drip from the end of the catheter tube. That was a good sign.

Volkov straightened up, took a deep breath. Beneath the mask he wore a thin smile. "Do you know the name of this patient?" he asked the nurse.

She scrolled through a list on her screen. "Not yet identified," she said, shaking her head.

"See if you can find out."

The nurse scurried away.

Volkov finished the procedure, suturing the catheter and the incision, stapling the scalp. He then attached the drainage system. He paused for a minute, remembering that he had caused all of this, that the bomb he exploded in a white van with a cell phone had injured this woman, almost killed her. Hundreds of other victims surrounded him. There was a lump in his throat. He didn't understand why. He had not felt this way when he'd labored over patients who survived his shooting spree at the country club. He cleared his throat and swallowed.

He went back to work on A-12. He covered the hole in the patient's head with a surgical patch. He re-set her fractured tibia and stitched up the wound. Volkov stepped back and stared down at her, as a mechanic might scan an engine that needs more tweaks. Even unconscious, her visage exhibited both a survivor's strength and a victim's frailty. She would need all of that strength when she woke up. If she woke up.

He foraged through two equipment lockers before he found the bone saw, then took it to the sink, rinsed it with water. There was no autoclave nearby to sterilize the blade, so he removed the oscillating blade and doused it with alcohol. That would have to do. He returned to his patient, who had not stirred. He snipped away the bandages lacing her arms and tossed the wrap into a bio-hazard bag. The whir of the saw, whose speed could be adjusted from a moderate buzz to a high whine, added to the racket. He made precise cuts at the shoulder and cauterized the wounds. Afterward, he tucked and folded the skin around her shoulder joints, stitched it in the back in a way that would minimize scarring. He slathered on abundant amounts of anti-bacterial salve. When finished, he admired his work, then placed sterilized pads over the wound sites. He stared down at her, at the tattered face that would need multiple reconstructive surgeries. Even with her wounds, she reminded him of someone. He had an intense need to learn this patient's name.

7

The room was a dark cave. Blackout curtains covered the lone window. Marcus Cunningham sat in a folding chair that was too small for him. He wore blue jeans and a navy shirt with US MARSHAL printed in yellow letters on the back. He'd been sitting in the chair for more than two hours. Waiting.

Finally, the figure on the bed stirred.

Cunningham looked up from his phone. "You are officially dead," he said in the voice he used to make courtroom announcements.

Abdul Alnoor turned beneath the sheet and sat up, blinking awake. "How can I be dead?"

"This death certificate proves it." Cunningham flipped on the lamp beside the bed, then handed a copy of the official document to Alnoor. The marshal wondered how many men had ever seen their own death certificates.

Alnoor fingered the raised seal at the bottom. "How did you make me dead? I don't understand."

"We paralyzed you and stopped your heart," Cunningham said. "Then we brought in a doctor, and he declared you dead. We revived you with epinephrine after he left. It was touch and go. You almost didn't come back. Lucky you."

Alnoor's eyes flickered with recognition. "You were the one who stabbed me in the chest."

"With a big needle."

Alnoor remembered the pain, the pierce of the needle into his chest. "What have you told my parents?"

"You died in your cell. In a few days they'll get an urn filled with ashes to remember you by." Cunningham had not forgotten that Alnoor had been the target of an assassin's bullet that had instead struck a fellow marshal in the neck. While Cunningham watched, Marshal Smathers had fallen to the courthouse sidewalk and bled out in less than a minute.

"Muslims are buried, not cremated. It is Allah's will," Alnoor said.

Cunningham shrugged. "Not in this case."

Alnoor swung his feet over the edge of the bed. "What about my trial?"

"Once you're dead, there's no trial."

"No trial," Alnoor whispered. He rubbed the tan fabric of his federal prison uniform and noticed the contraption strapped around his left ankle. He ran his fingers over it. "What is this?"

"It's an ankle monitor. So we know where you are at all times."

Alnoor glanced around the spartan room. The last thing he remembered was being attacked in his cell. "Where am I?"

"You're in protective custody. Somebody tried to kill you." Cunningham stepped to the window and pulled the heavy curtains aside. Dappled sunlight came into the room. "Take a look."

Alnoor stood from the bed and leaned toward the lone window. "Nothing but trees."

"That's right. No houses nearby, no paved roads. Nowhere to run. Rugged and steep terrain. Temperatures sometimes dip below freezing here at night. The windows are unbreakable and secured with double locks. There's one door. If you try to leave this house, that ankle monitor will go off and shock you. If you try to escape, you'll be moved to a less comfortable place. Or worse. Just remember that."

"How long do I have to stay here?"

"Not my call. Now get dressed. There are clothes in the dresser."

Alnoor went to the dresser and donned a pair of black jeans and a white T-shirt. He slipped on a pair of gray canvas shoes without laces. "Are we going somewhere?"

"Stop asking questions. Hand me your uniform."

Cunningham stuffed the tan prison uniform into a black vinyl bag. He would burn both later in a trash barrel. "Come on."

They emerged into a small living area furnished with a couch, a plastic table, and two upholstered chairs. A large window behind the couch was covered with a blackout curtain. All three windows in the house were made of bullet-resistant glass. The small house, acquired from FEMA, had one bedroom, one bath, a living area, and a galley kitchen. The wheels had been removed, and the house had been set on a low, concrete-block foundation that had no access panels. The safehouse was almost impenetrable.

"Go to the bathroom." Cunningham pointed at a white wooden door.

Alnoor stepped into the bathroom, flicked on the overhead light, and closed the door behind him. It was the first time he had used a bathroom with a door since he'd been arrested almost a year earlier. There was a small vanity with a molded sink, and a metal mirror above. He grasped the mirror in both hands and tried to budge it, but it was securely fastened to the wall.

Alnoor opened the bathroom door a crack. "I want to take a shower."

"No," Cunningham said. "Do your business and get out here."

While Alnoor was in the bathroom, Cunningham briefed the marshal on duty, a man with close-cropped gray hair, a former soldier. "We won't be gone long. I need to take him to meet someone."

"Fine by me," the marshal said, reclined in one of the chairs. "At least we've got cell service out here, if I sit in this chair."

"Only because of the booster on the roof," Cunningham said, pointing up. "Have you tested the ankle-monitor alarm?"

The other marshal nodded. "Goes off if he crosses the door threshold. Delivers a pretty good little jolt, too. It will knock him down, or worse."

"I'll disable the shocker before we take our ride, but leave the GPS on."

They heard the flush of the toilet.

Cunningham moved into the galley kitchen. He pulled open the three drawers, finding only rubber and plastic utensils. They could still be used as weapons, but they were less deadly than the metal alternative. He stepped to the kitchen window and pulled aside the curtain, eying the gravel driveway outside. Except for the unmarked van he had driven here, and the other marshal's plain black sedan, the driveway was empty. The house was in a remote location, at the end of a gravel road that wound around a mountain and stopped abruptly on the edge of a steep drop-off. The US Marshals Service had been using the safehouse for about two years to protect at-risk witnesses until they could testify. After they testified, they would be relocated and given new identities. Alnoor's status was less certain.

When Alnoor stepped into the kitchen, Cunningham slipped a pair of zip cuffs around Alnoor's wrists before he could resist.

"Am I still a prisoner?"

"Protective custody. But when we're transporting you anywhere, this is how you go." Cunningham knelt and, using the screwdriver from his multi-tool, removed the plastic cover from Alnoor's ankle monitor and flipped off the shocker switch. He screwed the cover back on.

Alnoor climbed into the back of a white van through double doors that had no windows. He nestled onto a metal bench bolted to the floor, his cuffed hands in his lap. It was not dissimilar from the van that had transported him from Butner Prison to the Asheville courthouse for his trial. Except this time there were no guards with semi-automatic weapons seated across from him.

Cunningham closed the metal doors and locked them from the outside, then settled in the driver's seat. Between the cargo compartment and the cab was a sheet-metal partition, separating the cargo bay from the cab. A small, sliding door was embedded in the panel, with steel mesh covering the opening on the driver's side. Cunningham slid the door open. He eyed Alnoor through the mesh. "Comfy?"

Alnoor looked around his confines. The metal floor and the hard bench had not been designed for comfort. "Can you turn on some music?"

Cunningham slid the partition closed, plunging Alnoor into total darkness. He started the van's engine. He found a country-music station and turned the volume up. He pulled his Glock from its holster and pulled the slide back, loaded the chamber, then released the slide with an audible snap. He laid the Glock on the plastic console between the front seats, within easy reach.

Cunningham arrived at the rendezvous point off Highway 441 as the sun dipped behind the Blue Ridge Mountains. An eighteen-wheeler was parked on a dirt road in the Pisgah National Forest, the engine running.

Cunningham backed the van up to the lift on the shipping trailer. Before leaving the van, he donned a thick, bulletproof vest and cinched the straps around his torso. He covered the vest with a black windbreaker. With binoculars he scanned the surrounding trees. The yellow-gold leaves of poplar trees fluttered like mittens in the breeze. The rendezvous spot was remote, more than ten miles from the ranger station and the nearest campground. Still, the dense trees provided ample cover for a voyeur, or a shooter.

At the back of the van, Cunningham opened one of the two hinged doors and climbed into the cargo bay. He strapped a dark Kevlar vest on Alnoor and ushered Alnoor toward the open door.

From inside the shipping trailer, Perez swung the large back doors open 90 degrees, blocking anyone from seeing between the two vehicles. He lowered the truck's electric lift to the height of the van's floor.

Cunningham and Alnoor stepped onto the lift platform and were soon in the back of the trailer, with the doors secured. The whole transfer took less than fifteen seconds.

Fluorescent ceiling lights illuminated the trailer with a harsh glare, an incessant buzz emanating from the bulbs. Three bunk beds lined one wall. A small refrigerator stood against the front wall, beside a wooden door that led to the bathroom and a shower. An oval table anchored the side wall opposite the bunks, surrounded by three chairs.

David Johnstone rose from a lower bunk and approached Alnoor. Johnstone's face was a mixture of happiness and relief. "Abdul, how are you doing?"

To Alnoor, this seemed like a crazy question, yet there was a tone of genuine concern in his attorney's voice. "I am hungry," he said.

"Of course," Johnstone said. He retrieved a white Styrofoam container from the refrigerator and handed it to his client.

Alnoor took the container with bound hands.

"Are those necessary?" Johnstone asked, pointing at the plastic cuffs.

Cunningham pulled a folding knife from his pocket and cut the cuffs without comment.

The Judge rose from his spot at the table, dressed in a pair of jeans and a denim shirt. He gestured to an empty chair at the wooden table.

Alnoor stared at him for a moment and swallowed hard. Both the prosecutor and the Judge worked for the United States government. He didn't understand why they were there, unless they intended to harm him. He slowly approached the table.

The Judge thrust out his hand. "Mr. Alnoor."

Abdul took his hand because he did not know what it would mean to not shake the offered hand of a federal judge.

"Please, sit."

Abdul placed his food container on the table and sat down in a folding metal chair.

"This is a highly unusual situation," the Judge began, his hands knitted together on the table. "I am sure you have lots of questions. But let me tell you first that you were brought out here, to this secure and secret place, because your life was in grave danger."

Abdul felt he had been in grave danger since the day the FBI stormed into his house and arrested him. He felt no safer now. He stifled a retort and ate a forkful of food.

"Yes, please eat," the Judge continued. "We believe the person who shot at you outside the courthouse intends to try to assassinate you again."

Abdul looked up from his meal with renewed interest. "Assassinate me?"

"That's correct," the Judge said. "We received a credible threat. That's why you have been declared dead—to protect you." Westlake told this half-lie without averting his eyes. There was no need to tell Alnoor that the threat had been levied against them.

"You faked my death and brought me into the woods to protect me?" Alnoor said with a hint of indignation.

"As odd as that sounds," David Johnstone interjected, "yes." Johnstone looked at the Judge and continued. "I know you didn't kill those people. I'd like you to help me convince the others of your innocence. Because the real shooter is still out there."

Abdul laid the plastic fork he was holding in the food container and straightened up. "I am innocent. I did not shoot up the country club. I told you that. I could have told everyone that at my trial."

"We do recognize the possibility that you have been framed," the Judge said, "and that the real shooter tried to silence you. But Mr. Johnstone and your other attorney are the only ones who have had a chance to discuss the facts with you. I and Ms. Bannister have not. You're here because Ms. Bannister requested you be placed in witness protection. We are hoping you can provide us with information so we can identify the real perpetrator."

"I was not there," Abdul said. "At the country club. How would I know who the shooter was?" He reached up and scratched his face, fingering old wounds.

The Judge looked at the maroon carpet for a moment. "You're saying someone planted your blood and skin tissue at the scene of the shooting. What is your explanation about how that could happen?"

Abdul began to shrug, but stopped halfway as he realized that insolence was not the best approach in this situation. "I know it is hard to explain, sir. I have thought long and hard about how my blood could be there, at the country club. I have never been there. Well . . . not inside the gates. I cannot explain it."

"All right," the Judge said, glancing at Johnstone. "Have you ever given blood?"

"I have given blood a few times to earn extra money." Abdul shrugged before he could stop himself.

"When did you give blood?" Johnstone asked, hoping to find something to implicate another suspect. He knew that persuading the others to fake Alnoor's death had gained his client only a temporary reprieve. With no one searching for an escaped prisoner, it would be easy for the Judge to order Alnoor's execution and dispose of his body in the wilderness.

"Several times. At a blood center near downtown. To earn money. Also, I have had Hijama."

"What is Hijama?" Johnstone asked.

"It's a practice recommended by Prophet Muhammad—peace and blessings upon him. They put these suction cups on your back and they take out blood that is bad."

"When?"

"Last November," Alnoor said.

"Who did this? What is the doctor's name?" Johnstone continued to probe.

"It wasn't a doctor. It was the Imam at the mosque."

"At your mosque? I didn't know about that." Johnstone cast glances at Caroline and the Judge. "That's a possibility we haven't explored."

"Because it's not plausible," Caroline replied. She said this with her arms crossed over her torso. "Blood degrades substantially after two or three weeks in refrigeration, in less than six weeks even if frozen."

"Yes, but you can extract DNA from blood that's ten years old," Johnstone countered. "So the DNA match to Abdul could have been from old blood."

It was an argument they had been having since Alnoor was arrested, an argument both were tired of making, but Caroline refused to relent. "The most likely explanation for how his blood was found at the scene of the massacre was that he was there. Period. He doesn't have an alibi. And don't forget thirty-six people are dead."

"The Hijama was very recent," Johnstone countered, looking at his client. "Abdul, do you think there's any possibility the Imam had anything to do with the shooting at the country club?"

Abdul considered this for a moment. "He does not condone violence," Abdul said.

"Do you know what he did with your blood after he removed it from your body for Hijama?"

"I don't know. I didn't ask."

"So your blood could have been kept, or stored, right?" Johnstone asked.

"Possibly," Abdul said.

"And if it was kept, you don't know whether it could have been taken by someone else, right? Someone other than the Imam?" Johnstone asked, trying to lead the others down the road past reasonable doubt.

Caroline shook her head. "Can I talk to you guys, privately?"

"I think we're making some progress here, Caroline . . ." Johnstone said.

"Let's talk outside. Now."

They exited the trailer and stood in the darkness on the dirt road. The trees loomed above them as deep shadows, no stars in the sky, as if they were inside a long tunnel. Caroline rearranged a few pebbles with the toe of her shoe. "I didn't agree to this. I understand we had to fake his death and put him in protective custody, but with all due respect, this is a futile exercise. It's not like we can renew the investigation, interview witnesses, or issue subpoenas. There's no case, no investigation. In the eyes of the justice system and the rest of the world, the shooter is dead. The crime has been solved."

"But we know he's innocent," Johnstone countered.

"We don't know that," Caroline said in a harsh voice. "Even if Alnoor didn't shoot up the country club, he admitted to planning an attack on a school or a mall, he just didn't have time to execute that plan. He bought a gun. He bought ammunition. This is a serious federal offense that gets him life in prison. You know that, David."

"Even if that's true, it doesn't get him the death penalty."

"It doesn't matter. We're not doing this to exonerate your client. And this isn't about searching for the terrorist who shot up the country club. This is about searching for the blackmailer. You're just using this . . . this incident . . . to try and save Alnoor. We have to focus on finding the blackmailer. Our freedom, maybe even our lives, depend on it."

"But the shooter and the blackmailer are probably the same person," Johnstone said, peering into her eyes. "The real perpetrator wants Abdul dead. Maybe we've fooled him; maybe we haven't. But if the blackmailer is just some random guy and not the shooter, why did he use the photographs to demand we murder Abdul before his trial? Ask yourself that. It's not coincidence. If we want to catch the guy who is blackmailing us, then we have to assume he was trying to shut Abdul up. He didn't want Abdul to testify, to profess his innocence from the witness stand. He didn't want the jury to find Abdul innocent, in which case the FBI would have to resume its search for the real shooter. That puts the real shooter at risk."

Caroline let out a sigh and cast her eyes to a place above the tree line. "Right or wrong, we made a decision, and with that the murder case ended. It doesn't matter now whether Alnoor is guilty or innocent" she said.

Johnstone closed his eyes and exhaled. "That's ridiculous. Listen to yourself. This has always been about guilt or innocence. Since the very beginning—Henry Lawter, Elise Rutherford, all of them. We don't secretly prosecute and execute innocent people. We go after the guilty who have escaped justice. Are you so blinded by fear that you've forgotten that?"

Westlake stepped between them and faced Johnstone. "Nobody's blind here, David. We see perfectly clearly what our purpose is. But you're confusing our agreement to spare Alnoor, temporarily, as consent to re-open an investigation. Caroline is right. That's not going to happen. There's no way, because it's too risky. We're presuming that the person blackmailing us has some connection to Alnoor."

"Then why fake his death? Why not just kill him in jail? Or shoot him right now?" Johnstone said, swinging his arm toward the woods.

Caroline shifted her feet, cut her eyes at Raleigh. She waited a minute, then took a cue from his silence. She stared into Johnstone's eyes. "He's alive because we need to use him as bait."

8

Viktor Volkov stared at the vibrating burner phone. "Unknown Caller" flashed on the screen. He pressed the answer icon but didn't say anything for a few moments. An unfamiliar voice, a Russian voice, said "hello." Volkov peered through the windshield of his SUV at the other vehicles in the hospital parking garage, trying to determine if the caller was nearby and spying on him. He couldn't see anyone else. Only his KGB handler, who had given him the burner phone, had this cell number.

"Text me the code," Volkov said. A few seconds later, he received a text with the proper alphanumeric code. "When can I go home?" Volkov asked in Russian.

There was a pause on the other end. "You are needed here."

"I was promised."

"Be patient. Did you handle the loose end?"

"Yes, it's taken care of. I have been very patient. I have done everything asked of me."

"We must meet. Later this month. I will send you details in the usual manner." The caller clicked off.

Volkov stared at the phone, as if it held a capsule of poisonous gas. It was not the call he had been expecting. He had been anticipating instructions on how and when he would leave the US and return to Russia. He slammed the phone down on the passenger seat. With a car key he pried the back off the phone, then removed the battery and SIM card. From his medical bag he pulled a pair of trauma shears, which he used to cut the SIM card into tiny shards.

He scanned the parking area for activity, grabbed his medical bag, and stepped onto the concrete. He dropped the phone carcass in a trash can at the garage elevator and dribbled the SIM card fragments onto the grass as he walked toward the hospital. As he dropped the last shard, he paused, realizing he was being careless. He should have disposed of the phone and the SIM card in a different manner, but it was too late now. Maybe the lawn mower would destroy the remnants. He would toss the phone battery into the small

30

pond on his farm.

Once inside the hospital, he rode the elevator to the sixth floor. The sixth floor was filled with bombing victims. As were several other floors in this hospital. And hospitals across the region. Thousands of them, most of them with serious injuries from which they would never fully recover. He had stopped keeping track of the number of dead.

He paused at the nurses' station, removed a tablet from its slot, and logged in. He was there to see patient A-12, whose arms he had amputated in the surgical tent on the hospital lawn. She now had a name: Ella Winslow.

Volkov entered her room for the second time since she had regained consciousness. The first visit had not gone well. He had asked her questions, using a routine protocol to test whether the intracranial pressure on her brain had caused any memory loss. He had started with easy questions—her name and address, whether she could identify her sister and mother, who were both in the room—then progressed to the night of the bombing. Did she remember anything about that night? Did she know why she was at the arena? Was she there to see the concert? She had answered every question "no," questioning why her memory of that night was completely blank.

"Trauma can produce amnesia," Dr. Volkov had told her. "There was a lot of pressure on your brain. The memory-loss could be permanent."

On this visit, Ella was awake. She appeared calm. Her head was swathed in white bandages, her body prone beneath the sheet. On the tablet, Dr. Volkov scrolled through her vital signs.

"What happened to me?" she said, her voice like the sound of a rasp on wood.

He looked up, scratching his chin where he had recently shaved off his beard. He tried to hold her eyes. He had rehearsed this. He willed calmness into his voice. "There was a bombing. Downtown. At the arena."

"I know. I mean later. After I was brought to the hospital."

He stepped back, retreating to the protocol he had learned in medical school to answer the hard questions. "What do you remember about being brought to the hospital?"

"Nothing. I was in a coma."

"What is the first thing you do remember, when you woke up?"

"Seeing my sister." She turned her head to her sister Mattie, who sat in a bedside chair, her arms folded across her chest.

"Yes. Of course. What do you want to know?" Volkov said.

She looked at the empty place where her arms used to be, first the right side, then the left. "Who cut off my arms?"

He did not hesitate. "I amputated your upper extremities. It was a necessary procedure to save your life. Your arms were infected with Necrotizing Fasciitis, flesh-eating bacteria. If I had not performed the amputation, you probably would have died from infection." He took a breath. "I also relieved the intracranial pressure caused by bleeding in your cranium. Without that, you could have suffered severe brain damage, or your vital functions could have ceased."

"So you saved my life?"

He paused, absently rubbing irritated skin beneath his jawline. "Yes. You are one of thousands of victims. I helped others as well." It was an unnecessary comment, one made in a swirl of anxiety blurring his reasoning, but something about her unnerved him.

"Do you know the original meaning of the word 'victim'?" The question came from the other side of the bed, from her sister Mattie.

Volkov looked at her as if she had appeared from thin air, not prepared for her intervention, or for a question that threatened to slice through his facade. He shook his head.

"It's Latin," Mattie said, stepping toward the hospital bed. "Originally from the fifteenth century, it means a creature killed as a sacrifice to a deity. Later, it came to include a person who is hurt or tortured by another."

"This is torture," Ella said, clenching her eyelids.

Volkov could not face her and instead glanced down at his tablet, scanning notes he had made about the reconstructive surgeries he planned to conduct. "But soon you should return to normal," he offered.

"Normal," Ella replied. "You call this normal?" She rocked from side to side on the bed to exhibit her incapacity. "I'm as helpless as a newborn. Look at me." Her voice scraped upward in her throat. He wondered if the blast had somehow damaged her vocal cords.

"It was a poor choice of words, perhaps." He ran the tips of the fingers of his left hand over his lips, as if to corral other words on the verge of escape.

"How dare you touch your face in front of me. Every time you touch your face, it's an insult to me. I don't have any goddamned hands." She raised her torso from the bed, as if to spit the words at him like bullets, her eyes beaded and angry.

The phone call had thrown him off. He had not been expecting that message. He didn't fully understand, after all he had accomplished, that they would demand he undertake another mission. He tried to re-focus. He had to mollify this patient, he had to regain control. "It might be time to remove the bandages from your face," he said evenly.

After a moment, Ella tried to smile, but only the left side of her mouth lifted in reaction to the news.

Volkov set his tablet in the rack at the end of the bed and approached her with bandage scissors in his right hand. He snipped away the bandages, unwrapping the gauze in a slow twirl. When he was done, he examined the scars on her face and scalp. Her skin was a fiery pink and glistened with antimicrobial ointment. Short, black bristles had emerged on her scalp, struggling to push through the gashes and stitches.

"You are healing well, right on schedule," he pronounced. "Skin grafts will be necessary."

"I want to see myself," Ella said.

"That might not be prudent," Volkov said. "It is too soon. I can show you pictures later."

"Bring me a mirror," Ella said, leaving no room for argument.

The nurse looked at Volkov, and he nodded. She produced a small hand mirror with a pink plastic frame and held it so Ella could see her face.

The shock of her own appearance was too great. For a moment, Ella could not speak. Her blue eyes grew wide beneath hairless eyebrows. Her lips quivered. "Oh my God," she whispered.

Volkov could not help but feel pity for her. Her life would be difficult, at best. And he was to blame. Perhaps he should have let her die in the triage tent. If he had tended to other patients for a few hours, the intracranial pressure or the flesh-eating bacteria would have killed her. They both would have been better off.

"Your scars will fade, Miss Winslow. Some of them may disappear entirely, in time. That is my hope, and my mission." He smiled the way he had been taught, with lips slightly parted, to convey a sense of optimism.

The nurse took the mirror away. Ella lay staring at the ceiling, her forehead furrowed, trying to replace the indelible images of the tattered face she barely recognized. Tears leaked from her eyes. Her sister Mattie dabbed them with sterile gauze.

After summarizing her treatment protocol, Volkov took a number of digital photographs with the tablet. Then he left her with the nurse. There was a moment when he wanted to lay a hand on Ella Winslow's wrist, to assure her of something, but he had amputated those wrists. Touching her in any other place would have brought him too close.

Volkov left the hospital and traversed wet sidewalks leading to the parking garage. He unlocked the door to his SUV with a trembling right hand. He got in and gripped the steering wheel in both palms, willed himself to calm, to shake off the image of her face. Once the bandages had been removed, he could see it clearly. There was no doubt. Ella Winslow bore a remarkable resemblance to his dead sister Anna.

9

Anna Volkov was born a Thalidomide baby. She'd had perfectly formed legs, but where her arms should have been, there was nothing, the deformity caused by the sedative given to her mother to ease morning sickness. A torso with no arms, as if the sculptor had died before he could finish.

She was older than Viktor by five years, and theirs was a house of accommodation. Viktor learned this when he visited the homes of his young friends, who had toilets with lids, doors that locked, clothes hung on hangers, and dressers for other things. Anna could navigate none of those ordinary furnishings, even though she was adept with her feet. And when he came into the world when his sister was five, his parents kept things the same. The bedroom he shared with Anna had no locks. Their clothes were folded on low shelves, out in the open. Their closet door had been removed. The door to the lone bathroom was also void of lock—in case Anna had an emergency in the tub, his parents explained.

As he entered kindergarten, his resentment toward his sister began to grow. Even in a deprived Soviet Union, he saw that some children had things he did not, all because of his sister. Anna could not ride a bicycle. So when he asked his parents to buy him a used bike he'd seen at a shop, they refused, concocting an excuse that they couldn't afford it and that it was unsafe to ride in the streets in their neighborhood because of truck traffic. Young Viktor knew the real reason he wasn't allowed a bike: they didn't want Anna, who had so little, to be constantly reminded of the things she would never be able to do.

He was angry that he suffered because of her. When his classmates chided Anna or made fun of her, he did not defend her, he joined in. She cast an odd shadow in sunlight, an awkwardly tall girl who resembled a thin tree whose limbs had been torn off in a violent storm. His clan of friends had a dozen or more nicknames for her, most of them vicious, none of them kind.

In her mid-teens, Anna entered a phase in which she refused to be fed by anyone. At mealtime, her plate often went untouched. She had learned something about embarrassment, perhaps because of the constant insults she received, and not even a remote table in the school cafeteria, to which she retreated to feed herself with her feet, was a safe haven. Her classmates often gathered around to watch the spectacle, hurling insults about her crooked toes or her greasy hair or a sleek torso they likened to a wriggling eel. If she had not already learned it, these episodes taught her the cruelty of children. On days when the weather was so bitter she had to wear boots she could not unlace to free her feet, she simply sipped milk through a straw. She disdained dipping her head to the plate to eat like a dog. That she would never do. Not in front of anyone. So, she slowly starved.

One morning she barged into the bathroom to take a shower. Viktor was brushing his teeth at the sink and saw her nakedness before she slipped behind the shower curtain. He had not seen a naked girl before, but he knew that his sister's protruding ribs and sunken chest were not normal. At the time, he was twelve; she was seventeen. To Viktor, she looked like the concentration camp inmates he had seen in state-sponsored documentaries from World War II, and her body repulsed him.

He was a voracious reader, even then, often buying books from the West for a few kopeks from a stash in a basement that wasn't supposed to exist. He read at night, a book propped upon his stomach, a dim halo from a candle lighting the pages, leaving the rest of their room in shadow.

"They censor those books brother," Anna said. Her voice, like her emaciated body, was thin and hollow.

He looked up. "Are you planning to turn me in? I don't care. I like reading about the West, even if it's maybe not all true."

After a time, she asked him to read to her, for although she was literate, sitting upright against the headboard and flipping pages with her toes proved an exhausting task. They both liked books about cowboys, the descriptions of gunfights and men riding horses across the plains, all depicting America as a vast and lawless place.

"Do you think you will ever go to America?" she asked as he finished one book and picked up another.

He raised his chin toward the ceiling. "I would like to," he said in a voice that had begun to deepen. "One day."

"I don't think I will live that long," she said.

He glanced at her on the other side of the room. Despite her emaciation, he had not contemplated this—her death. He somehow did not translate her protruding ribs or sunken cheeks into an irreversible physical decline. He was in a phase of his life where, despite the gray, cloying nature of life in the

Soviet Union, he chose not to acknowledge suffering.

"I would like to see America, or any other place, but . . ." she stopped abruptly.

He scanned her frail frame with something between pity and judgment. "You should eat more," he said. He then dropped his eyes to the new book, as if this pronouncement had solved all of his sister's problems.

Their reading sessions became something they both looked forward to. He narrated the stories as if he had witnessed the events, an air of authority in his voice. He embellished the whine of bullets and the whisper of arrows through the air before they plunged into flesh. Sometimes he added his own description or interpretation, highlighting the moans of the mortally wounded or the jubilation of those who inflicted the agony. These books were filled with death caused by man, famine, and disease. When an Indian or settler fell, from a bullet or arrow or tomahawk it did not matter, an undetected smile would emerge upon his lips.

When Anna turned 18, their parents threw her a birthday party, complete with unwrapped gifts. Viktor bought her a soft pillow filled with goose down, for her neck had become so weak that she could barely hold her head up. She blew out all 18 candles on the first try, and they all pulled her ears in Russian tradition. After their mother cut the cake into thin slices, Anna allowed Viktor to spoon cake into her mouth.

Two days later, she told him about the dreams she had been having. In some of the dreams she had arms and went dancing, her arms draped around the neck of a young man, or poised gracefully as she performed a perfect pirouette. She watched herself make a bed, wash her hair, and paint polish onto fingers so long and beautiful they should be in a magazine. In other dreams, in her state or armlessness, she was killed when she stepped in front of a bus, or fell from a roof, or drowned in a placid pond into which she had wandered.

During this recitation, Viktor heard a vague hope and longing in her voice. One kind of dream could never come true; the other type was possible.

On a Wednesday night—he would always remember it was Wednesday—Viktor finished reading at the usual time, then blew out the candle. A faint moon seeped through the thin curtain of their bedroom window. The curtain undulated on a breeze. He waited for a time, steeling himself, and then he approached her bed, tiptoeing in imaginary moccasins. He stood over her, the moonlight washing her face. Her black hair curled onto the pillow. Her eyes were open. She neither smiled nor frowned at him.

As he locked her eyes with his, he lifted her head with his left hand, pulled the down pillow from beneath it with his other, and gently laid her head back on the mattress. He held the pillow aloft with both hands, giving her time to decide, allowing her an opportunity to provide him a signal. They remained in pause for several minutes. Her eyes did not widen or narrow. She did not speak. When her lips parted slightly in an expression of anticipation, he lowered the pillow slowly onto her face.

Their parents found her in the morning, her eyes closed and her body prone, her skin a light shade of blue. Had his mother not seen a small, gray feather beneath Anna's tongue, they might have concluded she expired from starvation, or the weight of unhappiness. The pillow lay on the floor next to her bed. His mother turned toward him, her mouth wide, her eyebrows raised.

"Viktor, did you do this?"

"Yes," he replied without hesitation.

He was smart enough to know that, at 13, he would not be sent to a juvenile prison camp for his crime. Social services intervened, and he resided in a fetid and crowded dormitory for a few months, enduring rounds of electro-shock therapy and swallowing nameless pills, before he was returned to his parents. He was told there would be no inquiry, no trial.

As he recalled that distant night on the drive back to his farm, he remembered that Anna had not resisted. When he pressed the pillow down onto her face, she did not thrash or kick or otherwise try to escape. He had convinced himself that she had invited it, that he had relieved her suffering, that he had saved Anna from a living hell. And in some twisted way, when he saved Ella Winslow from almost certain death, he had resurrected his sister.

10

Caroline Bannister walked the several blocks from her office to the Charlotte arena, striding between glass and stone skyscrapers. As she approached from a distance, she began to sense the devastation. Flashing police lights greeted her at every corner, where barricades kept onlookers at least three blocks away. Even some of the neighboring buildings were closed because of blast damage. The bomb had blown out all of the windows in the arena and ripped off some of the roof, remnants of which lay on the sidewalks and in the streets. Bulldozers pushed the debris into huge piles.

She stood at one of the orange barricades, taking it all in. The air was acrid with hazy smoke. Her nose and eyes burned. The clang of heavy equipment and the shrill whine of emergency sirens was disorienting. She waved a policeman over and showed him her Justice Department badge. She was admitted around the barricade.

With her arms folded she walked to the top of the concrete ramp that descended to the loading dock beneath the arena. A line of idling ambulances snaked from the loading dock, up the ramp, and around a corner. Caroline showed her badge again at a security gate that had been recently erected. As she walked down the ramp beside the line of ambulances, she noticed the concrete retaining walls were pocked and marred. From shrapnel, she surmised.

When she entered the vast basement of the building, a basement that covered more than a city block, the air turned fetid. The decay of a crypt filled her nostrils. At the bottom of the ramp, she was provided a loose-fitting white coverall, nitrile gloves, a two-filter environmental mask, plastic goggles, a hard hat, and rubber boots. She donned the garb and followed her escort along a narrow path carved through the rubble. Twisted rebar jutted from hunks of concrete littering the floor. Cadaver dogs and their handlers roved over the mounds of debris, searching.

The concrete floor of the loading dock had been swept clean in one direction, as if ocean waves had rolled across it, leaving plastic evidence markers in their wake. The scorched and partially crushed shell of a delivery van was surrounded by yellow crime-scene tape and orange cones. A gaping hole in the ceiling of the loading dock revealed twisted steel girders and beams that had once supported a thick base of concrete. Temporary columns in newly poured concrete footers held up what was left of the ceiling. Still, it did not look entirely safe to Caroline.

She had seen digital photographs of the Murrah building in Oklahoma City after Tim McVeigh set off his bomb, and images of the Twin Towers after they had fallen. Seeing the devastation in person was different. Photographs couldn't capture it all—not the noise, or the odor, or the feeling of so much death trying to penetrate her safety suit.

As she stood looking through the hole in the floor at a small patch of blue sky, Eric Mullen touched her elbow. He was the Special Agent in Charge of the bombing investigation, and the man at the FBI largely responsible for identifying Abdul Alnoor as the perpetrator of the mass shooting at the Eagle's Nest Country Club. Mullen's goggles were fogged, as if he'd emerged from the night. He lifted the goggles to clear out the moisture.

Mullen introduced her to the site supervisor from Homeland Security—a man who had helped manage the recovery efforts after the twin towers toppled in New York on 9/11. She also met two explosives experts from the United States Army, and Mullen's second in command, Natalie Goodloe. Suited up and gloved, none of them shook hands. Through the breathing apparatus, conversation was muted and distorted. The din of saws and torches cutting through steel revved above them.

Mullen guided her to the van. "This is ground zero. We're certain of that," he shouted, leaning in. "We're still processing the van. We just got all of the concrete off of it last night."

"Can I look inside?" Caroline's voice came from a cave.

Mullen nodded.

She lifted the crime-scene tape, ducked under it, and stepped carefully between the evidence markers. She peered through a small, irregular opening that had once been the passenger window, now a misshapen slit in the twisted metal. All of the glass was missing, some of it in shards in the well of the bench seat. She noticed what looked like small puddles of water on the floor.

"What is that?" she pointed.

Mullen peered in beside here. "Glass that melted and then cooled. Had to have been 1600 degrees, according to the blast experts."

Caroline continued her inspection. The interior of the van was blackened. The vinyl dash had melted into a shape that could have been the subject of a

Dali painting. She could not tell what color the upholstery on the seats might have been. Only the metal framing and springs remained, charred and blistered.

Caroline did not have to imagine what the bomber thought as he drove down the ramp into the delivery area. From her experience, she knew what he felt—nothing. The moves were rehearsed. All of the emotion had been quelled beforehand, consumed in the planning. The bomber had acted in a robotic fashion. Once put in motion, the plan allowed for no hesitation, no second-guessing, no variations. She knew this because it was how she had ambushed and executed Judge Hal Manning in his barn. It was how she had been able to put a bolt gun to the head of Mayor Williams and pull the trigger while the rest of the team watched. It was cold and calculated. It came from a place within that was dark and icy. It could be no other way.

She noted evidence tags taped to the dashboard and to the door frames. "What are those marking?" she asked.

"Bone fragments," Agent Mullen said.

"Bone fragments? So . . ."

"There was someone, or something, inside the van. We know they are bone fragments, but we don't yet know if the fragments are human, or animal."

She stood up, edging closer to Mullen. "But you're certain these are bone fragments?"

"Yes."

"Embedded in the metal?"

Mullen nodded. "That's how powerful this blast was. Tore apart the body and embedded bone fragments in steel."

"How soon will you know if they're human bone fragments?"

"They're being analyzed in the mobile lab now."

"The bomber?" she said.

"We don't know." Mullen shook his head slowly.

Caroline turned and surveyed the scene, not able to fully comprehend the enormity of the investigative task. Dozens of evidence technicians scurried about under huge stanchions of LED lights. A large nylon tent had been erected in one corner of the basement. Through the hole in the arena floor she saw search teams on hands and knees, scouring the rubble.

"Why is the hole in the roof so much smaller than the hole in the floor?" she asked, pointing upward. "I thought the blast would expand."

"The experts say the design of the roof probably caused the blast energy to spread out, into the seating area of the arena, diverting some of the upward

41

energy and momentum. The same engineering design that keeps the curved roof from collapsing also helped to contain the blast. When the bomber selected this building, he knew what he was doing. He picked this site for maximum casualties."

"He? You're sure the bomber was male?"

Mullen shrugged his shoulders. "You know the profile."

In the command tent, dozens of FBI agents worked on computers, cataloguing and analyzing evidence. Others worked on victim identification and tracking body parts, which were placed in bags and bins in refrigerator trucks. With mask and goggles removed, Caroline sipped coffee from a paper cup. She flipped through a growing list of the victims, typed in neat columns on white paper. In these early stages, most were identified by number, with only a smattering of names appearing on the list. Beside each identifier was a summary of what had been found. Each entry was labeled with "DOA" or "HOSP." She flipped to the last page, page 256.

"How many dead so far?" she asked.

"We eclipsed two thousand this morning," Mullen said.

"I presume you're interviewing all survivors," Caroline said.

"Of course," Mullen replied. "Most of them are extremely traumatized. Many still in the hospital. So far, no concrete leads."

"What about the concert fans who weren't injured or treated?"

"We have a list of the patrons that night, and those working in the arena. But it's incomplete. We don't yet know how many on the list were victims, or how many escaped. As we find them, we interview them. For now, we're relying heavily on the tip line. Hundreds of tips so far, none of them leading anywhere."

"Do we have video?"

"Dozens of cameras captured video throughout the night. The main security center was directly above us. Heavily damaged in the blast. One server was completely destroyed, so we know some video is gone, but we haven't fully catalogued what's missing."

"They didn't have offsite backup?" Caroline asked.

Agent Mullen shook his head. "Uploads after midnight, after everything shuts down. But we do have this." He ushered her over to a computer screen. "Key it up," he said to an FBI technician.

They bent forward and watched as a white van entered the driveway from the street, slowly descending to the security station. The technicians had already pieced together the available footage from various cameras, so the video showed a continuous stream of the van's movement from different angles. The van stopped. On its side was painted the logo of a local beer distributor. The windows were tinted. A security guard stepped to the driver's side. The shot angle was oblique, capturing the security guard as he examined a piece of paper, but the van's driver was not on camera. Only the left arm of the driver could be seen. The driver was wearing a dark, long-sleeved shirt. A work glove covered the driver's left hand.

Caroline and Agent Mullen watched as the security guard opened the back doors of the van and peered at what appeared to be beer kegs stacked to the ceiling. He closed the doors, went back to the driver's side door, raised his cell phone and appeared to take a photograph of the driver. The driver's side window went up. The security guard stepped back. The van pulled toward the loading dock. Its license plate was fully in view. Then the video went to black.

"That's it," Mullen announced.

"No video at the loading dock?" Caroline said.

"Not that we've found. That might have been on the destroyed server."

"So no images of the driver?"

"Not yet. We don't know if he ever exited the van. The bomb went off at exactly 9:11 p.m. One theory, based on the existence of bone fragments inside the cab, is that he ignited the bomb and killed himself in the process."

Caroline mulled this over. It made some sense. A suicide bomber. That was the typical way in which Islamic Jihadists set off their explosives. Different from most.

"Has anyone claimed responsibility?"

"Nothing concrete. A few vague claims. ISIS claims they inspired the bomber, an attack on Western values and so on. A couple of other fringe groups have claimed responsibility. We're checking them out."

"You think this was ISIS?"

"Too early to tell. The 9:11 detonation time could be coincidence, but I doubt it. We'll follow the evidence, as we always do. But you see the breadth of the crime scene," Mullen said, gesturing with his left arm. "We have months of work to do here."

"And the security guard?"

Mullen glanced down at a notepad. "Terrence Thomas. He had worked at the arena for two years. Aged 29. Deceased."

"Killed in the bombing?"

"Yes. Once the rubble was cleared, we found his body inside the security booth, or what was left of it. Hard to tell if he died from the explosion, or the collapsed ceiling. And, before you ask, we did find remnants of a cell phone in the booth. Not much left to examine, but we're checking the cloud to see if he uploaded anything. So far, it looks like a dead end."

"Why would he take a photograph of the driver with his cell phone? That seems unnecessary with all of the video cameras."

"We don't know. It's strange. We're wondering if the video cameras in the loading area had been disabled, and perhaps Thomas had been notified."

"Could he be an accomplice?" asked Caroline.

"It's plausible, but if that's the case, why take a photograph of your co-conspirator? And if you know there's a bomb in the van, would you just stay put?"

11

Caroline replayed the voicemail message for the third time as she drove to FBI regional headquarters in south Charlotte. Agent Mullen's voice was clipped and urgent. She had never heard him sound so . . . unraveled.

At the security gate, two agents armed with semi-automatic weapons and body armor examined her car. They traversed the length of the car with long-handled mirrors, examining the undercarriage for devices. A third agent in the security booth watched the live video image from a moving camera on the track beneath her car. While she stood outside on the driveway, they searched the well where her spare tire was kept, and the interior of the car, including the glove box and the alcoves beneath the seats. A German Shepherd walked around her SUV, sniffing at the tires and hubcaps. The Shepherd stopped and sniffed Caroline's shoes and pant legs.

The steel gate slid back. Caroline drove up the driveway and parked in a visitor's space near the building. Though Agent Mullen's office was on the top floor, the security officer at the reception desk escorted her to an elevator that led to the basement. Only after the agent swiped his badge and bent down to eye the retina scanner affixed to the elevator wall did they begin to descend. She had not been in this elevator before, had never been to the basement of the FBI building. She noted there were no numbers or labels next to the three elevator buttons.

The doors opened to a vast space and a bustle of activity. To her left was a glass wall, behind which was an endless bank of computer servers, green lights blinking. Agents crisscrossed the open floor, darting between rows of cubicles and tables piled high with documents and evidence bags. Agent Natalie Goodloe, Mullen's second in command, emerged from a perimeter office and beckoned to her. Caroline entered the small office, which was filled by an oval table and three chairs. Agent Mullen moved from the corner where he had been standing and shook her hand.

"Have a seat, Caroline."

In the middle of the table was a laptop computer and a device she recognized as an audio blocker. It was designed to prevent listening devices from recording any conversations inside the room. She had one in her office, but she had never used it.

"This is Jason Bixby," Mullen indicated. "He's a forensic scientist and anthropologist. Specializes in bones and fossils and extracting DNA from them."

Bixby, sporting bloodshot eyes behind black-rimmed glasses, raised his hand in acknowledgment before returning his attention to the computer screen.

Mullen continued. "The bone shards in the van were human. Agent Bixby extracted DNA from those shards and ran it through our database, came up with a match. He's running a confirming search now."

"Okay, are you going to keep me in suspense?" Caroline said.

"Only until we confirm the match from another sample."

They waited a minute longer, maybe two.

"Confirmed," Bixby said. "The two bone fragments are from the same man."

Mullen turned to Caroline. "Carmelo Williams."

Caroline sucked in a breath. "Mayor Carmelo Williams?"

"One and the same. What's the potential error rate, Bixby?"

"About one in fourteen million."

"Holy shit," Caroline said. She tried to keep her eyes from darting about, absorbing this revelation that the man she had killed with a bolt gun after a secret trial had been framed by a terrorist for bombing the Charlotte arena. When the Mayor went missing, local law enforcement launched a massive search for him, but the search ended when emails purportedly sent by the Mayor from locations in Africa were discovered. Caroline and the other four vigilantes knew the emails were fake, but they constituted some evidence the Mayor was still alive, and when the search was called off she felt nothing but relief.

Now, she realized that the bomber, or a terrorist cell, had turned the tables on her and framed a dead man for the second-worst terrorist attack on American soil. Sweat trickled down her back. She had to keep her cool. Aside from the bomber, she was the only person out of seven billion in the world who held all the evidence in the chain: the Mayor had been dead for several weeks before the explosion.

"I've got to call the Director," Mullen said.

"Wait," Caroline said. "Was there any other DNA found in the van?"

"No," Bixby replied. "Just the bone fragments. If there had been hair or skin fragments in the van, they would have been incinerated in the blast."

She turned to Mullen. "Do you think the Mayor did this alone?"

"We haven't gotten that far, but we have a lot of questions. The bomb was made from ammonium nitrate fertilizer, nitromethane, and diesel fuel. All easy enough to get. We don't know what he used as a catalyst. Not yet. But catalysts are harder to obtain. You can't just walk into a store and buy something like that. So where did he get the catalyst? That's one question."

"The van. Any leads on that?"

"It wasn't stolen. It was purchased at a car auction in Florida about a week before the bombing. We've got agents down there interviewing the owner of the auction yard. But nothing so far."

"Eric, do you *think* he was working alone?"

He stared off through the wall of the room, perhaps trying to imagine something the evidence didn't yet point to. "I don't know."

"He was in Africa," Caroline said. She looked at Mullen in a measured way, watching his eyes as she spoke. "It looks like he spent his time in Africa planning this. Maybe he went there to train. Maybe that's where he got the catalyst." She was surprised at the agility with which she concocted this false theory.

Mullen nodded. "It's almost a copy of the McVeigh bombing in Oklahoma City, except this time the van wasn't rented. Maybe it's something one guy could pull off, but with the van, the cell phone ignition, probably forged paperwork to even get down to the loading dock, it would have been a lot easier with an accomplice. McVeigh had an accomplice."

"I know. Could Williams have learned how to make and explode a truck bomb in Africa? What do we know about his time there? Where did he go?" Caroline asked.

"We don't know anything about his travels. Until this moment, we had no idea he was dead. But we'll coordinate with NSA and CIA to see what info they might have about his activities."

So the FBI would keep looking. They would search for someone who, unknown to the FBI, was also blackmailing her, Judge Westlake, and the rest of the team because he had concrete evidence they had killed the Mayor. And if they found the real terrorist, he undoubtedly would be a font of information. He had damning evidence they had assassinated the Mayor, evidence they could never explain away. Evidence that would land them in a jail cell for the rest of their lives. Or worse.

12

From the bench perched above his courtroom, Raleigh Westlake looked down at his cell phone. The text from Caroline was simple and compelling: "**911**." He adjourned the afternoon session and descended three steps to the courtroom floor. He went to his chambers and hung his robe on the back of a chair. He tapped an icon on his cell phone and stood in front of the large plate-glass window behind his desk, gazing at the Blue Ridge Mountains to the west.

"What's the emergency?" he asked.

"We need to meet, tonight," Caroline said. "All of us. Here in Charlotte. It's urgent. I can't leave and come to you."

He glanced at the watch on his left wrist. "All right. Where?"

"My house. Pull in the alley and park in the back."

"Okay. Why so secretive?"

"I'll tell you when you get here."

Judge Westlake pulled a key from his pants pocket and unlocked the bottom right drawer of his desk. From the drawer he took an amber prescription bottle and shook two pills into his palm. He dropped the first pill in the back of his mouth, swallowing it dry. Then he swallowed the second. He put his robe back on and walked the short corridor from his chambers to the thick wooden door separating his suite of offices from the courtroom. Marcus Cunningham stood by the door in his uniform of gray slacks and navy blazer.

"Everything okay, Judge?"

"We need to go to Charlotte after court. To Caroline's house. I'll drive down separately. You and Iggy need to be there by eight o'clock. Please let Johnstone know. Park in the back of her house." He took a deep breath and straightened his shoulders.

"Anything we need to prepare for?" Cunningham said.

"She was cryptic, but it's an emergency of some sort. That's all I know."

Cunningham opened the door to the courtroom and stepped inside, leaving the door ajar. He made his announcement, and the two attorneys in the courtroom dutifully rose.

The Judge came through the door and ascended three steps to his bench. "Sorry for the interruption." He settled into the leather chair and leaned back, fingering his chin.

He spent the rest of the afternoon listening to pre-trial motions in a civil case filed by a man who had lost his business to a fire. The insurance company denied the claim, asserting that the man had burned down his building. The business owner denied it, noting that a building down the street had been torched by an arsonist the weekend after his fire. Trial was scheduled to begin in ten days. The attorneys argued about discovery that had not been timely produced, the admissibility of the opinions of experts as to the cause and origin of the fire, and testimony about the value of the building and the profitability of the plaintiff's business.

Westlake heard all of the arguments over the pounding of his heart and the rushing of blood in his ears. He had been this way since announcing Abdul Alnoor's death in open court. The anti-anxiety medication wasn't helping. Long and frequent runs in the woods didn't fully calm him, or calm him for long. Everything was out of control. Though they hadn't heard from the blackmailer in almost two weeks, the threat hovered above them like the sword of Damocles. At any moment, their lives could be shredded. He wondered if this is how Robert had felt as he climbed the steps to Chimney Rock and stood on the edge of the monolithic rock, contemplating a quick end to all of it.

Westlake wasn't depressed. His doctor had confirmed that. But being the target of a blackmailer, and the frustration of their unsuccessful hunt for him, had withered his resolve to a thin veil. It was all he could do to muster the patience to listen to arguments in cases he didn't care about, to attempt to dispense justice he no longer believed in.

He realized the attorneys had finished presenting their arguments. Both were seated, their faces raised to him in expectation. He turned his attention back to the case. He wanted this case to go away. He did not want to sit for two or three weeks listening to this dispute, overseeing a jury who would be even more bored and disinterested than he was.

He looked down at a yellow legal pad on which he had scrawled a few notes he didn't remember writing. He shuffled through the stack of motions filed by the parties, which one of his law clerks had annotated.

"I'm going to deny all of the pre-trial motions," he said. "On both sides." He startled himself with this pronouncement, resorting to inaction as opposed to decisiveness, which would only postpone his need to rule until a later time. "But I'm making the following observations. I don't know how the jury is going to decide this, but if the jury decides for the plaintiff, I'm going to impose treble damages on the insurance company for failing to conduct a thorough and objective investigation and improper handling of the claim. If the jury decides for the defendant, I'm going to refer this matter to the Buncombe County District Attorney to investigate for arson."

As he finished speaking, he watched the faces of the attorneys turn from bewilderment at his denial of all motions to deep concern that one of their clients was going to be in the shit. The lawyers twitched in their chairs and looked at each other for a moment.

"I strongly suggest you settle it," Judge Westlake said. "Emphasis on the word 'strongly'." He didn't rap his gavel, but sprung from his chair and hurried down the steps, reaching the courtroom door before Marcus Cunningham could get there. He pushed open the door and strode into his chambers, removing a bottle of bourbon from the cabinet. He tipped the bottle to his lips but pulled it down before drinking anything.

13

The five of them sat in upholstered chairs and on the striped couch in Caroline's living room, looking expectant and uncomfortable. A piebald cat wandered among their legs. The four men held tumblers of liquor. With both hands encircling a mug of tea, Caroline told them what she'd learned.

"The FBI has identified the Charlotte bomber as Carmelo Williams."

She left it there, a succinct announcement with no additional facts necessary, its starkness laid bare for all of them to see. The import landed upon them with the weight of an avalanche: the person who was blackmailing them had masterminded one of the deadliest terrorist attacks in the history of the country, killing at least two thousand people. And he had framed someone else for the crime.

"But that's impossible," Johnstone said after a period of silence.

"Yes and no," Caroline said. "His body was in the van. They've matched his DNA from bone fragments. Obviously, we know he was dead before the explosion, but the FBI doesn't know that. They don't have any way of knowing that. So Carmelo Williams was, officially, the man who bombed the Charlotte arena, killing almost three thousand people." There was no emotion in her voice, as if she were reading from a teleprompter.

"Okay," Johnstone said, sucking in breaths, on the verge of hyperventilating. He took a long slug of liquor from the glass and held it between his knees. "This is better for us, right? Now the blackmailer can't reveal our involvement in the Mayor's death without implicating himself."

Caroline scoffed and shook her head. "You've got it all wrong. If the blackmailer reveals the photos, us carrying the Mayor's body and burying him, that's evidence that we put the Mayor in the van. That's evidence that we bombed the arena. We are the terrorists. We murdered thousands of people."

"Shit," was the word Cunningham emitted involuntarily when he realized their predicament. Only he and Ignacio Perez were directly implicated in the Mayor's death—one of the photographs showed the two of them carrying Williams' body to his car.

"So maybe he has no need to blackmail us now," Johnstone said. The words fluttered in the air and died. "He thinks Abdul is dead."

"The FBI is looking for accomplices in the bombing," Caroline said. "They think it's unlikely the Mayor acted alone. We know the Mayor didn't act at all. If they find the real terrorist, he'll cut a deal, and we'll be the first casualties," Caroline said. "We have to find him before the FBI does. Not only is he an imminent threat to us, but a threat to thousands, or tens of thousands, of innocent people. We know what he's capable of."

There was a prolonged silence. Caroline picked up her cat and began to stroke the back of its head. It was the cat she had rescued from Hal Manning's barn as carbon monoxide filled the cab of his pickup. She had yet to name it.

"We have to assume this guy didn't act alone," she said.

"Why?" Judge Westlake asked.

"Because, the crime is too complicated. Manufacturing the fake emails from the Mayor in Africa, acquiring the bomb catalyst, purchasing the van, and the fertilizer, and the diesel fuel. And the Mayor's body was probably stored in a freezer for at least two weeks so it wouldn't smell when the bomber placed it in the van. This is not the work of one person. We're dealing with a terrorist cell."

Westlake's lips parted involuntarily. He took a moderate sip of bourbon. "I see your point. This is not a good development." He swirled the amber liquid in his glass for no apparent purpose. "I'm assuming the FBI will keep you informed every step of the way, so that if they get a lead on any suspect, you'll know immediately."

"Don't count on that," Caroline said. "That's not the way it usually works. I'm in the loop, but sometimes I find out only after the perp has been arrested. That's what happened with Alnoor. In this case, that would be too late. And deadly for us."

Westlake stood up and walked to the kitchen and back, like a convict pacing his cell. He stopped on the oriental carpet in the living room and broke the silence. "Look, we're in a predicament that's untenable. Whoever did this, they are highly skilled. Not only at pulling off the crime, but at leading the entire law enforcement community in the wrong direction." He gripped the tumbler of liquor more tightly to still his trembling hands. "I see no possibility that we can catch him, or them, before the FBI does. We simply don't have the manpower, or the tools."

"We don't have a choice," Caroline said without looking up.

Westlake stared at her. It would have been easy for him to initiate the accusations, which the others would join, blaming her for their predicament because of her blind rush to prosecute Carmelo Williams, her execution of an innocent man. But he knew it would solve nothing, and it was probably what the blackmailer hoped for—infighting—which would turn them against one another and all but seal their fates.

"I want to apologize for dragging all of you into this," he said. "I know I didn't force you, but it was my idea, starting with Henry Lawter. I thought we were doing the right thing, bringing justice to victims whom our legal system has failed. I never thought it would lead to this. Instead of chasing down criminals, we're the ones being hunted and manipulated by this madman, or his terrorist cell. I'm sorry." He glanced out Caroline's living room window at the darkness of the night. "They could be watching us right now. They know where Caroline lives. They know where I live." He downed the remaining bourbon in his glass. "I suggest everyone arm themselves. Be extremely careful. And there's one more thing—if anyone wants out of the group, you're free to leave now."

14

After an evening of fitful sleep on the day bed in Caroline's spare bedroom, Raleigh rose and stood before the picture window, looking out on Caroline's front yard. The grass shone emerald beneath a glitter of dew, and birds sang from two maple trees, their chirps an audible reminder that, in the world outside, nothing had really changed.

Inside, nothing had changed either. No one had left the group. Their conversation the night before had veered away from their predicament and the revelation that one of their victims had been framed as America's most reviled terrorist. The repercussions were too painful to contemplate, and even the smallest, well-intentioned comment sent a collective shiver through them. So the drinking had continued, with Caroline trading tea for a bottle of Pinot Noir, and everything but crime and justice became fair game. Cunningham and Perez told them about a fishing trip they had recently taken to the Gulf of Mexico, where they landed a limit of redfish. Perez promised to have them all over for a fish fry before the weather turned cold. David Johnstone talked about the major league baseball playoffs and his son's semi-promising baseball career in the minor leagues. This, coupled with the soothing effect of alcohol, lifted the corners of their mouths and unburdened them. Raleigh mentioned a marathon he might enter in the spring, but complained about old bones and sore muscles, even though he was probably in better physical shape than any of them.

Caroline refrained from the banter except for the occasional, well-constructed remark, content to pet her adopted cat with long strokes down its black and white body that soothed her as much as it did him.

"Does your cat have a name?" Perez said with one eyebrow arched.

"No, he doesn't," she said. "I haven't had time to name him yet."

"Astrophe," Raleigh said. When Caroline looked at him with a blank stare, he said, "You know—cat astrophe." He did not intend it to be funny, or morbid. He said it to distract Perez and the others from asking for details about the cat, which would inevitably lead them to discover Caroline had rescued the animal from Judge Manning's barn as he succumbed to carbon monoxide in the cab of his truck, which the local Sheriff classified as suicide. He said it to make sure they didn't know that Caroline had gone back to the Manning ranch and countermanded Raleigh's order that Manning not be touched. And yet, in the liquor-infused haze they had slipped into, his suggested name for the cat got a roar of approval from everyone and uninhibited laughter that somehow made their desperation wane.

As the morning light infused the living room in yellow and he finished picking up tumblers and wine glasses from the evening, he thought about going for a run in Caroline's neighborhood, but in some sense it seemed a cowardly move, even though he planned to return before Caroline rose, and he knew that this time, unlike the predecessors, running would bring him no solutions, no peace, no solace. Instead, he went to the kitchen and poured himself a glass of water from a pitcher in the refrigerator. Then he pulled out slices of ham and a half-empty carton of eggs, some cheese and mushrooms, and began to make breakfast.

Amid the clanging of the skillet and the drone of the hood fan, Caroline appeared at the edge of the kitchen, her bare toes twitching on the porcelain tile, her hair tousled. She stood in the doorway with a sanguine expression, and he wasn't sure if it was because he had stayed until morning, or she had come upon something resembling a solution to their dilemma. She took three steps toward him, reaching out with one hand as he shifted the iron skillet on the burner. She rubbed his forearm in ambiguous fashion, and then she had both arms around his neck, kissing him first on the cheek and then on the lips, moving away from him almost as quickly, as if a rogue gust of wind had blown across his cheek on an otherwise still morning.

She poured a cup of coffee from the pot he had brewed, even though he didn't drink coffee, and she settled back against the edge of the counter as wisps of steam rose from the cup. There was a smile playing on her lips as she watched him at the stove, a smile that was shy, as if she wanted to keep it to herself but share it with him at the same time. He alternated his attention between the sizzling ham and this woman he once knew, and maybe would know again, the door unlocked but not ajar, though about that he was anything but certain.

"I came up with something last night," she started, "or early this morning." She left it dangling there, her smile emerging in increments, then hiding in another sip of coffee.

He stuck a long-handled fork into a piece of ham that had browned on the edges and flipped it over in the skillet. He turned toward her so he could watch them both. Though he said nothing, content to allow the sounds of the kitchen to establish the mood, his eyes invited her to continue.

She took another sip of coffee, her eyes watching him over the cup. "Grand jury." She said it without explanation, as if he would instantly understand, the way people tell others about a vivid dream, its freshness descending into obscurity as they try to find the words to articulate the images.

Raleigh's face was blank, or he thought it was, his mind unwilling to undertake the effort to connect a dot to other dots not yet on the page. The smell of frying ham reminded him of something, an event from his childhood perhaps, a pleasant moment that enveloped him. He didn't fully understand that he had yielded, had allowed the fervent need to control to drop from the top of his menu. He felt relaxed and uncluttered. He pulled two plates from a cabinet and set them on the counter, filling them with ham, carving in halves the omelet he had stowed in the oven, covered with foil. He held one plate out to her and smiled enough to raise his cheek bones.

She took the plate and moved to the peninsula, pulling out one of the two wooden stools with high backs, the wooden legs scraping the tile with an unpleasant sound. She pulled out the other stool and patted its seat.

"I empanel a grand jury so I can investigate the bomber's accomplice, in secret, who we know is the real terrorist. That way I can issue subpoenas for records, get warrants from you and bypass the FBI, have them served by Marcus and Iggy." She seemed to have it wrapped tightly.

He didn't say anything at first, staring past her through the kitchen window to the back yard, noting a tangle of high weeds in the flower bed by the back fence. Something about the scene brought him back to the dream he'd had the night before, the image of a fawn, its hide still speckled with white dots, scurrying into a treeless canyon, bordered on three sides by steep cliffs, insurmountable and sheer, with the fourth side blocked by a pack of five snarling wolves. He thought he understood the message, but there was an uncertainty about whether he was part of the wolf pack or the lone deer shuddering against a boulder.

When he put down the glass of water, he said, "then others will know. There's no way to keep something like that secret."

She cocked her head to the side and stabbed a mouthful of ham. "It's how we get the tools. You said we don't have the tools to track down the terrorist. This is how we do it."

"I don't think so. A subpoena leaves a record. A warrant leaves a trail. In addition to the grand jury, the people on whom you serve the subpoena, the person whose premises you search, they'll know. If they're not the target, they'll be close, and then he, or the whole cell, will know exactly what you're doing. They go underground, or they accelerate their next act of terrorism, or they come after us while we're following legal procedures."

She huffed out a puff of air that lifted her bangs. "So what do you suggest?"

"We have to become as ruthless as he is, or they are. Due process goes out the window, the Fourth Amendment becomes an afterthought. You know it's the only way. It's what you did with Hal Manning, and with Carmelo Williams."

"Sure, but . . ."

"And with Robert," he said, scooping the last bit of the omelet into his mouth with a spoon.

She remained quiet for a time, feeling it was unnecessary for him to remind her of the lawless path she'd taken, executing three men with her own hand, all close and personal, no guns fired from a safe perch. At least he hadn't told the others what she'd done. "Last night, when Perez asked about my cat, you . . ."

"I know. I've kept it to myself. I don't know how they'd react if they knew you'd killed Robert and Manning, or that you concocted the Mayor's confession."

"It wouldn't be good, that's for sure. They might take me out."

"Maybe," he said. "In any event, it doesn't matter. I didn't divulge our secret."

"Why? Is it because of our relationship?"

"Frankly, I'm not sure, Caroline. I don't know exactly what our relationship has become." Before his eyes passed an image of a soggy red towel in the corner of the bathroom, which neither of them wanted to pick up. Perhaps he recalled the image from an argument he'd had with Heather some time back, or maybe it was something he conjured because he'd mixed Zoloft with three glasses of bourbon the night before. Whatever the reason, he thought the wet towel was likely to lie there for some time.

"I see. I can't say I'm surprised. I understand how you could be disappointed with me, or upset about our predicament. What can I do to re-earn your trust?"

He picked up both plates and took them to the sink, ran water from the tap over them and scraped the breakfast remnants into the drain. He spoke to her without turning around. "I don't know the answer to that. It's a secondary consideration at the moment."

"Then what's your primary consideration?"

"We, all of us, have to focus on one thing. We have to catch the bomber and kill him."

15

There had been innumerable press conferences in the aftermath of the Charlotte bombing, with officials pleading for assistance from witnesses or updating the media as to the tally of the dead and wounded. This one felt different from the start.

Special Agent Mullen stepped to the lectern on a podium set up across the street from the arena. He was flanked by the FBI Director, the Director of Homeland Security, and the United States Attorney General. Caroline Bannister stood behind them, near the edge of the plywood podium. A fleet of limousines and SUVs lined the curb, Secret Service Agents standing guard.

"Thank you all for coming on such short notice. I am pleased to report that we have identified the bomber of the Charlotte arena," Mullen said. He paused as the murmurs grew and then abated. "The FBI, Homeland Security, ATF and specialists from the US Army, as well as two private genetics testing labs, have been hard at work, sifting through the evidence. As you might imagine," Mullen turned to the charred hulk of the arena behind him, "this has been a monumental task. But we had to get it right. As you know from previous releases, the bomb was planted in a white delivery van that drove into the underground loading dock of the arena, just behind me. The bomb was made from diesel fuel and fertilizer, and ignited by a cell phone. It was a suicide bomb. And although the bomber himself died in the blast, multiple DNA testing confirms the identity of the bomber. It was former Charlotte Mayor Carmelo Williams."

The murmurs grew to shouts as the media hurled questions at Agent Mullen. He held up his hands for quiet, then dipped his head to the microphones arrayed on the wooden lectern with the blue FBI logo affixed to the front. "Please, please, hold your questions for later. We have a special guest joining us today. Please welcome the President of the United States."

President Danny Roberts, who had emerged from the unmarked armored limousine third in line, ascended the podium with an athletic stride. He shook hands with the dignitaries and Agent Mullen, then took control of the lectern. "This is a monumental day for law enforcement, from top to bottom," he said, "And for our country. Now this great city, and the entire nation, can truly begin to heal." He paused and unbuttoned his suit jacket. "All of the credit here goes to the hard, unceasing work put in by a lot of people, including first responders, search and rescue, recovery teams, the FBI, Homeland Security, the US Army, Mecklenburg County Sheriff's Office, the Charlotte Police Department, and hundreds of nurses and doctors and other medical professionals who have been caring for our wounded brothers and sisters. Let's give all of them a round of applause." President Roberts began the ovation that lasted more than one minute. "And the work continues. Right behind us. There are more grieving families who deserve to have their loved ones returned to them. Let's respect their rights." He then relinquished the lectern to Agent Mullen.

As Mullen began to field questions from the media, the President sidled next to the Attorney General. "Johnny, we're not needed here any longer. Let's meet in my limo. Bring Ms. Bannister with you." The President left the dais, immediately surrounded by a huddle of Secret Service Agents, who ushered him to the armored SUV second in line.

When Caroline descended the podium steps, she heard a shouted question about a terrorist cell and Agent Mullen's vague answer that there was no evidence to support such a theory.

Attorney General Franks led Caroline through a line of Agents, one of whom opened a rear door to the Presidential limousine. Once they were settled into the leather seats, the entire line of six armored vehicles, five of them decoys, pulled from the curbside. President Roberts leaned forward and extended his hand. "Ms. Bannister, nice to see you again."

Caroline leaned forward and took his hand firmly, as her father had taught her. "Mr. President, it's my pleasure, and my honor."

"We're heading to the airport," the President said. "We don't have a lot of time. Do you know why you're here?"

Caroline shook her head. "No, sir. Not a clue."

The President glanced at the Attorney General.

"She knows I'm retiring in a few months," Franks said.

"Plain and simple, I want you to be my next AG, Ms. Bannister."

"Caroline, please."

"All right, Caroline. I like your style. Are you ready to come to Washington?"

"Frankly, I'm a little stunned right now. Why select me for the AG's job?"

"Your father was a Charlotte cop for almost thirty years. You come from a law enforcement background. You're strong, smart, accomplished everything on your own. Distinguished tenure at UNC Law, successful career at a blue-chip firm, solid record as an ADA prosecuting domestic violence cases, no major blemishes as US Attorney."

"I'm not a politician, sir. I'm a prosecutor."

The President smiled broadly, revealing teeth so uniform they had to be capped. "Hell, Caroline, everybody's a politician. Most just don't know it. You're perfect for AG. You're a dedicated prosecutor. Your whole life has been about bringing criminals to justice. Are you saying you don't want the job?"

"No sir, I'm not saying that. It's just . . ."

"Fast, I know. But my people have been vetting you for a few weeks. We had some other candidates, but background checks revealed some things that removed them from consideration. You're squeaky clean. Plus, if I don't get re-elected, you'll be in the job little more than a year, and then you can write your own ticket. Law school dean, think tank, private sector, whatever you want."

Caroline smiled, creating a mask to cover the vivid images racing through her mind: Robert Crenshaw, lying prone on a dusty road with a gash in the back of his head; Judge Hal Manning, semi-drunk, succumbing to carbon monoxide she piped into the cab of his truck; and Carmelo Williams, now mistakenly identified as a terrorist, whom she had dispatched with a cattle gun. The President's vetting team had found none of that.

"You're pondering the offer," the President said

"It's just that I'm not done here, sir. The bomber has been caught, but none of us are certain he pulled this off by himself. He may have had an accomplice, or accomplices. If so, we're all still in danger. I want to find and prosecute everyone involved in this devastating crime."

"Well, if we don't round them up before your confirmation, then you'll oversee the investigation from Washington. Is that so bad?"

"This is my city, Mr. President. I grew up here. I've lived here my entire life. We've all been devastated by this calamity. Two thousand people are dead, more than four thousand injured. I . . . I don't feel like I can leave right now."

President Roberts looked out the window, his fingers drumming on his left thigh. "I'm not used to being turned down, Caroline. There a dozen candidates behind you who will jump at this opportunity the moment I ask."

"Yes, sir. I'm not turning you down. It's a big decision. I just need some time to think about it."

16

Caroline Bannister stood gazing out a bank of windows five hundred feet above the street. She'd once worked here, at this prestigious Charlotte law firm, before being appointed as the United States Attorney for the Western District of North Carolina. She liked the trappings, the polished wood, the shining brass, this perch from which she could look over the city.

She'd decided this was where she would start searching for the bomber. The FBI was consumed with the forensic evidence and investigating how the van and bombing materials had been acquired. The FBI knew Williams would have needed access to funds. Agent Mullen was more than willing to let her take charge of the financial side. They needed to know how Williams had financed the bombing.

Kendall Rohr strode into the room, his silver hair perfectly coiffed, a thin smile on his lips. The handshake was more than perfunctory, but less than sincere. They settled at the end of a table that could seat forty, in high-backed chairs covered with calfskin.

"These are new," Caroline said, rubbing her hands along the chair arms, the leather as soft and supple as new gloves.

"We've made a few upgrades since you were a partner," Rohr said.

"Business must be good."

"Business is good."

She smiled, the pleasantries necessary, softening the approach to a tough topic. "Kendall, I'm here as a friend and a colleague, not as United States Attorney," she began. "You represented the Mayor's election campaign. And, I presume you represented him in his personal affairs." She paused, gauging his reaction.

"Well, I can't disclose the identity of our clients, Caroline. You know that."

"It's not confidential, Kendall. The firm has represented the City and its Mayor for a long time."

"What are you looking for?"

"Campaign finance records. Not the summary reports that are public record, but the underlying financial data."

If he was surprised, Rohr didn't show it, maintaining an even countenance, his eyes steady. He'd had a lot of practice. "I imagine, Caroline, that those campaign finance records show that a very large number of people and groups contributed to Mayor Williams' election campaign, including most of the partners in this law firm."

"Yes, myself included," Caroline said. "But I have to look into this. I have to determine whether Mayor Williams used campaign funds to support terrorist activities." She held his eyes while she told this lie.

Rohr contemplated the backs of his hands for a moment. "What are you implying, Caroline?"

"We're just having a conversation, Kendall. A conversation off the record. A conversation that doesn't have to turn into a subpoena or a grand jury investigation."

Rohr nodded, analyzing the potential repercussions, but remained stoically silent. The law firm had an image, one honed and polished for more than a century. The firm had spawned trial and appellate judges, state lawmakers too numerous to count, seven United States Congressmen, two United States Senators, and five US Attorneys. Caroline Bannister was the fifth. Any hint of a link between Rohr's representation of the Mayor and an act of terrorism would devastate the law firm's reputation. If he stonewalled the investigation, the perception would be that the firm knew something about the Mayor's activities after he went missing.

"You're already looking into this, that's obvious. Have you empaneled a grand jury?"

"Oh, Kendall, you know I'm not at liberty to disclose something like that. Grand jury proceedings are secret. But if I had a grand jury looking into this, would I be here just for a conversation?" She smiled, allowing that gesture to replace words, letting the fire burn slowly beneath him.

Rohr shifted in his seat, crossed and uncrossed his legs. "Caroline, I can't disclose …"

"You can, Kendall. The crime-fraud exception to the attorney-client privilege. Rule 1.6 (b)(4)."

"Crime-fraud exception. What crime?"

"Do I need to say it out loud? You've already connected those dots, I'm quite sure. The only question is whether you connected those dots before the bombing. What did you know Kendall, and when did you know it?"

"I didn't … You can't be serious, Caroline. You know me better than that."

"I thought I did."

"You ..." he trailed off in a sign of capitulation.

Caroline leaned forward, put both elbows on the table and clasped her hands together. "You know how this works, Kendall. I don't want this to become public any more than you do. This is just you and me having a quiet conversation. Off the record. Whatever you need to tell the other four hundred attorneys here, that's your business."

"Five hundred and twenty-seven," he said.

"Congratulations, you crossed the five-hundred mark. Whatever you want to tell those attorneys, that's your decision. But I'm going to get the information, one way or the other. Cooperation begets leniency. All the way to the end."

"I don't know anything about the Mayor's nefarious activities," Rohr said, his face drained of color, his shoulders hunched so that his fitted shirt bunched in the front.

"Then I guess I'm wasting my time," she said. "Can you accept subpoenas on behalf of the firm? Sure you can. You're still on the management committee, right? Let's hope the media doesn't get wind of this." She rose from her chair, sliding the legs back on rotating casters, completing the bluff. She doubted the campaign finance records would lead her anywhere, but she had to look. If the person blackmailing them had followed the Mayor and witnessed his abduction and the aftermath of his trial, perhaps his name would appear somewhere in the documents. She knew Williams was not the bomber. But the man sitting across the table from her, his head in his hands, did not know that.

"Wait. I need some time. There are ethical considerations involved. Caroline this is ... this is overwhelming."

"Is Jerry still the firm's ethics advisor?"

Rohr nodded.

"Good. Go talk to him. Right now. I'll wait here."

Rohr left the room and closed the door.

Twenty minutes later, Caroline rode the elevator down, a thumb drive in the right pocket of her jacket, a thumb drive that contained six years of financial records for Mayor Williams' election campaigns.

17

Viktor Volkov drove toward a destination in the rolling hills of Virginia, where the Russians had a safehouse disguised as a horse farm. He could have flown to D.C. and driven down, as he usually did, but he had been overtaken by a sense of foreboding. There was no particular catalyst for this dread; rather, it was the absence of anything concrete. Things were too quiet. Nothingness made him nervous.

Since the authorities had declared they found their terrorist, in the bone fragments of the once-beloved Mayor, the buzz of law enforcement had subsided like cicadas quieted by sunrise. "Normal" was not the word he would have used to describe the changed atmosphere, but as he observed his patients, and other shoppers in the grocery store, and the nurses and doctors scurrying about in the hallways of the hospital, it was apparent that people had returned to their lives. Anxiety and fear had disappeared from their faces. Conversations once held in veiled whispers turned to celebration after the bomber was declared dead.

Volkov should have been relieved, but amid the quiet, he became more cautious. Airports and other places where he might be required to show identification, or that had networks of cameras, became too risky, for if *he* was able to mastermind a bombing of that magnitude and frame an innocent dead man as the terrorist, perhaps the FBI and Homeland Security were concocting a similar scheme to entrap him. He knew the investigation was not over. They would continue to piece together all of the story, trying to find where the Mayor had purchased the fertilizer and diesel fuel. They would trace the van to the auction yard in Florida. ATF would investigate the source of the Tovex, which they would not find because it had been smuggled into the United States in a diplomatic pouch. If the FBI had not already concluded there was an accomplice, the absence of a money trail in the Mayor's personal financial records would further their suspicions. If the FBI couldn't trace the purchases of the bomb-making materials and the van back to the Mayor, then there had to be a financier hiding in the shadows.

As he drove up the highway, Danya stood in the back compartment of the SUV, momentarily blocking his rear view. The Caucasian Mountain Dog turned around twice, pawed at his blankets, and settled onto a pallet behind the wire divider. Volkov had brought the dog along for . . . he wasn't sure why exactly, because the hassles of having a huge dog on this trip certainly outweighed the benefits. Perhaps Danya was extra security, security he did not normally need. Security he could summon with a sharp whistle.

As he drove, his mind drifted involuntarily to Ella Winslow. During the post-operation consults, she stared at him in silence with a look he could not identify, her eyes narrowed, her lips in a tight line. When he leaned over her, a surgical mask covering most of his face to minimize the risk of infection, she stared at him with eyes so dark they absorbed everything and reflected nothing.

The nightmares had begun shortly after the amputations. Nightmares of his sister Anna, whom he had not thought about in years. And in these visions, from which he bolted upright in his bed with sweat dripping down his back, Ella sometimes appeared, a mirror image of his sister, Ella's face tattered with scars he had promised to heal, and Anna's visage marked by the blue tinge of suffocation.

On the night he had lowered the pillow to Anna's face, she had succumbed to it, sending chills up his spine. In recent days, he had scanned old and creased photographs of his sister onto his laptop. One showed her reclining on grass next to a river, her head against a large rock, her face turned to the sun. He arranged this photograph side-by-side with a digital photograph of Ella's healing face. Their bone structure was almost identical, including the cheekbones, brow, and curve of their jawline. Their mouths were wide, their noses narrow, their eyes darkly defiant. When he studied the digital enhancements of Ella's future features—the scars erased, the skin healthy—he realized he was resurrecting Anna.

He pulled into a rest stop in rural Virginia, the area surrounded by dense forest. After snapping a stout leather leash to Danya's collar, he allowed the dog to roam the grounds tenuously tethered. Other owners pulled their dogs in close as his two-hundred-pound bear dog bounded by, pulling him along. When Danya had finished his dog business, Volkov urged the dog into the back compartment of the SUV with a treat and then went inside the building. Volkov returned to the car, took out his phone, scrolled through the search results, and found a place nearby.

When he arrived, Volkov parked his SUV against a wooden fence, the rear license place obscured from the parking lot and the mildly curious. He removed two hard-sided cases from the front passenger seat of the car and carried them to a wooden bench. Only one other person was at the range, and they gave each other a wide berth. From the small case he removed a Makarov pistol, snapped in a magazine, and pulled the slide back to load the first copper-headed bullet in the chamber. He spread his feet wide, took a deep breath, and aimed down-range at a target twenty-five yards out. He emptied the magazine, the bullets piercing the target in a grouping the size of a grapefruit. He removed his safety glasses and wiped his brow with his shirt sleeve, then replaced the pistol in the plastic case, unloaded.

Volkov unlocked the larger case and removed the AR-15. It was similar to the rifle he had used at the country club, a rifle whose parts he had disassembled and disposed of in unconnected places. He inserted a banana clip holding thirty Remington .223 cartridges, then settled on the shooting bench. He bent to the scope, his left elbow on a bean bag, and sighted a target 100 yards out.

The first shot pierced the center of a circle the size of a deer's heart, the blast loud even through his ear protectors. He shot eleven more times, his trigger tempo increasing as he no longer cared much about his aim. Still, he put all twelve bullets into a grouping the size of a basketball. He stood and moved away from the bench and onto an open expanse of trampled grass, pressed the gun to his shoulder, and eyed a rusted barrel fifty yards away. The remaining 18 bullets in the magazine left the gun in less than ten seconds, creating a staccato thunk as each hit the metal barrel like hail on a tin roof.

Enveloped by the acrid smell of gunpowder, Volkov laid the gun on the bench, the barrel still smoking. He pulled off his ear protectors and his yellow-tinted shooting glasses and stuffed them in a nylon bag. The other shooter had left. For a few minutes all Volkov heard was a ringing in his ears, until the chatter of birds resumed in the trees bordering the range. He stashed the gun cases and the nylon bag in the floor of the passenger compartment of the SUV and drove off.

He arrived at the safehouse, a meeting place in the countryside surrounded by a white board fence, where a handful of horses grazed. Danya bounded from the back of the vehicle without invitation, racing through the grounds like a wild bear. He sniffed at the horses but did not provoke them, keeping his nose to the ground and searching the perimeter, as he was trained to do. Volkov followed him at a distance close enough to whistle a command, if necessary. With sniffs and snorts, Danya completed his inspection of the farm without straying far from his master and returned at the piercing command of the dog whistle, bounding into the back of the SUV and plopping down on his pallet of blankets.

Alexei Perchenko, a KGB officer portraying a diplomat stationed at the Russian Consulate in Washington, D.C., greeted Volkov on the front sidewalk. In a living room adorned with Russian furniture and artwork, Perchenko set out glasses of black tea and a plate of brown crackers topped with cream cheese and caviar. Volkov scanned the room, noting several electronic devices designed to stymie outside microphones, and other devices that blocked transmissions from within the house. It was the only reason he had been allowed to keep his cell phone. Volkov pulled his cell phone from his pants pocket. Though he had passed a cell tower less than a mile away, he had zero service bars.

After a few minutes of idle conversation that never veered toward the real reason for this meeting, they ventured out into the back yard, forty yards or so from the house in a small grove of trees, and opened a hatch disguised as the cover of a septic tank. They descended an aluminum ladder into a large space furnished with camp chairs and a folding table. Shelves of food and bottled water lined two walls, enough provisions for a handful of people to survive for six months or more.

"This was built during the height of the Cold War, by a tobacco magnate who feared a Russian nuclear attack," Perchenko said in Russian. "Ironic, isn't it?"

Volkov scanned the space, which was buttressed with thick concrete walls and ceiling. In the corner was a composting toilet sectioned off by a portable partition, painted black. Next to the sink was a shower wand for quick rinses. Two chartreuse-colored radiation suits hung behind the metal ladder. A lower shelf held a row of novels. He noted the titles of a dozen spines listing Russian authors. This space resembled his own bunker, tucked beneath his metal barn, though his bunker was more spacious and had a better stock of weaponry. Perchenko's bunker was not designed as a place to launch attacks; it was built as a place to hide out, temporarily.

"Faraday cage?" Volkov asked.

"Of course. We are fully protected."

Perchenko was new to him, his fourth handler in a dozen years, and Volkov maintained a cautious demeanor, saying little, smiling when appropriate. He knew little about Perchenko's background except that Perchenko knew the timing and mode of their clandestine communications, something he could have learned only from the previous handler. Volkov sipped water from a plastic bottle and, when his inspection of the bunker was complete, plopped into a red canvas chair.

"The President is most pleased with your latest mission, Comrade Volkov," Perchenko said, referring obliquely to the bombing of the Charlotte arena.

"*Spasibo*," Volkov replied.

"The second highest number of casualties ever on American soil, engineered by a Russian agent and made to look like the act of a madman American politician. Brilliant in all of its facets."

"*Spasibo*." Volkov shifted in the chair. "What do you know of my retirement?"

Perchenko shrugged and smiled at the same time. "The most prized Russian operative in America is still needed. You are too valuable to leave America just yet. We have even bigger plans for you."

After all he had done for the Motherland, he deserved to go home. He had presumed this meeting was called to discuss the details of his return, but that was not the case. He was perturbed, but he managed to mask his frustration.

"You deserve a parade in Moscow, in my opinion," Perchenko said. "You have been here for almost three decades, yes?"

"Twenty-eight years," Volkov said. "But inactive until four years ago."

The KGB recruited him when he turned fifteen. Not in a way that included an option to decline, but with unsubtle threats, both to Viktor and to his parents. Viktor's murder of his sister had captured their attention. The recruiter showed the family a picture of a prison camp in Siberia, sooty buildings in the snow, bleak faces of men verifying the desperation of their doomed lives. Viktor was shipped by train to a school in Moscow where his indoctrination began. He was neither large nor small, but a lean teenager, with intense eyes that come only from doing things other people would never attempt. His talent was that he lacked compunction, the capacity for empathy or remorse.

Young Viktor also had an aptitude for science, especially biology and anatomy. And in an era when the rest of the world saw the toppling of the Berlin wall as a sign that the Soviet Union's power would disappear like steam rising from a sidewalk grate, the KGB altered its mission to survive. When communism was officially abolished in the Soviet Union by Mikhail Gorbachev, and the Soviet Union itself was dissolved, immigration policies in the United States were relaxed, especially when it came to immigration from the Soviet Bloc. Scientists, political refugees and young men like Viktor Volkov were among the half million migrants from the former Soviet Union granted immigration visas. A dozen years later, he became an American citizen.

He had gone to medical school in the northeast and relocated to Charlotte because he preferred warm weather. A stint in a medical practice specializing in cosmetic surgery had trained him well. He remained a sleeper agent all of this time, learning his craft, biding his time, waiting for a contact that might never come. And when it did, he resigned from the practice and started his own, where he could work mostly in solitude, away from the prying eyes of his doctor partners, without scrutiny.

"So what is this bigger plan I am needed for, Comrade?" Volkov asked.

"You have researched viruses, yes?"

Volkov nodded. "During medical school."

"Your experience will be a great asset." Perchenko broke into a broad smile, unable to contain his enthusiasm. "This has been approved at the highest levels," he said.

"What are they planning?" Volkov asked in a blunt tone.

Perchenko leaned forward. "An engineered virus. Unleashed on America. Delivered through the flu vaccine." Perchenko sat back in the canvas chair and clasped his hands together behind his head.

"Influenza vaccine isn't a biological weapon," Volkov said. "Flu vaccine doesn't cause people to get the flu."

"Do you think we are ignorant, Comrade Volkov?" Perchenko's eyes bore into him. "Our best scientists have been working on this for years. They've recently had a break-through. The flu vaccine is merely the delivery system."

Volkov nodded, feigning agreement, the scope of it just beginning to register. He remembered that the Spanish Flu of 1918 killed an estimated 50 million people worldwide, more than 675,000 in the US. "So what is the biological agent?" Volkov said.

"It will be provided when it is time," Perchenko replied.

"You don't know," Volkov said. "They haven't told you. They don't trust you with that information."

Perchenko forced a smile, the muscles in his jaw bulging. "It is not necessary that we know all of the details, Comrade. It should be sufficient for us that when this is over, Russia will be the world's only superpower, returned to her rightful glory."

Volkov steepled his fingers beneath his chin. "This plan is beyond ambitious. Retaliation by the United States will be swift and furious."

"Furious perhaps, but not likely swift. Our hackers will disrupt the communications systems, both internet and satellite, which will slow the Americans' response to the epidemic."

Volkov contemplated this. He now saw that his missions at the country club and sports arena were merely preludes, designed to gauge his capabilities and loyalty for a mission that was almost unfathomable in scope. "It might start a third World War," he said.

"We are prepared for that."

"For mutual destruction?"

"The Americans will stand down before it gets to that," Perchenko said.

"There are at least a dozen places where we could fail."

"We will not fail," Perchenko said. "That is not an option."

Volkov knew his reservations didn't matter. He and Perchenko were both pawns in a game of chess played by masters who didn't care about what happened to their soldiers. He would never go home. He could see that now. Promises, whether ancient or recent, would never be met. As he stared at Perchenko, he realized that at some point while he was carrying out this complicated and ambitious mission, he would be killed by this man whose face could not keep a secret.

18

Caroline Bannister unlocked the safe in the back wall of her kitchen pantry, its door hidden by a tiered plastic shelf filled with cans of soup and vegetables. Some of the cans were several years old. She pulled a thumb drive from the safe, closed the door with a thud that sounded loud in the quiet house, and replaced the riser and the cans. She shut the pantry door with a click, then opened it again, plucked a can of chicken-noodle soup from the shelf, and set it on the counter. While the soup began to warm in a pot on the gas range, she opened her laptop and plugged in the thumb drive. After peering into the retina scanner and unlocking the computer, she pressed a piece of gray tape over the camera eye above the screen.

She opened files that were labeled by year, clicking through the innocuous public filings and reports, until she came to the financial ledgers. She scanned the list of donor deposits that exceeded four hundred pages for a single year, and then the list of payees, which was much shorter. She had access to software programs that would cull through and analyze this data, though she was no expert at using the software. She preferred the same methods her dad had used when he was reviewing case evidence as a detective. He always told her there was no substitute for the subliminal mind, which would hold information that was seemingly unimportant, only to reveal it at the appropriate time, sometimes during a dream, or while peering into the refrigerator for the last can of beer, or while making love. He had not said that last part. That was her contribution, and it was sometimes true.

She returned to the soup only when she heard the rattle of the pot lid on the stove. She removed the pot from the burner and let it cool. She placed the soup pot on a trivet next to the laptop and ate directly from the pot with a teaspoon. She followed the soup with a glass of burgundy, one glass only, because she wanted her mind relaxed yet ready, not murky or asleep. As she worked, Astrophe jumped into her lap and settled.

She was two and a half hours into the next day when she closed the laptop. She had found nothing. Well, that was not true. It was there, in little unconnected segments, bits that needed to be linked to make them into bytes.

She thought of it in that digital way only because she was working on a computer, and tired, but she knew that the better metaphor involved jumbled letters that needed to be arranged into words. She examined the yellow legal pad on the table, flipping the pages, reading notes that might settle into her brain somewhere, which she hoped would connect in the night. It had worked for her innumerable times before, and she had to trust that process.

She rose at dawn, poured herself a cup of coffee and stepped into the backyard. The grass was higher than it should have been, and the planting beds were overgrown with weeds. Though her father had promised to take care of her yard, he obviously had not. She shouldn't have expected he could handle it. She should have recognized that his promises were solely for him now, little goals that might provide daily accomplishments, something to seize upon as he was losing his mind. She knelt by a bed of lilies and gathered a handful of mulch. It was cool and dry. Perhaps it was time to bring the carnivorous plants inside. If she could find the time.

She went to the bathroom and stared in the mirror. She tousled her hair, which was mostly auburn. A few renegade grey hairs had emerged near her part, and she made a mental note to set up an appointment with her stylist for a cut and color. She pulled open the glass door on the shower, marked with the white outlines of dried water droplets, and turned on the water. She washed sleep from her eyes, then allowed the water to cascade over her head.

She stood there for a time, in this makeshift sensory deprivation chamber, sound constant, the tactile sensation of warmth enveloping her, tasting nothing, seeing nothing, smelling the non-odor of water. She stepped away from the water and lathered her underarms and legs with shaving cream. As she ran a razor beneath her arms and up her shins and over her knees, she watched the suds, diluted by the water but still floating like tiny cumulus clouds. Many raindrops coming from the sky, collecting in a lake somewhere, sucked into a system that filtered it, sanitized it and pumped it into a labyrinth of pipes too complex to contemplate, then under her yard and into her house, released by a simple turning of a knob, washing over her and collecting on a tile floor, then funneled into a single drain so it could eventually return to that lake.

She dressed in a hurry and padded to the kitchen in bare feet, flipped through the pages of the legal pad and clicked on her laptop. Back and forth from the notes to the accounting records, from the records to the notes, she finally discerned the labyrinth of pipes too complex to see. Money from thousands of donors, accumulating raindrops that filled the cisterns, originating from political donors local and national, cleaned and sanitized, and much of it returned to a reservoir in the guise of a nonprofit company called New View Democracy, LLC. The company was organized in Nevada.

Kendall Rohr's law firm, the firm where she had once been a partner, had a Las Vegas office. Using her computer, she checked the company filings on the Nevada Secretary of State's website. New View had been organized four years earlier. The registered agent was an attorney in the law firm's Vegas office. Caroline did not recognize her name. The annual filings listed a single manager for the limited liability company—Kendall Rohr.

As she stood in her bare feet in the kitchen, fingers drumming the counter top, she hatched a theory. Carmelo Williams' donor lists included individuals who made small contributions, as well as political action committees. By federal law, no donor can contribute more than $5,000 per year directly to a candidate or a candidate's campaign. While that law caps donations to a campaign, it does not limit amounts that can be spent on issue campaigns, a result of the Supreme Court's decision in *Citizens United*, which spawned the rise of Super PACs. The law also does not limit the flow of money *out* of a candidate's campaign.

She opened her laptop again and scanned the campaign's payment records for the last year. There were regular payments to New View. In the week before they put Mayor Williams on trial in secret, there was a final electronic transfer from the campaign's account of $10,000, also to New View. Though it was murky, Caroline had discovered what looked like a money trail.

19

"I've been looking into Mayor Williams' campaign finance records," Caroline said from a rocking chair in front of the stone fireplace at the Judge's lake house. Flames crackled the seasoned oak logs, throwing much needed warmth on all five of them. "I traced a large number of financial disbursements from Mayor Williams' campaign to a company called New View Democracy, LLC. It's a Nevada company. Kendall Rohr is its sole manager."

"Kendall Rohr?" the Judge asked. "Isn't he the managing partner of your old law firm?"

"Not managing partner, but he's on the firm's management committee. Rohr was the attorney for Mayor Williams' election campaign. His firm does a lot of legal work for the City of Charlotte."

"He's appeared before me on a few matters," Westlake said. "Always seemed like a straight-up guy."

Caroline continued. "The State of Nevada doesn't require public disclosure of LLC members or corporate shareholders, so there's no public information on who owns New View. And New View hasn't filed any reports with the Federal Elections Commission regarding its donors. It has reported limited information to the FEC regarding its expenditures."

"So is this a dead-end?" Johnstone asked.

"Unless I issue a grand jury subpoena, or I get a warrant. But I'm not inclined to do either." She glanced at Raleigh, then continued. "Here's why. I undertook the review of the financial records for Williams' campaign because, if there was something there, I could find it and control the release of that information. I can truthfully report to the FBI that I didn't find anything in the records that would support the theory that Williams had an accomplice. I can also report that there are undocumented cash disbursements from the campaign in various amounts that would have been sufficient to purchase diesel fuel, fertilizer and the van the bomber used. It's not much of a paper trail, but it's a paper trail that leads back to Williams. That might be enough for the FBI to conclude there was no accomplice, and close the investigation."

Caroline rose from the rocking chair and went to the bar, poured herself a glass of wine and returned. She sat down on the warm rocks of the hearth and faced them as she might a jury of four. "The more I look into these records, the more suspicious I've become that Williams was involved in something nefarious. I don't know what—maybe money laundering—but if everything was aboveboard, why have such large expenditures going to a dark money company where nothing is transparent?"

"It looks suspicious to me," Westlake said. "I'd issue a warrant on that evidence but we can't go that route. So where does that leave us?"

"Kendall Rohr designed this web, and I have little doubt that he did it in a way that we'll never know who's behind the companies, or what the money was used for. He probably doesn't even know where the money went. He's a manager in name only. Rohr's not even a signatory on any of the bank accounts. The company has a Vegas accountant. But even if I keep probing, I'm not going to find checks or cash receipts for bomb-making materials."

"So you don't foresee finding anything that will help us identify our blackmailer?" Westlake asked.

"Unfortunately, no."

"I know you guys don't agree with me, but I think Volkov is the one blackmailing us," Johnstone said. "He had access to Abdul's blood and tissue, and he could have planted it at the country club. He'd have a strong motive to want Abdul eliminated so he couldn't testify at the trial."

"We've been over this, David," Caroline said. "Even if Volkov did keep Alnoor's blood and tissue, which is a big stretch, that doesn't mean he's our blackmailer. Besides, he has an alibi for the night of the shooting. He was on duty at the hospital. We checked and triple-checked the hospital records. And all of the medical waste from Alnoor's surgeries was accounted for and incinerated. That eliminates Volkov as a suspect. If our evidence points to anyone other than Alnoor, it's someone at the mosque who had access to his blood. But I've said it before, and I'll say it again, we had the shooter in custody, and I was about to convict him and give him the needle."

"You're still bitter that you didn't get to try him, that you didn't get your big win," Johnstone spat. "You can't be objective anymore."

"And you can, David?"

Judge Westlake intervened. "This squabbling isn't getting us any closer to finding out who is blackmailing us. What about the emails that were sent under the Mayor's name from Africa? Whoever did that obviously knew the Mayor was dead and created the fake accounts to make everyone think he was alive. Can't we trace the emails back to the source?"

"Sock puppets," Caroline said.

"What?" asked Westlake.

"The fake accounts are called sock puppets. We don't know who created the accounts, and we can't find out because the messages were routed through a VPN, probably using Tor or a similar router that sends the messages through hundreds of stations to mask the origin. The emails look like they came from Africa, but could have originated anywhere in the world. The FBI has reached a dead end on that one."

"So we're operating in the dark," Westlake said. "Do we have any leads on the person who shot Marshal Smathers?"

Perez spoke up. "No, sir. All of the security footage, both from the courthouse and surrounding buildings, has been rounded up and reviewed. There's no video of the shooter. No fingerprints near the scene. No DNA evidence, which isn't surprising, given that this happened in the middle of a storm. There weren't a lot of people on the street that morning. We've found a handful of witnesses, none of whom saw or heard anything. Someone mentioned seeing a nun that morning, walking in the direction of the Basilica, but we haven't been able to get a good description of her."

"So what's the consensus at the Marshal's Service?" Westlake asked.

"The shooter is in the wind," Perez said. "Nobody's saying it, but without some luck, we'll never find him."

"We're not going to find the perp who shot Marshal Smathers," Caroline said. "And if Alnoor didn't commit the massacre at the country club—which is a big 'if' in my opinion—then we probably won't catch the guy who did it. Thirty-eight percent of murders are never solved. After 48 hours, the odds of solving a murder drop dramatically. Samuel Little killed more than 90 people and got away with it for 42 years. We catch killers when a victim is murdered by a family member, or we have an eyewitness. We don't have either in this case. Not to be pessimistic, but I hear it all the time from my dad and others in law enforcement: 'We only catch the dumb ones.' And this one isn't dumb; he's very smart."

"But we can't stop looking," Johnstone said.

They let this hang in the air like rain clouds threatening to burst.

"There's something else," Caroline said. She turned and stared out the large windows at the gray waters of Fontana Lake. "Just after the press conference announcing Williams was the bomber, the President asked me to be his new Attorney General."

From his chair, Westlake looked at her, his eyebrows arched. He opened his mouth to speak, but his voice caught. He rarely showed hesitation. "So you've decided to accept?" he asked.

"I haven't decided. Part of me wants to stay in Charlotte, near my parents, to be the good daughter and help my mother care for my dad and his Alzheimer's. Another part of me knows that becoming AG is the logical next step. It would be hard to pass up. I can do a lot of things in that position, make big policy changes that will impact the system of justice in our entire country, not just a small swath of the western part of our state."

"If you move to D.C., you won't be trying cases anymore," Westlake countered. "And you won't really be able to help us seek justice for the victims who don't have a voice. At least not the way we do it." At the meeting at her house, he had given her, and all the rest of them, an explicit out. As he tried to read her eyes, to see if she'd already decided, she kept her gaze fixed on some indeterminate point in the dusk.

20

The white marble gravestone gleamed in the sunlight. Caroline and Herb Bannister stood before her sister's grave. Her father seemed to not know where they were. He leaned forward and silently read the headstone. A flicker of recognition lit his eyes, then faded away.

"Daddy, do you know where we are?"

Herb Bannister glanced around, unable to find the word.

"We're in a cemetery. And this is Catherine's grave," she said.

"Oh, yes. Catherine . . ." he said in an uncertain voice. "She was your cousin, right?"

Herb Bannister had been a Charlotte cop for almost thirty years, rising to detective in the homicide division in a city with plenty of murders to investigate. His decline had been slow, its start almost imperceptible—a forgotten name, an appointment missed. At the firing range, his aim, once tight and focused, had begun to wander across the paper targets. And with it, a frustration rose in him like flood waters approaching his house, threatening to destroy everything. As the Alzheimer's overtook him, his speech had become this way, most statements a guess, utterances punctuated as questions.

"No, daddy. Catherine was my sister. She was your daughter. I'm wearing her necklace," Caroline said, pulling the locket from beneath her blouse. "See, it has her initials on it."

At this he tilted his head to the side, eyeing the piece of jewelry. "Catherine," he said, his lips parted. "She was my daughter."

They sat down on grass that was soft and spongy. The day was unseasonably warm, the ground cool. "Do you remember when she died?" Caroline asked him in a soothing voice.

"It says right there 1992," Herb pointed. "That was . . ."

"No. I mean, do you remember the night she was killed?"

Her father leaned back, his arms supporting him, looking at a sky pocked with wispy clouds, as if the answer could be discerned there. "I thought . . ." He drifted away again. In other circumstances, Caroline might have thought the man who had accidentally killed his own daughter was feigning a memory lapse, but Herb Bannister was not faking. His disease had been confirmed by two doctors, and these memory gaps were occurring more frequently. There were times when he was totally lucid, and there were days when he could not remember his wife's name, could not recall that Caroline was alive and Catherine dead, did not know who they were to him. Sometimes he could not remember his doctor's name, or where he kept the medication prescribed to combat his decline. Yesterday, he had been unable to find the bathroom in the hallway of his home.

Caroline pulled out her cell phone, swiped the screen, then punched the icon for video. She scrolled down to the video she had labeled as: "Catherine's Truth." It was the video Raleigh had shown her the night they received the blackmailer's demand. She'd copied the video from Robert Crenshaw's cell phone, a clandestine interview between Robert and her father, secretly recording Herb Bannister admitting he had accidentally shot his own daughter while trying to rescue her from a heroin den. The video proved that Carmelo Williams had not killed her sister. Caroline had replayed the video dozens of times, imprinting in her own mind the tilt of her father's head, his neck stretched yet wrinkled, as he acknowledged the killing in the unabashed voice of a man who had tried unsuccessfully to forget what he'd done. There had been no tears from him at this revelation, confirming to Caroline that her father was gone. In his stead was left an incomplete version of him, mostly bones and withering tissue and a decrepit mind. His smile had faded because he did not remember how to smile.

Sitting upon the verdant expanse of grass in the cemetery, with squirrels skittering about in the trees, she muted the sound and tapped the play button. Her father's image was stoic but jerky at times, as he and Robert moved about Herb's vegetable garden. She didn't want her father to know she was watching a video, didn't know why she was watching it at that time and place. After Raleigh revealed it to her, she had planned to show her father the video, to let him know that she had finally solved the mystery of Catherine's death. Viewing it for the first time, she'd been haunted by the revelation that her quarter-century quest to hunt down her sister's murderer had been in vain, that she had executed an innocent man. The man responsible for her sister's death had been right next to her all along.

She went back to the beginning of the video and poised her finger over the mute button, ready to activate the sound. Would her father recognize his own voice? What did she expect from him if he did remember that night? Would the video only send him deeper into darkness? She looked over at him and grasped his hand, a hand that had once wiped away her childhood tears, a hand that had held a smoking pistol in an abandoned house, a hand that had cradled the head of his dead daughter. His hand was bony, crossed by blue veins, and the flesh was thin and the texture of faded newspaper.

She could only imagine what a map of the electrical activity in her father's brain would look like in these moments—perhaps like a dark sky on a cloudy night, the light of recognition only occasionally shining through. Or, a heavy black curtain.

She turned off the video and slipped the cell phone back into her pocket. She decided she would never show the video to him. She owed him that.

"Daddy, when you were stuck on a case, had reached a dead end, what did you do?"

Herb plucked a handful of grass and rubbed the blades between his fingers, retreating to memories still barely held. "We went over everything again. We put photographs and news articles and witness statements on a board. Sometimes me and my partner would sit there and stare at the evidence for hours without talking. Sometimes we'd interview witnesses again, or watch video tape if we had it. We did a lot of brainstorming, but we didn't always solve it. When I left, there were dozens of cold cases in the department."

"But you didn't give up," Caroline said.

"No, we didn't give up. The victims—the victims and their families—they deserved justice. We just couldn't always give it to them."

"Do you remember any particular case, a case where you were stuck, and you kept investigating, and going over the evidence, and something clicked into place, and you caught the perp?"

He turned to her, put a frail hand on her forearm. "I don't remember a lot of my cases, honey. It's been too long. I just know that you have to keep at it. Go back and interview the witnesses again. People forget things, and then they remember. They know things but don't realize they have any significance."

She thought about that, about the thousands of witness interviews the FBI had conducted, though they had slowed since identifying Mayor Williams as the bomber. No one remembered seeing that particular van on the street, or driving into the loading dock. No one remembered anything amiss or out of place that night. Some of the victims had no memory of that night, nothing at all, that place in their minds swept clean by the blast.

She drove her father home and led him into the house.

He turned to her and drew his lips open with considerable effort. "This disease I have is the worst. Some days I don't know who your mother is. Some days I don't know who I am."

Caroline put her arm around his shoulder. "You were a good cop. And you're my dad. Don't forget that." She kissed him on his furrowed cheek.

After crinkling his eyes with recognition, he wandered through the kitchen and into the back yard, heading toward the vegetable garden where he had made his ominous admission, the tomato plants bending toward the ground with the weight of unpicked fruit.

Caroline found her mother asleep on the couch in the den. She plopped into a leather chair facing the television, emitting a sigh just loud enough.

"You're back," her mother said in the clear voice of someone who was not fully asleep. "How did it go?"

Caroline shrugged. "He didn't remember Catherine at first, thought she was my cousin. But then there was some recognition."

"It's the Alzheimer's. He has good days and bad. Not so many of the good anymore."

"Can you handle him, mom? Can you take care of him in his condition?"

Barbara Bannister sat up, smoothing her slacks at the knees. "Not for much longer, to be honest. I've been looking into hiring someone to come in to help, at least during the day. I want to keep him at home as long as I can."

Caroline appraised her mother, the dark circles beneath her eyes, the red veins at the corners that never fully went away. "I want to help, mom. I . . ."

Her mother emitted a smile that mixed gratitude and dismissal. "You can't, Caroline. It's not your responsibility. You have a busy career, and he won't even know you're here most of the time."

"I know. It's just . . . I don't want you to have to deal with it alone."

"I'm not alone. I've joined a support group, and we have meetings on-line. One of the things we keep reminding each other is that we're not alone, and we have to take care of ourselves, too."

Caroline nodded, knowing she'd lost the argument, remembering that she'd gotten some of her determination from her mother, even if she sometimes stretched it to stoicism. "I've been offered an opportunity, mom. It's a great opportunity, but I'd have to move. To D.C."

"The Supreme Court?" Barbara Bannister asked.

"No. Attorney General. Heading up the Justice Department."

"That's great, Caroline. And you're wondering if you take it if your father, or I, will resent you for it? You're wondering if we'll think you're abandoning us?"

"Yes. Exactly."

"Not in the least. We lost a daughter a long time ago, Caroline. Maybe because we kept her too close, maybe because we made too many decisions for her, and she didn't learn soon enough to make good decisions for herself. If your father thought for a second that you were hesitating in taking this position because of him, he couldn't live with it. It's hard enough for him to live with the knowledge that Catherine died from his gun."

"You know about that?" Caroline said. "You know how Catherine died?"

"Sure," her mother said, rising from the sofa. "He told me where he was going that night, what he was going to do. And when he came home, I'm the one who washed my daughter's blood out of his clothes. If we can handle that tragedy, we can deal with this. You go to Washington and put all of your focus and energy into your new position. Your father will be very proud of you."

21

Caroline picked up the desk phone in her office and punched in the number for the White House. She was routed through the switchboard and, after a few minutes, she was informed the Chief of Staff would take her call and was put on hold. She listened to most of "Amarillo By Morning" before the President himself picked up.

"Afternoon, Caroline. I'm presuming you're calling with good news. If it's bad news, you need to tell Carly," he said, referring to his Chief of Staff.

"It's good news, Mr. President. I'm accepting the nomination. And I want to thank you. I greatly appreciate this opportunity to serve my country."

"Wonderful. When can you get here?"

"How about Thursday?"

"That sounds fine. Carly or someone on her staff will be in touch about the arrangements. I'm looking forward to working with you, Caroline."

"Same here, Mr. President."

She put the phone in the cradle, satisfied she was doing the right thing, for any number of reasons. After she'd announced she's been offered the Attorney General nomination, Cunningham and Perez and Johnstone had left the lake house, leaving her alone with Raleigh for the night, his sullenness descending upon both of them like a gray, winter storm. He stomped about the house with his hands thrust into his pockets and stood for a long time looking out at the lake, though it was too dark to see the water, which was just an inky void in the distance.

She had settled down on the floor with Shiloh, on the braided rug in front of the fireplace, stroking the dog's ears, flicking the tip of Shiloh's tongue with a finger as it lolled from the dog's mouth. The dog's wiry hair, the color of dried apricots, coupled with the warmth of the logs sighing in the fireplace, gave her a sense of comfort she had not felt since before the night of the blackmailer's demand. Caroline fell asleep, only vaguely aware that Raleigh had left the room.

She found him in the basement, riding a stationary bicycle. They had once exercised together in this room while snow fell outside, she wearing a green leotard that his deceased wife Heather had once worn. Afterward, she had joined him in the shower. He had seemed surprised but did not resist, and they had what . . . made love? Was that the proper term? It seemed an inappropriate description of a complex situation. There was certainly no love involved, at least not on her side, and Raleigh was undoubtedly still angry at her for causing Robert Crenshaw's death. Since then, what had they become? Vigilantes and liars, for sure, but also indelibly bound to one another through their secrets, as if the secret trials were children they had raised together in a happier part of their relationship.

When he finished on the bike and stepped off, she snapped him with a large white towel, engendering something of a smile from him, though he tried to mask it.

"This might be our last night together," she said.

"So you've decided," he said. "You're going to D.C.?"

"I've got one last reservation to resolve."

"Not us, then? Not the group?"

"No. I know you understand, even if you don't want to admit it. You can't be angry over this."

"You're awfully presumptuous, telling me how I should feel."

She wasn't certain she understood his tone, whether it contained an acerbic taint, whether his mouth turned up at the corners with a hint of playfulness. She'd decided to take a risk, the ramifications of being wrong not dangerous. "You remember the time we worked out together down here?"

He nodded. "Not something I'd forget."

"Good. I'll meet you in the shower," she said.

When she had departed the next morning, he had been better, perhaps merely mollified, and they made concrete promises that he would come to D.C. after the dust from her confirmation hearing settled. She felt relief that she had not hurt him deeply with her announcement, or that if she had hurt him it was only temporary and would leave no permanent scar. But this conundrum over what to do about their relationship had been solved with a four-hundred-mile move, smoothing out weeks of discontent, mistrust and atrophy.

Caroline's desk phone buzzed, and her assistant let her know that Special Agent Mullen was waiting to see her. They settled in a conference room with an electronic signal blocker in the middle of the table, something she once thought she would never use but which now seemed indispensable.

She summarized her research into the Mayor's financial records, telling Agent Mullen that there were a few undocumented cash withdrawals that could have been used to purchase any number of items, but nothing in the records indicating that funds had specifically been funneled to illicit purposes or terrorist activities. There was nothing in the records to indicate that the Mayor had an accomplice, either.

Agent Mullen received this information with a firm nod, then summarized the Bureau's findings. "The white van was purchased with cash at a wholesale auction yard near Ft. Lauderdale, Florida, by a man roughly matching the Mayor's physical description. The purchase was made a week before the bombing. We've had no luck tracing the cell phones used to ignite the bomb, which could have been bought almost anywhere. The arena security guard who appeared to have taken a photograph of the van's driver did not upload anything to the cloud, and no images could be recovered from his destroyed cell phone. The most-accepted theory within the Bureau is that the guard recognized the Mayor was making a delivery and took a picture of a local celebrity. The video of the van driving down the ramp is the only video we've recovered. The rest was destroyed in the bombing, and there's no off-site backup. Enhancements of those images neither confirmed nor contradicted that the Mayor drove the van into the loading dock. The Mayor had rented a self-storage unit not far from his home, in which he kept boxes of campaign signs, buttons and other paraphernalia. We found traces of diesel fuel and fertilizer in the storage unit. We're pretty sure that's where he stored the bomb materials."

Caroline listened intently to the summary, looking for any missing shred. "What about motive?"

"We've interviewed his wife, his friends, City employees, and all the City Council Members," Mullen said. "To a person they were shocked that the Mayor could do something like this. But he left a typed suicide note in a steel box in the trunk of his car, which we found parked in a lot at the docks in Fort Lauderdale. We've been over it hundreds of times, analyzed every detail. His fingerprints are on the note, but he didn't sign it. I wouldn't call it a manifesto. It's rambling and doesn't make much sense. Talks about his disenchantment with politics and how money has ruined everything, but it doesn't lead us anywhere."

"So where does that leave us?" Caroline asked.

"We're tying up a few loose ends, but there's nothing to suggest that the Mayor had an accomplice. I talked to the Director, and to the AG, this morning. The long and short of it is, we've concluded that the Mayor acted alone." He closed the file and placed his hand on top of it. "Do you concur?"

Caroline nodded solemnly, trying to conceal from her features the niggling knowledge that the Mayor had not acted at all, that the bomb had exploded long after the Mayor had been murdered. "Are you going to make a public announcement?" she asked.

"There's a victims' conference at the hospital in two days. I've been asked to give a summary report to the bombing victims. It's an unusual request, but it seems appropriate, telling the victims first. We can issue a press release simultaneously so the press won't seem left out. Can you join me at the conference, Caroline?"

Her lips parted for a moment in surprise, then she regained her composure. "Sure. It will be one of my last acts as United States Attorney."

22

Agent Mullen stood behind a nondescript lectern in the auditorium at the hospital. In front of him were rows of doctors and nurses, seated at white tables. Behind the medical teams, approximately two thousand victims filled the seats in the amphitheater.

Mullen started by acknowledging it was rare to be addressing the victims of a terrorist attack, but this was a unique situation for everyone. He promised to provide details that had not been released to the public, and the details would not be gory. He asked for a show of hands from anyone who didn't want to hear details. Then, gazing out at the audience and recognizing that many could not raise their hands, he also asked that anyone who didn't want to hear about the bombing please say so. No one voiced an objection.

Agent Mullen recited the facts in a monotone, as if reading from a history book about an event none of them had witnessed. "A white van entered the loading dock of the Charlotte arena at 8:58 p.m. that night." On the large screen behind him, he put up a video of the van, taken from the front, as it descended the arena driveway. A timer in the corner tracked the scene in seconds. "For those of you who cannot see the screen, it is showing a video of the white delivery van coming down the ramp beneath the arena. The windshield and windows are heavily tinted, so the video doesn't show anything inside the van but a shadow behind the wheel."

"The cargo compartment didn't have any windows. On the side was painted the name of a local beer distributor. It wasn't their van. The delivery van was purchased by the perpetrator at a car auction in Florida about a week earlier, then painted to look like the van of a local beverage distributor." The video showed an oblique view of the driver's side window coming down, and the left arm of the driver, covered by a shirt, resting on the door sill. The video ended when the van passed beneath a camera. "That's the only video we have of the van. The video from other cameras in the arena was destroyed."

"We do know that the van backed up to the loading dock, with the front pointing back up the ramp. The concert was in full swing by this time. The perpetrator used what's called a burner cell phone, something you throw away, to call his wife's cell phone at precisely 9:03 p.m. That detail hasn't been previously released. She didn't pick up, and he didn't leave a message. Eight minutes later, the perpetrator ignited the bomb with that same cell phone."

Mullen took a deep breath and exhaled forcefully enough that everyone heard it over the microphone clipped to his tie. "Okay. This next bit of information hasn't been released publicly. You're the first to hear it. The perpetrator acted alone. There were no accomplices. We're sure of that."

Mullen paused, pulled a handkerchief from an inside pocket of his coat, and wiped it across his brow. Then he dabbed the cloth beneath his eyes and upon the slopes of his nose. "I want you to know," Agent Mullen said, "that seeing all of you here inspires me. You are incredibly brave and courageous. You are working to heal. You are working to resume your lives. That inspires me to stop this madness. To stop the random killing of innocent people. It is the Bureau's top priority. And mine too. And I want you to know from the deepest recesses of my heart, that I am truly sorry for what has happened to all of you. Those who survived, and those who didn't. I know that's not enough. It will never be enough, not until we stop every terrorist before . . . before they can act. The Bureau, and me personally, will help in any way we can. So feel free to call us. Feel free to come visit us at our regional office here in Charlotte. You will not be turned away. I promise you that. Now, Caroline Bannister, the US Attorney for the Western District of North Carolina, would like to say a few words."

Caroline approached the wooden lectern and gripped its edges, preparing to tell the biggest lie of her life. "First, let me thank you for this opportunity to speak to you, from my heart. When Agent Mullen first suggested it, I didn't know what to think. I'm used to issuing press releases and talking to the media. I didn't know how hard this would be, to stand here in front of you. Most of you were there, and I can only imagine what you went through, and what you're going through now. I had friends who were in the arena that night. Most of them didn't make it out." She bowed her head, looking down at her notes.

When she looked up, her eyes landed on Dr. Volkov, who was sitting at the second row of tables in the auditorium, stroking his beard. He gazed back at her with a countenance that gave nothing away. She returned to her notes. "I have separately reviewed all of the evidence in the case and concur that the . . . the perpetrator acted alone. I spoke to the Attorney General this morning, and the President. They both asked me to convey to you their deep sorrow over what has happened here in Charlotte, and to let you know that they are committed more than ever to utilizing every resource we have to stop these senseless acts of terrorism. I know that nothing I say can bring back those we have lost, or help the rest of you heal, but if you need anything at all, I invite you to call me and tell me how I can help."

Viktor Volkov listened to the speeches about what he—not the Mayor—had done. It was not a perfect crime, but when Mullen confirmed that the bomber had acted alone, Volkov quietly exhaled. The search for an accomplice was over. There were details the FBI would never discover. After the Mayor was executed and buried in a roadside ditch by the cabal headed by Judge Raleigh Westlake, Volkov had dug up the body, transported it to his barn, and stored it in a walk-in industrial cooler in the bunker. To stop the search for the missing Mayor, a group of Russian hackers known as Fancy Bear created fake social media and email accounts in the Mayor's name, and posted messages from various places in Africa. The Mayor's car had been abandoned in a state forest by the Mayor's executioners. Volkov had moved it to his barn, and then driven it to Ft. Lauderdale. After powdering the door handle and steering wheel with traces of Tovex, he left the Mayor's car in a parking lot at a cruise ship terminal. Roughly disguised as the Mayor, he had purchased the white van with cash at an auction yard and driven it back to Charlotte. Volkov had purchased the diesel fuel and fertilizer in small increments from various locations around Charlotte, over a period of many months, usually dressed as a woman, sometimes wearing a habib. He stored the diesel fuel in an underground tank at his farm, and stashed the fertilizer bags in the metal barn behind his house.

Volkov had typed the suicide note himself and left it in the metal box where the Mayor kept his handgun, in the trunk of the Mayor's car. It was a rambling note, a note written by someone who didn't understand what he was doing, who didn't truly understand himself. He had smudged the Mayor's dead fingers upon the paper to leave prints.

On the night of the bombing, he had placed the Mayor's body, with frost still upon his hair and eyebrows from the cooler, in front of the water-filled beer kegs, then pulled the body into the front seat after parking at the loading dock beneath the arena. Volkov then called the cell phone of the Mayor's wife, thankful that she had not answered the call from the unknown number. After making the call, he wedged the cell phone in the Mayor's dead hand. Traces of diesel fuel and fertilizer planted in the Mayor's storage unit, and all of the other evidence, pointed to only one person—the Mayor.

But Caroline Bannister knew otherwise, didn't she? He had taken the photographs of her standing outside of a tractor-trailer rig with the Judge and David Johnstone as the Mayor, obviously dead, was carried to the trunk of his own car. As Volkov watched her speaking at the lectern, perpetuating the lie with a straight face, he locked eyes with her only once. A brief, fleeting glance that he hoped would convey his attentiveness to her words, and nothing more. He had not expected her to be here, but as she spoke he felt safer, more assured about his secret. But there were still two unresolved issues. First, knowing that the Mayor was not the bomber, was she going to let the truth remain buried forever, or was she going to keep looking? And second, if she found him, what was he going to do with the photographs that linked them to the Mayor's death?

After Mullen and Bannister left the auditorium, the doctors began their presentations to the victims, focusing on how they might help their patients return to some semblance of a normal life. Normal was not possible for many of those in attendance, but the promises were designed to imbue this group with hope, a key asset in their recovery.

Volkov spoke near the end, his sympathetic voice a running commentary over still photographs of a hypothetical patient. The images showed her progression from a badly scarred victim lying on a hospital cot to a completely rehabilitated and rebuilt young woman with a gleaming smile. Shrapnel scars and burns glowed red-orange on her badly bruised face and, with the magic of digital imaging, gradually subsided to thin pale lines. Her visage progressed from shaved head, to wig, to a full head of hair enhanced by plug transplants.

When the presentations were over, the tables were rearranged into pods, allowing the patients to wander as they might at a convention for new tech products. In contrast to the sterile solitude of a treatment room, this setup bred an atmosphere of enthusiasm, both among the specialists and their patients. The organizers hoped the patients would interact and encourage each other.

Ella Winslow stood in a short line of patients waiting to see Dr. Volkov, who took photographs of each patient from several angles with a digital camera, loading them into a software program that produced before and after images. The transformation was striking in almost every case. In an instant, the patients were able to see their notable improvement from his future surgeries, something they could not easily visualize when they were talking about infections and ceramic joints and healing of the mind.

When Ella worked her way to the front, she plopped into a chair next to Volkov's table. He had not seen her since her discharge from the hospital. She looked pale. She turned her face to the right and left when asked so he could take additional photographs, even though he already had a trove of photographs of her.

On the computer screen facing her she watched her own image as he moved a stylus about on his side. Her scars faded and her eyebrows returned and thickened. The thin lines at the corners of her mouth disappeared, and the worry creases on her forehead, which had become wider and deeper over the past few weeks, relaxed. She had seen this miracle before while still in the hospital, but seeing it again proved she made the right decision in coming to the conference.

"Would you like to be a blonde?" Volkov asked. With the touch of a stylus, her imagined hair turned blonde. "How about a redhead?" Her hair turned to the color of deep fire.

"I like black just fine," she said.

He liked it, too. It was the color of Anna's hair, though Anna's hair never had this luster. He switched her hair back to black on the image, then made some adjustments, and Ella's lips became full. A few more tweaks and the faint scars on her neck disappeared completely.

"How confident are you my scars will go away?" she asked.

His eyes narrowed and his lips pursed within his beard, speckled with gray. "Ninety-eight percent." He reached across the corner of the table and ran his bare thumb across her cheeks and forehead, pulled a bit at the corners of her mouth. "You've made remarkable progress. With new surgical techniques and better skin-tone matching, and if you will diligently follow the recovery protocol I lay out for you, the scars will fade enough that they won't be noticeable with makeup."

Hope. It was easy for him to produce. The other doctors had a more difficult task ahead of them. Human beings were fatefully attached to their own self-image, their emotions falling with every mark and wrinkle, rising when tanned skin hid the flaws and dyes covered the gray. He had debated with his psychology cohorts, a long-running debate recently resurrected, whether he or they had a more positive impact on their patients. The psychologists argued that with the rehabilitation of a victim's mind came confidence and optimism and the will to make themselves better. He countered that he could provide the incentive for recovery in an almost instantaneous fashion, a few hours of surgery transforming the person's visage and, by extension, their own self-image. "You can't make them pretty or handsome, but I can," he said to finish the debate. It didn't matter who was right. These patients believed in his powers.

Ella stared at him as he finished his examination of her face. "When did you grow the beard?"

"A couple of weeks ago," he said. "Do you like it?"

"It changes your face." She rose from the chair to make room for the next patient. She stood there for a time, studying his face like someone planning to paint it from memory.

23

Raleigh Westlake drove Caroline to the Charlotte airport for her flight to Washington, D.C. Her cat was in a pet carrier in the backseat of his Lexus, next to Shiloh, who occasionally raised her large head to stare at the cat's paw that kept jutting through the slats of the carrier.

"They'll get along fine," he said. "Shiloh hasn't been exposed to cats, but she won't hurt Astrophe."

"In case he goes outside, will you get him one of those little metal tags with his name engraved on it?"

"Does he stay outside?" Westlake asked.

"During the day, not at night. Oh, I forgot to bring his litter box."

"I'll buy one for him," Westlake said.

At the airport he dropped her off, popping the trunk and pulling out her two suitcases. There was an awkward moment when she picked up both suitcases at once, occupying her hands, but when he cocked his head to the side she set the suitcases on the concrete, wrapped her arms around his neck, and kissed him. And then she snatched up the suitcases and hurried into the terminal.

He spent most of the drive back to his lake house thinking about something else they had talked about. Though she was distracted by her upcoming confirmation hearing, she had concurred they needed to trap their blackmailer somehow, if they could only narrow the list of potential suspects.

"Usually we wait for him to make a mistake," Caroline said. "That's why we don't catch some of the serial killers for decades."

"We don't have the luxury of waiting that long," Westlake countered. "This quiet period has been going on for a few months. It's gnawing at me. I think he's planning something. Maybe it's how to leverage us, or maybe it's another terrorist attack. I doubt he's simply sitting around doing nothing."

"I haven't heard about anything suspicious," she said.

"Nobody heard anything about the bombing before it happened," he reminded her.

"True. When I get to D.C. and have a chance, I'll poke around. Maybe the NSA has something on the radar."

"Are you in that loop?"

"I'd better be. Being invited to every National Security Council meeting was one of my requirements for accepting the nomination. That should give me inside information on any issue threatening the security of the United States, and planned acts of terrorism are high on that list." She said this with a certain solemnity, as if she couldn't imagine it being any other way.

This mollified him, stitching something positive into the dark and ominous mood that had cloaked him since Caroline's announcement that she was moving to D.C. His initial thought, on which he dwelled until it made him melancholy, was that she was running away, abandoning him and the team at a crucial juncture, when they needed her most. But as he gazed out at the blue haze of approaching mountains, he reflected on her assurance and began to see it as positive. Caroline could become an early warning detection system, alerting them to any coming peril.

He stopped at a store and picked up a cat box and litter. Upon arriving home, he decided the tile floor of the laundry room was a good place to put the litter box and let the cat sleep. He put both the box and the crate next to the dryer, then returned to the living room. He watched for about ten minutes as Astrophe explored the house, with Shiloh never far behind. He got down on the floor, and Shiloh came to him. He petted his dog, scratched her behind the ears and on her belly, while the cat remained at a distance.

This ordinariness had a calming effect on him, distracting him from the jeopardy that stalked him every day, not knowing when the blackmailer would release his damning evidence, or if the FBI would walk into his courtroom one morning and arrest him. He couldn't tolerate the waiting, devolving into the role of a condemned prisoner awaiting the outcome of endless appeals with no timetable. He recalled with a wry smile a client for whom he had filed a complex and contentious lawsuit in Atlanta, a business dispute that stalled as it ran into roadblock after roadblock. At one point when he had run out of suggestions to move the case forward, the client implored him to "do something, even if it's wrong."

It was good advice, if for no reason other than the damaging impact of stasis, especially to a man accustomed to moving through his life and career with sustained momentum. He stood by the windows looking out on the lake, its pewter surface rippled by a breeze. Beyond, on the opposite hillside, the leaves were half gone, the rest of the landscape blurred, a smattering of yellow and red and rust patterned on a background of pine green.

He changed into his running clothes, the need for physical movement acute, thinking vaguely that Caroline had probably arrived at her D.C. hotel by now. He made sure the dog and cat bowls were full of food and water. He refrained from looking at his cell phone for a message, leaving it on the kitchen counter.

He veered from the asphalt road onto a steep path that was little more than a game trail, traversed by animals stalking food or water. He followed a series of narrow switchbacks up the slope, jutting rocks and exposed roots in his way. His breathing became labored, his legs heavy, and a sheen of sweat soon covered his face and stained his shirt.

He stopped at a granite outcropping that had a winter's view of the valley. At the higher elevation, few leaves still dangled from the hickories, oaks and poplars that rose from the thin soil. The lake was a silver sliver, the sun reflecting off placid waters an hour before dusk. To his left he caught a glint of metal. When he knelt and peered through naked limbs he could make out the ruined roof of a cabin.

He ran farther up the game trail and found what might have once been a foot path, now overgrown and covered with leaves. It looked more like a natural culvert for rain and snowmelt than a path. As he descended the slope he braced himself on the trunks of saplings, at one point turning his feet sideways to the hill to keep from falling.

The cabin stood on a flatish piece of land that had taken someone a long time to carve out of the mountain. Saplings grew close to the foundation, some of the trees almost twenty feet tall, eclipsing the eave line and shooting above the roof. The cabin's two windows were broken, with shards of glass scattered inside and out. One of the leather hinges holding the front door had rotted and cleaved, leaving the door sagging. Westlake peered inside, seeing that Mother Nature had taken up residence in this hunting cabin that had not seen a human occupant in five years or longer. Vines had invaded the spaces between logs and the gaps between the wall and roof. Guano covered one wall and a section of floor, giving off the acrid smell of ammonia, though there were no bats hanging in the rafters. The cabin had no electricity and no running water. It was perfect for what he had in mind.

24

The sun was high when Westlake and his team began to climb the trail. Caroline, unable to get away from her confirmation hearing preparation in Washington, was not with them. Westlake took the lead, with Johnstone next in line. Perez and Cunningham bracketed Abdul Alnoor at the rear.

Alnoor wore jeans and a light green jacket, with hiking boots purchased from Goodwill, and a black knit cap on his head. His hands were not tied. Cunningham had detached the ankle monitor and left it in the van so the GPS would not record their trek. As Cunningham watched Alnoor's back, he kept his hand close to the Glock holstered on his right hip.

They hiked steadily, brushing past rhododendrons whose leaves had begun to curl against the cold. Aside from their footfalls and Johnstone's wheezy breathing, the forest was silent. At a turn in the trail marked by a flat rock, Johnstone requested a break. He sat down and lit a cigarette.

Westlake tipped a water bottle to his mouth. When sated, he stepped back along the line to Alnoor. "Do you want water?"

Alnoor nodded, then opened his mouth.

Westlake squeezed a stream of water into Alnoor's mouth. He swallowed, then nodded for another squirt. He swallowed again. "Thank you."

Westlake sat next to Johnstone on the exposed granite, looking south. The huddle of buildings that made up Bryson City was visible in the distance.

"Where are we?" Johnstone asked.

"Just outside of Great Smoky Mountains National Park," Westlake said. "The Park is behind us, no more than a quarter mile."

"This is your stomping ground, then," Johnstone said.

"I've done a lot of hiking and fishing in these woods. There are still native trout in some of these streams. I've ridden horses out here a few times."

Johnstone flicked a length of ash to the ground and glanced at Alnoor, who was sitting on the ground beneath an Eastern hemlock. Johnstone leaned toward Westlake. "What's the future look like for Abdul?" Johnstone whispered.

Westlake shifted on the rock. "If he's innocent, and he leads us to the shooter at the country club, he probably goes free." He looked at the flare of

Johnstone's cigarette, then back at the view of the valley, unwilling to meet Johnstone's eyes.

"Probably?"

"It's not my call," Westlake said. "He's a protected witness. Ultimately, Caroline makes the decision."

Johnstone nodded and dropped his cigarette, stubbing it out with the toe of his boot.

Westlake glanced at the smoldering butt. "We don't want to leave any sign of our presence up here."

Johnstone ground the cigarette until it was completely out, then leaned down and picked up the cigarette, stuffing the butt in his back pocket.

They resumed their journey, the progress slower on the steeper part of the trail. They wound their way past tree trunks that seemed to grow out of the rock, and around huge granite boulders that had been cleaved from giant slabs centuries before. The trail was littered with leaves and tree roots.

The trail leveled out as it intersected the foot path to the cabin, and they descended one-by-one, Westlake showing the others where to put their feet and which vegetation could hold their weight. Cunningham kept a hand on the collar of Alnoor's shirt, though the teenager proved to be nimble as they descended in tandem to the cabin site.

In a dusty corner of the cabin rife with cobwebs, Cunningham and Perez unrolled an old sleeping bag. A family of rats scurried out one window. The marshals scattered empty food bags and plastic water bottles around to replicate the hideaway of an escaped prisoner. They brought in a gray plastic bucket, its rim scarred, undefined stains on the sides.

Westlake and Johnstone stood outside while the marshals made the preparations. From his backpack, Westlake pulled a small, zippered case and, from the case, a palm-sized video camera. He flipped open the screen and pushed the power button. He turned to Johnstone, who had spent nearly an hour privately rehearsing with his client in the van.

"He knows what to say?" Westlake asked.

"Yes."

"You're sure? It's getting cold, and we don't have much light left."

"I'm sure, Judge. He knows what to do. He knows his freedom depends on it."

They exchanged a look over the unsettled issue.

Alnoor leaned against the cabin. The fabric at the knees of his jeans was bare. His green flannel shirt, with the top two buttons missing, was too large by two sizes. Both pants and shirt could have been ripped from a clothesline.

Perez took Alnoor by the arm to a seep on the hillside and rubbed mud and damp moss across the jeans and shirt, smudged mud on Alnoor's hands, front and back. Then he told Alnoor to wipe his cheek with his forearm, which left a dim streak of dirt on Alnoor's face. Alnoor had a month's worth of beard, giving him the disheveled look of someone who had lived in the woods for weeks.

Westlake looked Alnoor over as they came back to the cabin. "Are we ready?"

"Yes, sir," Perez replied.

With Perez's hand on his elbow, Alnoor stepped into the cabin, his boots shuffling across the litter-strewn boards. When Perez commanded him to sit on the sleeping bag, Alnoor complied, crossing his legs and arms.

Westlake approached Alnoor with the camera. "All you have to do is move this switch down to record," Westlake showed him. "And then put it over here on this windowsill, point it at you, and say what David rehearsed with you. You can see on the screen what the camera is recording. Do you understand?"

"Yes, sir."

"And no mention of me, or David, or any court personnel, or Ms. Bannister. Agreed?"

"Yes, sir."

Westlake handed Alnoor a copy of the Smoky Mountain Times, a weekly edition that had been published two days earlier. "Hold this up to the camera so you can see the date." Westlake locked eyes with Alnoor, trying to read him. He was not convinced Alnoor was completely innocent. The semi-automatic AR-15 the FBI found buried in Alnoor's backyard was suited for one purpose. Alnoor's eyes remained impassive.

Alnoor flipped the switch on the camcorder and set it down on the rotted wood sill, then leaned back against the cabin wall, about five feet from the camera. A shaft of light from the window illuminated his face.

He took a deep breath and began. "I am Abdul Alnoor. I know you are surprised to see me alive. I was in witness protection, but I escaped." He held up the newspaper. "Since then I've been living in an abandoned cabin in the woods. I didn't shoot up the country club. I am innocent. I need your help to prove it."

Alnoor leaned forward to turn off the recorder, but Judge Westlake snatched the camera from the sill.

"I don't believe you. You're not convincing. Not in the least. If you came into my courtroom with a story like that, I wouldn't accept it. You need to make them believe that we faked your death, that you escaped from witness protection, and you are on the run. You need help, and you don't know where to turn."

"How am I supposed to make anyone believe that I escaped, when I am being held like a prisoner?"

"Look. The federal government was about to try you for a mass murder you claim you did not commit. Then they kidnapped you right before you could testify and clear your name. They kept you in a safehouse in the middle of nowhere against your will, and refused to tell you why. You're angry. You're incensed. They killed your mother in Iraq, and they won't quit persecuting you. Use that anger. Direct it at me if you need to. Now, do it again." Westlake erased the first video and handed the camera back to Alnoor.

Alnoor took a deep breath and closed his eyes. He took himself back to that day, fifteen years earlier. He heard the explosion at the oil refinery in Najef, less than fifty meters from where he and his mother were standing in line to get their daily supply of clean water. His mother urged him to run, and when he fell behind she snatched him up and carried him. And then she tripped and fell. And as he lay beneath his mother, he felt this great heat sweep past them as another explosion erupted. A searing heat scorched the sand, his face, and everything he could see. His mother screamed for a few minutes, and then she became silent. He said her name, over and over, and when she refused to answer, he lay there crying. When night fell, his thirst and his terror compelled him to crawl out from under her, where he stood in the street, looking at her still body. Until someone found him and took him to the hospital.

In the abandoned cabin, Abdul opened his eyes again, and there was seething in those eyes. His mouth and jaw were firm. He had turned into the anger-fed young man that lurked within. The vengeful one who had purchased an AR-15 at a gun show so it could not be traced. He eyed the Judge, an enemy. He glared at the two US marshals who had faked his death. They might not have killed his mother, but they were part of the government that had done it.

He pushed the red record button, aimed the lens at his face, and set the camera on the sill with a rap.

"I am Abdul Alnoor," he began. His voice had dropped an octave. "I have been falsely accused of shooting people at a Christmas party in Charlotte. I did not do it. I was nowhere near the country club that night. I have been framed by someone, and the murderer is still out there. The federal government faked my death and told me I was in witness protection. But I was still a prisoner, being held in a secret place, until I escaped. I had to escape, because they were going to kill me eventually, after they got what they wanted. I know that. I am hiding out near here." He held the front page of the newspaper beside his head so the masthead and date were captured by the camera. He put the newspaper aside in a crackle of pages. "They are looking for me. I have seen them. I have to keep moving. I am hungry, and I am cold. If they catch me again, they will kill me. I need your help. Please contact me by email before it is too late."

Alnoor reached for the recorder and turned it off, then sat back on his mattress, his arms encircling his knees. He stared through the window at an undefined spot above the trees. His breath came in heavy gasps.

25

When Perez approached him with a zip tie for his hands, Alnoor said, "I need to go to the bathroom."

"Go pee over there," Perez pointed toward a poplar tree.

"I don't need to pee," Alnoor said, staring at Perez with defiance.

"I'll go with him," Johnstone offered. "Come on, Abdul." Johnstone shouldered his backpack and escorted Abdul to the privy twenty yards behind the cabin, a structure with weathered gray boards, some of them cracked and falling apart.

Perez peered around the corner of the cabin and watched them until Alnoor went inside the privy and closed the rickety door.

Cunningham glanced at the horizon, the sun dipping to the blue-hazed range, shadows beginning to creep up the face of the mountain. "What's the play here, Judge?"

"The play?"

"With the video?"

Perez joined them at the front of the cabin, arms crossed over his torso.

"We need to lure our blackmailer," Westlake said. "This is the first step. If he responds, we'll have Alnoor rendezvous with him, set a trap, and catch him."

Cunningham looked down at his feet. "You're going to just email this to some target, out of the blue?"

"Probably multiple suspects, unless we can narrow it down. Caroline is working on that. There's a technology that will erase the video and the email so it can't be traced, and the recipient has nothing to prove any of it ever existed. If the recipient goes to the police, he'll just look like a crackpot with a crazy conspiracy theory."

"That seems risky."

"It is risky. But David and I talked about it. He's on board," the Judge said.

Johnstone came running back to them, blood streaking his forehead. "Abdul escaped," he said between gasps.

"Escaped? How?" Westlake said.

Cunningham and Perez were already running toward the back of the cabin, pulling their guns. Westlake and Johnstone followed.

The marshals stopped at the door to the outhouse, one on either side, leaning against the corners.

"Alnoor, get out here," Cunningham ordered. Nothing happened. Cunningham reached for the door handle and pulled it open. The back wall of the privy was destroyed, half a dozen boards missing, leaving a huge hole through which Alnoor had escaped.

"Johnstone, which way did he go?" Cunningham shouted. He scanned the surrounding landscape, moving a few steps left and right, attempting to see through the tree branches and a thicket of rhododendrons, trying to spot movement.

"He headed that way." Johnstone pointed down the slope, toward the tangled thicket. With his other hand he rubbed an emerging knot on his forehead, just below the hairline. The knot was an angry shade of red.

"Tell me what happened, David," Westlake said.

"He hit me with a rock."

"You'll need to put some cold water on that. There's a stream not far from the trail."

"We have to go after him," Johnstone said.

"I agree," Westlake said. "We can't have a witness in federal custody, one who is supposed to be dead to the rest of the world, on the loose. Iggy, Marcus, how do we deal with this?"

Perez took the lead. "We don't have enough manpower for a grid search, but Marcus and I can try to follow his trail, look for signs—broken branches, shoe prints, maybe torn clothing if we get lucky. You guys should head back to the van, in case he goes there. We don't have much daylight left. It will be dark soon. We stay in communication via cell phones."

"Cell phones might not work up here," Westlake said. "But we might be able to text. Give me the keys to the van."

Perez handed them over, and then he and Cunningham scrambled down the slope, into the trees, searching for signs and sounds of a man running through the woods.

Johnstone closed his eyes for a moment. "I can't believe I let this happen."

Westlake put his hand on Johnstone's back. "Let's head down. We need to get to the van before Alnoor, if he's heading that way."

They found the white van where they had left it. The sun had disappeared behind the mountain ridge, turning the light a murky purple. They walked behind the van, scanning the trees beside the road in case Alnoor was lurking there. Westlake got down on his stomach and peered under the van, seeing nothing suspicious. Westlake unlocked the driver's door, got in and started the engine. He slid open the metal window concealing the cargo bay. He tapped the flashlight icon on his phone and shone it into the storage area. There was nothing back there except Alnoor's ankle monitor.

Westlake checked his phone and saw he had no signal bars. Instead, he sent a text to Marcus and Iggy.

Raleigh: We're in the van. No sign of him.

Johnstone climbed into the passenger seat. Westlake handed him a bottle of water from a mini-cooler and flipped on the dome light in the cab. Johnstone rolled the bottle across his forehead, leaving droplets on his brow.

"You need ice," Westlake said. His phone chimed with a text.

Marcus: Nothing here. Too dark. Heading your way.

"They didn't find him."

Johnstone uncapped the water bottle and took a long swig, then touched the plastic bottle again to the lump on his forehead.

"Makes sense that he would have headed back to the trail," Westlake said. "That's the only thing he knows in these woods."

"Makes sense to me that he ran in the opposite direction," Johnstone said. "I'm sure he's trying to put as much distance as he can between him and us."

"Why? We don't constitute a threat to him. Not anymore."

"I don't think he sees it that way. You're using him as bait."

"*We're* using him as bait," Westlake corrected. "You agreed to do it this way. In fact, it was your idea, David."

Johnstone turned to the passenger window, seeing his reflection, the goose egg above his right eye, the film of dirt in the creases of his nose.

"David, look at me. What did you tell him?"

Johnstone turned his face to the Judge, trying to meet his eyes. "I told him we were being blackmailed, probably by the guy that shot up the country club, by someone who wanted him dead."

"You said what?"

"I only told him the truth."

Westlake glared at Johnstone, trying to pry something from him by sheer will. "Tell me again how he hit you with the rock, David."

Johnstone stared through the windshield at the dark shroud of trees covering a road he could barely distinguish against the backdrop. "He jumped me, knocked me down, picked up the rock and hit me in the forehead with it while I was on the ground. Then he ran off."

"Where were you standing at the time?"

"I was turned away from the outhouse, taking a leak myself."

"So he knocked you down with your fly unzipped?"

"Well, I was finished, I guess."

"So after he hit you with the rock, you took the time to zip up?"

"Yeah. I got up as quickly as I could, zipped up and came to tell you guys."

Westlake finished his water, screwed the cap back on. He tucked the plastic bottle in his backpack. "There's no way you could not have heard him coming through the back of the privy, David. Did you help him pry the boards off?"

"No, Raleigh, he surprised me. Plain and simple. He hit me with a rock. I was dazed. Maybe I'm still not thinking clearly." He rubbed his index finger across the welt.

"He didn't knock you down, David. There are no leaves or dirt on your jacket. I was behind you on the way back down the trail. There are no stains on your pants. Why did you help him?"

Johnstone looked at his boots, his head bent. He wiped his sleeve across his nose. "Now that he's made the video, you don't need him anymore. Caroline won't ever agree to release him. He'll be a prisoner in a secret location for the rest of his life. Or, he'll have an accident and quietly disappear."

Westlake took a deep breath, trying to still his rising anger. "Where did he go, David?"

Johnstone pulled a cigarette from the pack in his shirt pocket and put it between his lips.

Westlake reached over and grabbed Johnstone's left wrist, stared intensely into his eyes. "Where did he go?" he said with his jaw clenched.

"He hid under the cabin."

"So Marcus and Iggy are traipsing around in the woods, in the dark, looking for an escaped prisoner in the wrong place."

"You said he wasn't a prisoner, but yes. Now let go of my wrist."

For a moment, Westlake wanted to push Johnstone out of the van, take him down into the woods, and exact some type of retribution. With Alnoor on the loose, Johnstone had put them all in danger. The repercussions were catastrophic, too numerous and vile to contemplate. But he had to keep his cool. If he lost it, let rage overtake him, he wouldn't be able to think clearly. His stomach roiled as his wolves awakened. He released Johnstone's wrist.

"Did you arrange for transportation for him? Did you give him money? A cell phone?"

"Transportation, no; yes on the money and the phone."

Westlake pondered this. "So you planned this? It wasn't spur of the moment."

Johnstone remained silent for a time. "He's still my client, Raleigh. Not like the other ones you appointed me to defend, who had no defense. This is real."

"Where is he going, David?"

"I have no idea. That's the honest truth."

"So *now* you're being honest with me. How can I trust you?"

"I don't know."

Westlake stared at Johnstone, trying to determine if he was lying, if the disclosure that Alnoor was hiding beneath the cabin was just another ruse. "Do you know what you've done?" He picked up his phone and typed a text to his marshals.

Raleigh: He's hiding under the cabin.

26

Alnoor stayed underneath the cabin, curled in a tight ball against the chill, for about twenty minutes. From his hiding place, he had seen four pairs of legs, at least from the knee down. Two of the men ran into the woods behind the privy. The other two went up the path toward the trail.

Alnoor crawled from beneath the cabin and swiped the dirt from his clothes. He did not know where he was, only that he was in the wilderness. He had been surprised that Mr. Johnstone helped him escape. There had been no explanation. Maybe there was no need for one. He was innocent, after all, and Mr. Johnstone seemed to believe that.

He felt for the lump of money in his right pocket. He had not counted the bills, but it would be enough for food and water for a long time. The bulge of a cell phone slept in his left pocket. He had not turned the phone on. Mr. Johnstone told him not to until he was safely away, because they might be able to track his location through the phone.

The sun had been going down for almost an hour. The cabin was in deep shadow. Alnoor pulled his jacket tighter around him. The temperature was plummeting, and he needed to find a hiding place. Mr. Johnstone had told him to climb to the top of the mountain, where he would run into the Appalachian Trail. His instinct was to find a path, or a route where there was little underbrush, but he had to fight against that. He was an accused terrorist, a terrorist who had escaped trial by faking his own death. If he was caught again, that's the story they would tell. No one would believe his side. No one would believe that a federal judge and the US Attorney and two US Marshals had engineered his escape from the jail cell. No one would think he was innocent. He couldn't be caught again.

He had no place to turn, no one to call. He was on his own. Mr. Johnstone said if he could call, once things had settled down, that he would. But he didn't know if that call would ever come.

As they'd talked alone in the trailer that morning, Mr. Johnstone had given him a stern warning: "You can't go to your family, or to your friends, or to the police, Abdul. If you do, they will catch you. You might not even get to a trial. Either way, they will kill you." Mr. Johnstone had said this firmly so there could be no misunderstanding. In his shock, Abdul did not think to ask any questions.

He went up the foot path and found the narrow trail they had taken to get to the abandoned cabin. Knowing the van was down the trail to his left, he went right and began to climb. He had not gone very far when the visibility dimmed to a few feet. He walked through the woods, his hands in front of him to avoid slamming into trees, but in his panic it didn't help that much. He fell several times. Dry briars nipped his exposed skin like pointed teeth.

"Eric Rudolph survived in these woods for five years," Mr. Johnstone had told him. Abdul had no idea who Eric Rudolph was. Five years seemed like forever.

"The winter will be tough. You have to be careful."

He might have hit Mr. Johnstone a little too hard with the rock. He had fallen back against the privy. But it was necessary, or so Mr. Johnstone said, to help provide a cover story.

Abdul needed food. It had been more than twelve hours since he'd last eaten. He had seen some berries along the trail, red berries. He didn't know anything about berries except that he'd once watched a movie about a young guy who had mistakenly eaten poisonous berries in Alaska and died. He tried to subdue the growling in his stomach. He could go through the night without food. He had practiced that while in prison, and he fasted during Ramadan every year.

But he couldn't go long without water. He knew that. As he moved upward through the woods, he sometimes heard the gurgle of a stream close by. He was thirsty, but he had to keep going, at least for a little while. He had to put more distance between himself and the people chasing him. They had to be chasing him. They couldn't simply let him get away. He continued on for another half hour, hoping the clouds would move away so he could see the moon and its light could guide him.

His breathing became labored as he climbed, and his mouth grew dry. He had to find water. His eyes had adjusted somewhat to the fading light. He hiked down a slope, vaguely thinking there might be a stream at the bottom because water ran downhill. He could see a shadowy line of bushes and thought that was a good sign. He paused and stilled his breathing. Somewhere in front of him he heard the gurgle of water. As he approached the sound, he slowed down, looking carefully in all directions. He squinted into the woods, looking for the movement of animals feeding at night.

When he got close enough that he could see the water through the underbrush, he knelt down and crawled to it on his hands and knees. He came to the edge of the stream. It was narrow, but the water wasn't stagnant. He leaned forward and dipped his hands into the clear water. It was cold, shockingly cold. He dipped his head to his hands and sipped. He cupped more water and slurped. He did it again and again. Sating his thirst would only be temporary. There might not be another stream for miles. He needed a water bottle, but he didn't have one. This would have to do.

He leaned back on his haunches and let out a sigh. He closed his eyes and tried to think of how to find a place to hide. He thought about climbing a tree, or finding a cave and crawling inside. Maybe he could make a fire, but he'd have to find a cave or someplace hidden by rocks so the fire and smoke wouldn't be visible. As he began to stand up, he heard a sound. It was not the wind, and it was not the creaking of tree trunks. The rustle of movement in the brush behind him was very close.

27

Marcus Cunningham shined his flashlight under the cabin, which was supported at the corners with dry-stack rubble. He approached one of the broken windows and peered inside. The beam of light reflected off the mist of descending cold. The interior of the cabin was as they left it, with a few rodents investigating the empty food bags, pushing them around on the floor, making a scratching sound like tree limbs against glass.

Dew already had formed on stalks of dead grass the color of burnt butter, and as Cunningham circled the cabin, the cuffs of his pants became wet, his cammies wicking the moisture. The sun had been down an hour, lost clouds descending into the valley, and the beam of his halogen light seemed absorbed by the fog.

Perez came up the trail, the white fuzz of his light announcing him, his footsteps muted by the weather.

"Fuck this, Iggy. There's no way we're finding that little asshole in this muck."

"Agreed," Perez said. "We need the beams just to keep from falling off the mountain. He can see us before we see him."

"Let's head back to the van."

"I've got an infrared scope on the sniper rifle."

"You brought it?"

"In the truck, back at the rendezvous point."

"Makes a lot of noise," Cunningham said. "What would we tell the Chief?" He typed a text on his cell phone, then hit send.

Marcus: Nothing at the cabin. Heading your way.

They began to descend the trail, flashlights pointed a few feet in front of them, occasionally directing the beams into the woods, glancing off trees the color of old ashes, the light swallowed by thickets with no bottom. A seep crossed the path, its water clear, the source a cascade of boulders encrusted with lichen graying from the first frost.

"He's going to need water," Perez said.

"How do you know Johnstone didn't give him some?"

"He didn't bring any up the mountain. He was dry."

"So it wasn't thought out that well."

"It was a rag plan from a guy who's never spent any time in the wilderness."

They let this settle for a few strides, their breaths pluming like horses snorting in a pasture with ice in the water trough. "When did Johnstone decide to help him escape, you think?" Cunningham said.

"The night before we took him to the safehouse."

"That early?"

"He's a bleeding heart. Sees no way his boy could be Ali Baba. He's a terrorist. I saw kids younger than him strap on suicide vests."

"Me too."

"They always look innocent. That's their play. That's how they get close."

"Maybe he'll freeze to death tonight. That would save us a lot of trouble."

"We ain't that lucky, Marcus."

Below them, on a road that snaked out from the twinkling lights of the town, headlights approached at moderate speed. Both men cut their flashlights and crouched.

"They looking for something?" Perez whispered.

"Can't tell. I don't see a search light. You think somebody else knows?"

"Could be Alnoor's coach."

"You think Johnstone arranged a ride?"

"He's not concerned with the repercussions, Marcus. Best thing that could happen would be for both of them to get permanently lost. No more worry about loose lips."

"I agree, but the Judge will never allow it."

They approached the white van from the rear with lights out, crunching gravel even though they crept forward heel to toe, with knees bent, as if stalking wounded game. The van's engine rumbled in the night. They were standing on opposite sides of the van, at the side windows, before they were noticed by the occupants.

At the sight of Perez at the passenger window, Johnstone startled, his torso jerking against the seat belt.

Perez pulled the door open.

Westlake got out the driver's side. "We drove up the road a little ways, looking for him, then turned around. Thought he might come down the mountain," Westlake said.

"No sign of him near the cabin," Cunningham said, eyeing Johnstone through the windshield. Cunningham swept around the front of the van, grabbed Johnstone by the collar of his jacket, and wrestled him out of the van.

They were eye-to-eye, Johnstone's boots a few inches off the ground. "Do you know how bad you fucked up, Johnstone?"

"Yes. I realize what I've done," Johnstone said, trying to wriggle free. "It was stupid, I know, but I thought after the video you guys were going to kill Abdul. I only did it to save him." His breath smelled of stale smoke.

"Because you think he's innocent?" Cunningham challenged. "You have no idea what you've done. What do you want me to tell our Chief? That we lost a terrorist?"

Johnstone said nothing.

"When are you going to realize that our number one priority is to keep it safe for our team? Fuck everybody else." He tossed Johnstone against the side of the van, his body making the sound of an axe striking a stump. Johnstone's face was beet red as he slumped to the ground.

Cunningham remained standing, defiant, his fists clenched. "You think this is some kind of game? If we can't trust each other, we have nothing. This is what gets people killed. Iggy and I have seen it. Firsthand." His holstered gun was inches away from his balled right fist. "Without trust, the whole thing falls apart. I'm not sticking my neck out . . . I'm not putting my ass on the line one more time, unless I know to a certainty that I can trust everyone. Not anymore."

Westlake had inched his way around the front of the van. "And how do we do that, Marcus?" the Judge said in a quiet tone. He was as agitated as his two marshals, but if he let his anger rise, Johnstone would likely wind up in a shallow grave, or at the bottom of Fontana Lake, before the sun rose. Westlake's head shifted from side to side. "How do we rebuild your trust?"

"I'm not worried about you, Judge. You've never betrayed your unit," Cunningham said.

"I'm not a traitor," Johnstone said, rubbing his throat, trying to stand. His voice was raw, full of gravel. "I get that. I screwed up. I have to re-earn your trust. All of you," he said, trying to meet their eyes. "I want to. How do I do that? Rebuild your trust?"

"Bring Alnoor in," Cunningham said without hesitation.

"It's the only way to save your ass," Perez said.

"And if I do that, will you promise to keep him safe?" Johnstone said.

"Nope," Cunningham said. "I'm not even going to promise that I won't kill both of you." He looked around at their surroundings, at woods that went on for miles, at the fog descending upon them. "This is a perfect place to hide two bodies. Forever."

28

Abdul turned to the sound. It was something big, but he couldn't see anything through the dense underbrush. He rose slowly from his haunches and hopped across the stream, then crouched on the other side, making himself small but not invisible. Waiting. Watching.

The clamor grew louder. Something crashing through the brush, something not concerned with being silent. Coming toward the stream. Coming directly toward him. Then he saw it.

The bear saw him in the same instant. It raised up and stamped the ground with its front paws, letting out a loud huff, the equivalent of a dog's snarl. It was less than thirty feet away. There was only brush between them. Brush that would not thwart the bear if it decided to attack. They stared at each other for a moment, the bear swinging its head from side to side, sniffing the air. Another movement in the underbrush, quieter and hesitant. Two cubs emerged from behind their mother and approached the edge of the stream, watching him with steady eyes.

Alnoor placed his hands behind him and crab-walked away, keeping his eyes fixed on the big bear. He'd read somewhere that bears were incredibly fast, faster than a man could run. He scrambled through the brush, staying low. He put another ten feet between them, then twenty. The bear was still there, though he could no longer see her eyes, merely a dark, dense blur in the brush. He bumped into a tree, hitting his back and his head. Hard. He felt his way around the tree, then stood up. The bear was still there.

He walked away, slowly, turning frequently to check that the bear was not pursuing him. His heart beat in his throat. His mouth was cotton. He was prepared mentally for the two-legged hunters, had successfully eluded them for a few hours, but the four-legged kind might be more deadly. He needed to find a place to hide. Away from everything and everybody. A cave. No, a cave might be a bear's den. A tree. Bears could climb trees, right? Where could he go to escape?

With all of these thoughts spinning in his head, he didn't see the hole. As he turned to watch the bear, his right leg went straight into it, down to the top of his thigh, and he crashed face down in the leaves. The ground punched his chest, knocking the air out of him. He wheezed for breath and clawed at the ground. He tried to roll onto his back, but his leg was wedged in a tangle of roots and dirt. He was stuck. He lay on his stomach, turned his head to the side, and retched. He looked for a sapling or a root to grab so he could pull himself out of the hole. The closest tree was more than arms-length away. He dug with his fingers, trying to uncover anything solid. He scrabbled through the dirt, digging deeper, but all he uncovered was dirt and old leaves.

He laid there and shivered. His fingertips throbbed with scratches and bruises. The sound of animals at night filled the forest. The bear was behind him, somewhere.

His fragile state of mind began to unravel. He twisted his body and his leg in an attempt to free himself. He had been trying for hours to free himself. All he'd managed to do was find exhaustion. He'd had no food for more than a day, no water for several hours. Not since the bear had scared him away from the creek.

He tried to draw on his mother's strength and courage. She had saved him and sacrificed herself for a reason. She was looking down on him from *Al-Firdaws*, the highest level of heaven. He was not ready to join her, not yet. With considerable effort, he rolled onto his right side and bent the leg that was not trapped. Reaching into the front pocket of his jeans, he extracted the cell phone and the battery. Mr. Johnstone had told him not to install the battery until he was far away and safe, but if he didn't do something now, he might never get free.

The battery snapped into place, silencing the forest. He heard the pulse of blood in his ears. He hesitated for a breath, then two. The forest resumed its hum. Something was moving off to the side, crunching leaves and snapping twigs. It had to be the bear. Coming for him. He had no choice but to turn on the phone.

He pushed the power button, and the screen came to life. In the impenetrable darkness of the forest, the light from the screen seemed intolerably bright. He turned the screen away and laid the phone among the leaves. He put his forehead down upon his hands to ease the strain in his neck. He prayed to Allah.

The din of night insects became disorienting, like a wave moving over him. To his left he heard an owl hoot. He twisted his head to the side, scanning shadowy shapes in the trees. He could see nothing. Whatever had been moving toward him had stopped. He wondered if it was watching him. Hunting him.

He returned his attention to the phone. There was only one number in the contacts list. But there were other numbers he could call. His adoptive parents, for one. His parents would welcome his voice, the fact that he was still alive. They would be relieved to know that the urn of ashes delivered to them was not their son. His mother would cry when she heard his voice. But they would have questions. And a call to them would put them at risk. They would feel compelled to come search for him, to rescue him. He didn't even know where he was, just somewhere in a valley in the wilderness. And if, by some miracle of Allah, they found him, then what?

He could call 911. It happened all the time. Hikers got lost. Trained men and women came to their rescue, no matter the circumstances. Perhaps they could locate his cell signal. But if he chose that route, if he tapped in those three numbers, that would guarantee his return to prison, and he would be ensnared once again in a federal web whose only aim was to kill him.

He tapped the icon for David Johnstone's cell number. The screen brightened. A few seconds later, a span that seemed much longer, he was greeted with a message that said the call could not be completed as dialed. He tried again. He got the same announcement. He was afraid Mr. Johnstone had put in the wrong phone number. He could not have made that mistake, could he? He must be in an area so remote that his call would not go through. That was it. He looked at the signal bars and had none. No phone service. He had to do something. He couldn't simply lie there in the woods until someone . . . or something . . . found him. He could imagine no more painful death than dying from a bear's claws and teeth.

He texted a simple message: **I need help**

He had no way of knowing whether the message went through. He had no way of knowing if Mr. Johnstone even had his phone turned on. While he waited, the sounds of scrambling animals came closer, then veered away. He could not see these animals. He could not tell how close they were. But he knew they could see him. He listened for a grunt or a snarl or a heavy breath.

From a distant place came the howl of a wolf. He thought that wolves howled only at the moon. Tonight there was no moon. Only clouds. From the other side of the valley another wolf answered. He wondered if they were stalking him. He wondered if they could smell him. Could they smell his sweat? Could they smell his fear?

He laid his head on the ground, felt the coolness of the dirt on his cheek. He had almost fallen asleep when the phone chimed with a text: **Where are you?**

29

The map lay before them, depicting in green the vast Great Smoky Mountains National Park. The Park covers 812 square miles, straddling the North Carolina-Tennessee border, most of it wilderness without roads, paved or otherwise. The terrain is steep and perilous. And somewhere in the middle of it was Abdul Alnoor.

They stood around the dining table, at one side of the great room at the lake house, scanning the map. Westlake pointed to a spot at the end of a paved road marked by a squiggly red line. "This is where we parked the van. On the Road to Nowhere. It's labeled Lakeview Drive, but none of the locals call it that. The abandoned cabin is about here." He put his finger on a spot just outside the Park boundary. "It's been four hours since he took off. If he was moving fast, which would be tough in the dark on this steep terrain, he could have covered six to eight miles. In any direction."

"That's an area of 110 to 200 square miles," Perez said, calculating the search area in his head.

Westlake nodded. "And as you guys saw, there's dense undergrowth. He could be anywhere."

"What if we don't find him?" Johnstone asked, his hands gripping the edge of the maple table.

Westlake turned to him. "You should have thought of that before you helped him escape, David. The conditions are bad. The temperature is going to drop below freezing tonight."

"So he could freeze to death?" Johnstone asked.

The other three stared at him without comment.

"We've got another problem," Cunningham said. "Our chief is expecting us to bring Alnoor back to the safehouse. Now. We need a good reason to keep him out overnight. And we sure as hell can't say he escaped."

"What's a good reason?" Westlake asked.

"I can't say for sure," Cunningham said. "I've never had to do this before. But I'm guessing if Ms. Bannister says she's questioning Alnoor and needs to keep working through the night, that would suffice."

Westlake pulled out his cell phone. "I'll call her right now. Does she know your supervisor's number, or who she's supposed to call about something like this?"

Cunningham nodded. "She should."

Westlake stepped to the other end of the room and stood before the windows that looked out onto Fontana Lake. The fog had descended to the ground, obscuring the view, drifting across the expanse like a massive ghost. He thought it was ironically fitting. He paused for a minute, thinking about how to break the news to Caroline.

The call rang through to voicemail. He checked his watch. It was too early for her to be in bed. Perhaps she was having dinner at a restaurant, or was away from the phone. He didn't leave a message. There was no way to phrase it right. He texted her "911," instead.

She called back in a few minutes, after he had returned to the dining table and the map.

"I'm glad you called me back," Westlake said. "We have a situation here."

"Well, hello to you too, Raleigh."

"Sorry. It's pretty hectic here. I need you to call your contact at WITSEC and tell them you need to keep Abdul Alnoor overnight for interrogation."

"Interrogation? I don't . . . what happened?"

"Better for you not to know details right now. You've got the confirmation hearing coming up."

There was a pause on the other end, and Raleigh knew Caroline's mind was running through the possibilities, trying to understand the situation with limited facts. "Tell me this," she said, "do you have everything under control?"

"Yes," he said in as firm a voice as he could muster. Caroline's cat hopped off an upholstered chair, padded to the dining area, and jumped up on the table. It traipsed across their map, meowing.

"I hear a cat. Is that Astrophe?"

"Yes," he replied.

"How is he?"

"Oblivious."

"All right, the circle on this is tight. Only a handful of people in WITSEC even know Alnoor is alive. I'll make the call."

They secured a reprieve from WITSEC, though there were questions about why the GPS on Alnoor's ankle monitor had stopped working. In fact, the GPS tracking system was working, but as the monitor lay in the back of the van, it had been stationary for most of the day. Cunningham lied that the battery had gone dead and promised to replace it before they returned Alnoor to the safehouse the next day.

"We dodged a bullet," Cunningham said when he finished his calls. "We've got 24 hours, but no more than that. If Alnoor's phone keeps working, potentially he can help us pin down his location, which will narrow the search area. Maybe. But until we can narrow it down, there's no reason to go back out there."

"But we can't just sit here," Johnstone said.

"This is what we do," Perez said. "Track down fugitives. But there are four of us. That's the extent of the search party. You want to go traipsing around in 200 square miles of forest, in the dark, looking for a needle in a haystack, be my guest. But if you get lost, or hurt, we're not coming to look for you."

"Get your phone out, Johnstone," Cunningham said in a tone that was not a suggestion. He and Iggy were now in charge. The capture of Alnoor was their mission. "Ask him if he's still in the woods," Cunningham said.

Are you still in the woods?

Yes

How far do you think you traveled from the cabin?

IDK maybe 2-3 miles

Why do you need help?

Fell in a hole and am stuck Animals all around A bear too

Johnstone looked up from his phone, his eyebrows arched.

"Ask him if he can see any lights," Cunningham said.

Johnstone typed in a question.

Too dark but I hear a stream

Cunningham looked down at the map, seeing a myriad of creeks marked in blue. Some of them were named; others were not. Undoubtedly there were tributaries and rivulets that didn't appear on the map at all.

"Ask him how big the stream is, how wide."

Johnstone texted the question.

A few feet I jumped over it

"Judge, you know these woods pretty well," Cunningham said. "How many streams that size are within the search area?"

"Dozens," Westlake said. "Most of them aren't marked. Depending on which way he went, it's even possible he wandered onto the Cherokee Reservation."

A collective frustration spread through them like a contagion. The variables were too immense. They couldn't call in a helicopter for an aerial search, and they couldn't ask the National Park Service or local law enforcement for assistance in a ground search for a man who was supposed to be dead.

Westlake stared down at the map, tracing his fingers along the laminated features. He'd been hiking these woods since he was a kid. There were two natural barriers that may have hemmed Alnoor in—the Tuckaseegee River and Fontana Lake to the south, and the Noland Divide to the east.

"David, ask him if he came across any wide streams, something he had to wade across or cross by going over a log," Westlake said.

Johnstone sent the text, and they waited.

Cunningham drummed his fingers on the table. "His phone may have died."

"Maybe," Westlake said, "but more than likely this fog is blocking the cell signal. There are no cell towers in the Park."

They waited a few more minutes, a wait that built in them the worst of suspicions.

"He could be faking it," Cunningham said. "Maybe he's on the run and doesn't need help at all, and this is just a way of putting more distance between him and us."

"He wouldn't do that," Johnstone said. "I told him not to turn his cell phone on unless it was an emergency."

"Yeah, well, we're past being able to believe anything you say Johnstone," Perez said.

To stave off additional infighting, Westlake said, "Try calling him again."

Johnstone did so and received the same announcement he had on all previous attempts. The call could not go through.

"Give me your phone," Cunningham said.

Johnstone handed it over.

Cunningham began to text, reading the message aloud as he did so.

If U need help better respond. Now.

I did not cross any wide water

Westlake returned to the map and checked the legend. He pulled a felt-tip pen and a Leatherman from a kitchen drawer. He measured out from the cabin six miles, then eight, and drew an ellipse around the area where Alnoor most likely had become lost. "Look, based on the location of the cabin and these natural barriers to the east and west, he's probably in here. That's more manageable."

"With dense underbrush, at night, in the fog?" Cunningham said.

"What choice do we have, Marcus?" the Judge said.

"Wait until morning. If the fog lifts, visibility will be much better."

"We might even be able to hear him," Perez suggested. "Sound carries a long way in these mountains."

"That's true," Westlake said. He turned to look out the windows again, to stare into the fog that had them surrounded like a thick curtain. He started to ask Johnstone's opinion but refrained. "All right, it's settled then. We'll stay here tonight, go back out a little before dawn when we can see what we're doing. Let me see what I've got to eat."

Cunningham texted a final message: **Stay put. Coming to find U.**

During the night, a northwesterly breeze emerged, and in the morning the fog had dissipated to a thin gauze. They drove the van back to the Road to Nowhere, Perez at the wheel and Judge Westlake in the passenger seat. Johnstone sat on a hard bench in the cargo bay, Cunningham across from him. Cunningham's eyes were alert, even though the cargo bay was dark, save for a dim rectangle of light emitted by the dashboard through the window slit in the divider. Johnstone's cell phone was nestled in a pocket of Cunningham's jeans.

They emerged from the van into darkness, for even though sunrise officially occurred in four minutes, the first rays of light had yet to hit the valley. Cunningham leaned against the shell of the van, watching a pink hue develop on the eastern horizon. The ridge of mountains running from southwest to northeast was a shadow.

"Can I have my phone back, now?" Johnstone asked.

"Not on your life," Cunningham said, his breath forming a small vapor cloud. He pulled the phone from his pocket and scrolled through the text chain with Alnoor, which listed only a phone number and no name. He then tapped other icons and read the texts Johnstone had sent earlier in the day. There was nothing hinting that he was planning to engineer Alnoor's escape.

Cunningham sent a text to Alnoor: **We R hiking in from lake**. He didn't ask Alnoor's condition. Whether he received a response, and how quickly, would tell him enough.

Come soon I am very cold

RU you still in hole?

Yes animals close by

"He's fine," Cunningham said.

They embarked in pairs. Cunningham and Johnstone would follow the Nolan Creek Trail, heading north and up the mountain. Perez and Westlake would hike a parallel route two miles to the east. An hour in, the sun emerged over the ridge, bathing them in sunlight, starting to burn away the frost.

"I need to stop," Johnstone said, pulling a pack of cigarettes from his shirt pocket.

"Fine. Five minutes," Cunningham said, studying him. Johnstone's face was red from exertion. The hair peeking from under the bill of his cap, borrowed from the Judge, was damp with perspiration. In the crisp morning, his eyes were dull.

Cunningham turned back to the phone and sent another text to Alnoor: **Look for flash of light**. From his pack he pulled the rearview mirror from the van and angled it so it caught the sun. Standing along the creek bank, he slowly turned in a circle so that the flash could be seen from 360 degrees.

Did U see anything?

No

Can U see landmarks?

All I can C R trees

Do U see mountain peak, or ridge?

Yes. I am in valley can C mountains 2 sides

Is sun coming up over one mountain?

Yes

Cunningham pulled from the mesh pocket of his pack a folded paper version of Westlake's laminated map. It was damp with dew, flimsy in his hands. He unfolded the map and held it up, studying it, changing the orientation, finally deciding that Westlake was right. Alnoor had not breached the boundary formed by the creek to the west or the ridge trail to the east. Still, he could be anywhere between the Lake and the Appalachian Trail, ten miles to the north.

He checked the bars on his cell phone, then tried to call Perez. The call did not go through. He texted Perez: **Cell contact with A. Is in search area east to west. Not confirm north to south. Can U get high and send signal?**

Perez: 10-4

"Come on Johnstone, we're moving out."

"How much farther?" Johnstone said. "I'm not feeling great."

Cunningham looked back at Johnstone until he rose to his feet. "We keep moving until we find Alnoor, or you have a heart attack."

30

Perez and Westlake headed east and began to climb the steep slope to the Noland Divide Trail, a trail that would provide them a high vantage point, with views into the valleys east and west. Each step was labor. They pulled themselves up the hardest sections by grabbing trees and vines, winding a path around thickets and giant granite outcroppings. A few hundred feet below the ridge, they stopped, planting themselves on the uphill side of two trees that leaned down the slope.

"This was a mistake," Westlake said, his breath coming in gasps. "We should have dropped them off and then backtracked to Deep Creek."

"At least you're a runner," Perez said, bent over, his hands on his knees.

"You're almost twenty years younger than I am."

"Well, that's not helping at the moment."

They rested a few minutes against the grayish bark of the tulip poplars, which had established themselves with rigid permanence on the slope. When finally they arrived at the trail on the ridge, they rested again, looking out at the vistas, first to the east and the Cherokee Reservation, a dun landscape with dots of evergreens, and then to the west, where Alnoor lay in a hole somewhere, out of sight.

Perez drafted a group text to Cunningham and Alnoor: **On ridge to east. Sun is behind me. Flashing signal now. Look toward sun.**

Perez stood, angling a hand mirror so that it caught the sun and flashed like a beacon. He kept adjusting the angle so the reflection flashed toward the deep forest across 180 degrees. His phone chimed with a text.

Alnoor: I see it

Perez: Picture a clock face. Sun is at 12. Where is flash coming from?

Alnoor: Around 1 oclock

Perez: How far away?

Alnoor: Guess 2 miles

Perez: Turn your phone screen to bright. Catch sun with your screen and reflect it back

Perez gazed into the distance.

"I see a flash. A dull one," Westlake said, pointing down into the forest.

Perez handed his phone to Westlake, then slipped the rifle strap off his shoulder. He peered through the 24X scope at a dull reflection that became a corona as he zoomed in. "Tell him to hold the phone still."

Westlake texted the message. About twenty seconds later, Alnoor's illuminated cell phone became stationary, and the image through the scope became a twinkle. Perez could see Alnoor's torso through the leafless trees, but not his legs. Using the mil-dot reticle, Perez calculated the distance. "He's about three miles out," he said.

Perez retrieved his phone from the Judge, then sent a private text to Cunningham.

Perez: See my flash on ridge?

Cunningham: Yes

Perez: See A's cell phone flash?

Cunningham: No

Perez: Est A six klicks from me. I'll fix on U then triangulate

They repeated the procedure, Perez sighting through the scope, finding the mirror flash, then Cunningham's large form. He took the measurement, then calculated the approximate distance between Cunningham and Alnoor. Fortunately, it was the short leg of the triangle.

Perez: Estimate UR three klicks from A

Cunningham: On our way

Perez: Careful, rock climbers on face to northwest

In the low land near the creek, Cunningham could not see the wall of granite which three or four climbers were ascending. He thought it likely the climbers had seen the flashes from the mirrors, and they might be curious enough to investigate. The trail wound up the creek, packed wet leaves beneath them, their steps hushed by the forest. Johnstone trudged along behind, his breathing labored, sweat dripping off his forehead. They climbed a hill, threading their way through glossy green rhododendrons, and came to a waterfall that spilled into a deep pool.

A black bear and two cubs appeared on the path, not twenty yards ahead. The big bear, which Cunningham assumed to be the mother, raised her head and sniffed the air. Cunningham held up his fist. Johnstone, with his head down, stumbled into Cunningham's back and fell. The mother bear rose on her hind legs and stamped her front paws on the trail, huffing a warning.

Cunningham pulled his pistol from the holster, then helped Johnstone struggle to his feet. He did not want to fire at the bear, did not want to attract attention with a gunshot that would be heard for miles. They backed away from the path, away from the creek, keeping the sow in sight. Cunningham watched her big front paws for a signal. The bear charged, bounding toward him five yards, then stopped. She eyed Cunningham for a few seconds, then tossed her head and huffed, and the two cubs descended the creek embankment. She took a last glance toward Cunningham, then followed the cubs into the water.

Johnstone sat at the base of a hemlock tree whose limbs were tattered and without needles. He pulled a cigarette from the pack and lit it with shaking hands. He exhaled a large cloud of smoke.

"Calm down. They're gone," Cunningham said.

"That's what I'm trying to do," Johnstone said, exhaling through pursed lips another burst of smoke.

Cunningham stepped back on the trail, surveying the surroundings, confirming the bears were gone. He estimated they had walked half the distance to Alnoor, putting them less than a mile away. He sent a joint text notifying the others of their position. Perez responded they were still on the ridge. Alnoor did not reply. Cunningham had a fleeting thought that maybe the black bear had attacked Alnoor. Cunningham had an emergency medical kit in his pack, but not supplies for treating injuries from a bear attack. If that had happened, their mission would turn from search and rescue into recovery and disposal. He looked up at the sun, dappled rays warming his face. The sun had passed its zenith. With the ridge to the west, it would begin to cool soon. He didn't want to spend the night in the woods.

"Moving out, Johnstone."

Johnstone tucked the cigarette pack back in his pocket and rose unsteadily.

Cunningham watched him, trying to forecast if Johnstone was going to turn into a foe when they located Alnoor. He couldn't tell. With his gun still drawn, he said, "you lead the way."

Johnstone hesitated, until Cunningham's firm hand on his back propelled him forward. Up the trail they walked, Johnstone in front, with Cunningham behind his left shoulder. "You better hope we find him before nightfall."

Johnstone turned his head to the words but did not respond.

The trail became steeper, the rush of water white noise in their ears. Near the creek, the trees were dense, and the path was filled with roots. Thick lines of rhododendrons, their leaves vibrant and glossy, separated them from the water. They came to a stream that emptied into Holland Creek. Cunningham holstered his gun and reached for the folded map. "Stop," he said to Johnstone.

While Johnstone slumped against a tree, Cunningham scanned the map for streams in their approximated location, keeping one eye on Johnstone. He found none.

He sent a text to Perez: **Found another stream. Have the climbers moved?**

Perez: They're off the face. Don't know where.

Cunningham studied the stream. There was no path beside it. Dense underbrush crowded the bank, sometimes arching over it. The stream was narrow, maybe three feet wide. In places they couldn't see the water, could only hear its burble and hiss. It could be the stream Alnoor crossed before he fell into the hole, or not.

"In the water," Cunningham commanded.

"But . . ." was all Johnstone could utter before he was flung forward. He landed in the stream and fell to his knees. "There's no reason for that," he said loudly.

Cunningham picked him up by the shirt collar, set him on his feet. They marched forward, a march Cunningham had engineered on dozens of occasions, the last time down a winding path with Henry Lawter as his prisoner, a march that ended with Lawter dead on the beach, a needle dangling from his arm. Johnstone wasn't a prisoner. Well, yes he was, because he wasn't free until . . . unless . . . Marcus declared him free.

They sloshed through the water for a hundred yards, Cunningham counting the steps, then stopped. He stuck two fingers in his mouth and whistled, a shrill sound that could not be mistaken for any animal.

Cunningham texted Alnoor: **Did U hear whistle?**

Yes

Toward the ridge or away?

Toward

That put Alnoor somewhere in the "V" between the larger creek and the stream they were standing in. Cunningham climbed out of the water, and Johnstone followed. They took a few steps away from the water. Cunningham pulled himself through a thicket of bushes, dried branches scratching at his face. He came into a stand of high trees where the underbrush was sparse. It was only then that he realized Johnstone was not behind him. He scanned the thicket and the spaces between trees, but saw nothing.

Cunningham crouched to reduce his profile and duck-walked a few yards to his right. "Alnoor," he said in a voice less than a shout.

126

"I am here," Alnoor responded from a spot not far away.

Cunningham sent a text to Perez.

Found A. Johnstone disappeared.

Need help?

I've got my Glock.

He moved in the direction from which Alnoor had answered, his knees bent, setting his weight on the outside of his boots and rolling inward across the terrain, trying to be silent. He had two hands on the pistol thrust in front of him. A bullet was already in the chamber.

Cunningham stepped between two white trunks and saw him. Alnoor was on his stomach, holding the cell phone between his palms like a prize. Cunningham scanned the area. A thicket of vines anchored one side. Evergreens, maples and oaks littered the other, dense with underbrush in places. Insects buzzed in the trees, as if singing at his approach.

Where is Johnstone?

Cunningham slid forward in a crouch. He didn't know if Alnoor had been given a gun or another weapon. He didn't know how far Johnstone's treachery might reach. "Alnoor, I'm right behind you. Coming in," Cunningham announced. "Don't move, son. Not a twitch."

He inched his way around Alnoor, watching for movement in the brush. He scrutinized Alnoor for a reach or a sudden jerk, or eyes darting to a location. Ambush was on his mind. He had seen it before—a seemingly innocent kid with the heart of a killer. Waiting. Waiting for soldiers to come in range.

Now in front of Alnoor, he spoke again. "Put the phone on the ground."

Alnoor submitted. One cheek was cut, and his right eye was swollen. He was a trapped animal, and all of the fight had bled from him.

Cunningham approached and plucked the phone from the leaves. "Keep your hands still." Cunningham pulled a zip tie from his front pocket and looped it around Alnoor's wrists. "You're safe now." Cunningham had said this before when he didn't mean it. He stood up and scanned the area, a quick rotation at first, then more slowly.

He guessed Johnstone was nearby, hovering in the bush. "Johnstone, come out from behind that tree. Now."

There was no movement, no stirring. With human voices in their midst, the insect cacophony had abated. The forest wore an eerie silence. Alnoor was panting. Cunningham's own breath had become sharp and ragged.

"If you don't come out now, I'll kill the kid. I can bury him in this hole. Grave's already dug." Cunningham aimed the Glock at the top of Alnoor's head. Alnoor didn't try to squirm away, just kept his face to the ground.

Johnstone emerged from behind a stout hemlock.

Cunningham shifted, training the Glock on Johnstone's torso.

Johnstone stood with his legs apart, his arms crossed over his chest. As he worked a dead cigarette between his lips, a certain defiance emanated from his eyes. "What are you going to do, Marcus, shoot both of us?"

31

Cunningham did not shoot either of them, though the temptation was great. The sound of gunshots would have been heard by somebody, somewhere. Park Rangers would be alerted. People would come. And there was no need. Despite Johnstone's disappearance and re-appearance during the hunt for Alnoor, he had done nothing more to thwart the search or capture. That fact earned him a modicum of trust.

Alnoor's injuries were minor—cuts and bruises. Having laid so long in the woods, he also was dehydrated. Cunningham and Johnstone, working together, were able to free him from his snare in a few minutes. Cunningham cleaned the scratches on Alnoor's face and arms while he drank two bottles of water. Then they marched in a line back down the trail, Johnstone leading the way. They arrived back at the van a short time after sunset, hustled into it, and drove away.

At the lake house, Westlake watched Johnstone's ministrations—the application of an unguent to the cuts on Alnoor's face, the dispensing of anti-inflammatory medication—and realized there was something deeper between the two. Alnoor was not just Johnstone's client, he was an *innocent* client. For a criminal defense attorney, that was a rarity. Where Westlake had birthed his plan of vigilantism to bring justice to the innocent victims of evil deeds, Johnstone had risked himself to protect the innocent accused. Westlake vowed to remember this, already altering his description of their 24-hour ordeal from the hunt for an escaped murderer, to the search and rescue of a possibly innocent man.

As they boarded the van to return Alnoor to the safehouse, Cunningham shackled Alnoor's wrists, replaced the batteries in the ankle monitor, and snapped the monitor in place. Alnoor, freshly showered, sat on the cargo bench in khakis and a blue button-down shirt, holding a bottle of water.

"You've been in a hotel room being questioned by the United States Attorney," Cunningham said. "With your attorney present."

Alnoor looked at him with confusion.

"There was no cabin, no video, no escape into the woods. Do you understand?"

Alnoor nodded.

Cunningham delivered Alnoor to the safehouse at the end of the gravel road. Alnoor went into the bedroom, without comment, to sleep.

Cunningham settled in the living area, slumping on the cushioned couch. He had not slept in forty hours.

His fellow marshal, the man charged with guarding Alnoor for the next shift, sat beside him. "She get anything out of him?" the marshal said.

"Who?"

"Bannister, the US Attorney."

Cunningham sighed. "I wasn't in the room," he said.

"How did he get those cuts and bruises?" the marshal asked.

"How do you think? The guy's a clam. Somebody had to open him up." Cunningham managed a tired smile, then left the couch and the safehouse and the simmering situation, not confident that Alnoor would stay quiet, not certain that it would matter. He returned to the Judge's house.

Their meeting, if it could be termed that, was uneasy. They had spent an arduous day making a video and then hunting Alnoor down in a massive area of forest. They had taken no sleep and eaten little food. Though Alnoor had been recaptured, they all acknowledged it had been by luck. Had Alnoor not stepped into a deep hole, he would still be on the loose, a dangerous font of information in search of an ear.

Westlake piled wood upon the grate. He'd carried an unabated chill since Alnoor's escape. He flicked a long-nosed lighter and held it against split pine thick with sap. When the flame caught, he returned to his favorite rocker, with Shiloh at his feet.

Johnstone occupied the next rocker, his toe on the floor, moving the rocker in slow motion, as if something faster would destroy his tenuous equilibrium. He had not had a cigarette since seeing the bears on the trail. Cunningham would not allow him to smoke on the long trip back to the van.

"So where do we stand?" Johnstone said. It was an ambiguous question, designed so.

The Judge took a sip of amber liquid, needing it to induce sleep, because exhaustion was not quite enough. "As far as the video, nothing's changed. We'll have to decide when and how, then carefully plan it out. It's going to be a waiting game."

"And Abdul?"

"I can see why you did it, David, but having a well-intentioned motive doesn't excuse what you did. We don't even know how close we came to disaster. You need to go back to your other clients, forget about Alnoor."

Johnstone stopped rocking, leaned forward in the chair, his eyes fixed on the flames. "I haven't regained your trust."

"No."

"Will Abdul be safe?"

"He'll never see the inside of a courtroom again," the Judge said. "That's the only assurance you get."

Johnstone rose and trudged toward his bedroom.

Westlake pulled the empty chair back from the fireplace and settled it next to a low, wooden table made from an old door with metal strap hinges. Caroline's usual rocker was on the table's other side.

He pulled his rocker toward the fire, anchoring one end of a crescent. His marshals dragged their chairs together.

"Thank you for what you both did today." His hands had just stopped shaking. "It was monumental."

"It's what we're trained to do," Perez said.

"Yes, but . . ." The Judge stopped, knowing words were inadequate, and just nodded. He had not been prepared for this, for the push toward the precipice, the shoving hands coming from so many directions. The chaos had spread beyond the borders of his control. He felt like a fish in a leaky plastic bag half-filled with water, watching the water and its precious oxygen seeping from the seam.

They all stayed the night. Judge Westlake retired to his bedroom, Shiloh at his heels. The apricot-colored dog jumped onto the bed and curled up on the spread. Westlake picked up his phone.

Caroline answered in a voice full of sleep. "What time is it?"

"After midnight. Sorry for calling so late. But I needed to tell you ..."

"Is it bad news?" she said.

He pictured her green eyes blinking awake, her torso sliding up the headboard. "No. It's good news. Alnoor got loose for a day, but we caught him."

"Got loose? How did that happen?"

Westlake sighed. "We hiked up to a remote cabin and made a video. A plea for help from Alnoor, to send anonymously to whatever suspects we can target. To lure them out. Afterward, David helped him escape into the forest. Fortunately, Alnoor fell into a hole, and we found him this afternoon. If he hadn't become trapped, I doubt we would have caught him."

There was silence on the other end, then a rustling sound as Caroline propped pillows behind her back. "Who do you plan to send the video to?"

"While we were searching for Alnoor, I thought about it a lot. I'm not sure what to do. What do you think?"

"Don't send it, Raleigh. We can't know how any recipient will react to it."

"I can use a technology that will destroy the email and the attached video, leaving no trace."

"Still, someone could report it to the police. We don't need any scrutiny right now. Give it some time. We'll find another way to fix this mess. When I'm done with the confirmation hearing, whatever the outcome, I'll put my attention back on this, try to find some leads we can really use."

"You're right. I'll bank the video. I'm not thinking straight, Caroline. The aborted trial, Alnoor's escape, the bombing, the scheme to make us look like the terrorists. I wonder whether the bomber would have gone through with it if he hadn't had someone else to pin it on."

There was silence on the other end.

"Goodnight Caroline," he said. As he turned off his phone for the night and laid it on the bedside table, he heard someone walking down the hallway toward the dining room.

32

Scrolling through the usual jumble of spam and other worthless emails, Viktor Volkov came across an email with Antiqam Wahid in the subject line. It was the moniker Abdul Alnoor had used when posting in jihadist chat rooms before his arrest. The name translated from Arabic as "Vengeful One." The sender's email address was JWSmythe39748@aol.com. Volkov didn't know anyone by the name of JW Smythe. He looked up 39748 as a zip code and found it could apply to Acapulco, Mexico or the Military City in Saudi Arabia.

Curious, Volkov opened the email. It contained the following message: "This email will delete itself in sixty seconds - Abdul." There was an attachment at the bottom. Volkov hesitated, unsure if he might be about to unleash a computer virus or malware. This laptop, the only one through which he accessed the internet, was equipped with the latest security and anti-hacking software, but one never knew if the malware defenders were ahead of the hackers, or vice versa. As the clock ticked down on his one minute, he decided to take a chance. He opened the attachment.

Abdul Alnoor's face appeared on the screen. His cheeks were hollow, his complexion pale, his eyes those of an exhausted man on the run. He spoke with a frantic but stern cadence. The whitish scars on his face, from the skin grafts Volkov had performed, left no doubt the man on the screen was not an imposter.

Volkov watched the video to the end. It appeared he was hiding in some sort of cabin. According to the newspaper Alnoor held up to the camera, the video had been made not more than a week earlier.

Volkov tried to download the video to his hard drive, but the video disappeared. He tried to save the email, but it also disappeared. He clicked into his spam file. The email wasn't there. He went to his trash bin. No email from that address. He had heard about this technology that evaporated emails and attachments, but had never used it. He wondered if his internet provider would have a copy of the email. He could contact the company and see if an IT expert could retrieve the email from his archives. After thinking about the content of the video, he realized his request might spark curiosity in someone at the internet company, so he decided against it.

He pulled out a spiral pad and a pen and began to write down everything he could remember about the video. He summarized Alnoor's message, the empty water bottles and food bags strewn about, the bare wooden planks in the background. Rewinding the video in his mind, he tried to capture Alnoor's expression, his tone of voice, his gestures. The light source behind the camera had appeared natural, not artificial. He made a note: "Cabin might not have electricity." He wrote down the name of the newspaper and the date. He knew these could be faked and planned to research the paper for validation.

He made two pages of notes. Tapping the pen on the lined paper, he flipped the page and began sketching the scene. He was not an artist, but his work in rebuilding damaged faces had bred in him an eye for detail, and when he finished shading the beard on Alnoor's face, he stared down at a man he did not recognize. It was Alnoor of course, but a changed Alnoor. Beneath the eyes were dark, deep hollows, and the fine white scar lines almost flashed against the contrast of the unkempt beard. Alnoor's eyes were dead.

Volkov looked up from the sketch, staring out into his yard and to the barn beyond. A part of him urged that he do something, that he plot a strategy to tie up the loose end now unraveled. Alnoor had invited him— no, pleaded with him—to make contact. But contact would put Volkov in peril, for in Alnoor's tone was embedded a faint hint of accusation. He wondered if Alnoor had made the connection to him through the hastily scribbled note he had stashed in Alnoor's backpack while they were both in the Mosque, one kneeling on the floor in prayer, the other feigning tardiness while sowing the seeds of anger. Volkov had written the note in block letters with his left hand, hoping the jerky lettering with his offhand would prevent anyone from identifying him as the author. He had named a website, a site on the dark web, where posters inflamed one another to hatred and violence. He had unzipped Alnoor's pack and slipped the note in the top, where it could not be missed. Had Alnoor somehow discovered that he was the one who had shoved Alnoor down this path?

Volkov realized the video could be a hoax. He supposed someone adept with editing software could fake the video. He searched the internet and found the newspaper on-line. It was published weekly in a town called Bryson City. The on-line issue had the same date and the same lead article touting the local football team's surge into the playoffs. That part, at least, was authentic.

Alnoor had taken some risk to get the newspaper. Volkov wondered where he had gotten a video camera. He could have stolen the camera, but that too was risky. Or perhaps the video had been recorded and emailed from a cell phone. Could Alnoor have accomplished either of those things without help?

Volkov unlocked the back door and went outside. Danya followed him into the yard. When Volkov commanded the dog in Russian to search, Danya dipped his nose to the ground and headed toward the fence line. Volkov scanned the sky. Clouds the color of old pewter were pushing in from the north, the sun soon to be obscured. He looked toward the barn, the dormant orchard behind it, the grassy field on which he had once planted vegetables. He wasn't looking for anything in particular, just something amiss, a movement or a sound that didn't belong on the farm. His Makarov was tucked in a shoulder holster beneath his left arm. He unzipped his windbreaker, just in case.

He worked his jaw without realizing it, the portent of the video gnawing at him. He had no concrete sense of the risk Alnoor might pose. Undoubtedly, the Judge and the others had faked Alnoor's death. Alnoor couldn't have been clever enough to fool them. But had Alnoor really escaped? If so, they must be quietly looking for him, and they had some idea where he might be hiding. Volkov did not. But if he could arrange a meeting with Alnoor, that might be the easiest way of mitigating the danger, and if he was cooperating with the people who had killed the Mayor, it might bring all of them within his circle, and the encounter could end only one way.

Danya's ears perked, and the big dog bounded to the wire fence that faced the road. He stood peering at something in front of the house, his front legs flexing as if he were about to leap. Volkov flattened himself against the back brick wall of the house, inching toward the corner and a vantage point. Two steps from the corner, he slipped his right hand onto the butt of his pistol. Danya gave him a furtive look as Volkov canted his head around the corner.

Four children jumped down the steps of the school bus. The kids were middle-school age, backpacks half their size hoisted on their bent backs, an exuberant babble coming from them. They paused in front of his house because that was their bus stop, a place where the grass near the edge of the road was worn thin by their feet, a spot where on warm days they kicked a soccer ball in Volkov's front yard. He could hear their voices, if not their words.

The bus idled a few more seconds, its door open, before another child descended the stairs. She had a long metal brace from hip to ankle and had to lean her body to the side to swing her leg down the stairs. At the bottom, she turned and reached back into the bus, and the driver handed her a pink backpack. She shouldered the pack and worked the straps, then hobbled off in the other direction, the stainless steel of her brace glinting in the sunlight.

Volkov let out a deep breath, dropped his hand from the pistol butt. He wondered whether the girl could have been at the concert in the arena the night of the bombing. He didn't know why his mind went there, why random sights and sounds linked back to that night. But something had shifted inside of him.

He had to get back to his former state of mind. His safety depended on it. He realized that Alnoor was not the threat, that the danger lurked in deep shadows where agents worked to trap men like him. Whether Judge Westlake and US Attorney Caroline Bannister were part of the plot, or simply vigilantes on a renegade mission of their own, he couldn't answer, but he understood it was probable they were using Alnoor as bait to lure him in.

They had deceived him and faked Alnoor's death. But when the email and video vanished, the evidence of their treachery was lost. Volkov's face turned darker, his eyes narrowed, the line between his lips tightened. He was not a fool. He could not be caught so easily.

Back in the house, Danya curled up on his pallet. Volkov pulled up a map of the western section of North Carolina, a triangle of space dominated by mile-high mountains, deep river gorges, and vast wilderness. Bryson City was surrounded by the Cherokee Reservation, the Nantahala National Forest, and the Great Smokey Mountains National Park. The area was remote, most of it uninhabited. The Judge's lake house, where Volkov had mailed three photographs to initiate the blackmail scheme, was close by. If Alnoor was nearby, he was there on purpose, exposed on a video but hidden nonetheless. With more research, Volkov discovered that Eric Rudolph had eluded the FBI for more than five years by hiding in this same wilderness. This confirmed to Volkov that searching for Alnoor would be futile.

He opened a different laptop, one never connected to the internet, and perused the photographs he had taken of Judge Westlake, Caroline Bannister, and the others. Pictures of them standing outside a tractor-trailer rig, of two US Marshals carrying Mayor Williams' prone body to the trunk of his own car. Images of one Marshal digging a roadside grave, a close-up of the Mayor's mortal head wound, of his unearthed body beside the road in the dark. Volkov had used the photographs once as a threat, a threat to which they had acceded by killing Abdul Alnoor in his cell, a death he now knew was faked.

He wondered if he should use them again. These photographs could be leaked to the press or the FBI, but without context they constituted isolated images only, perhaps evidence of a crime, but the search for the photographer might be more intense than the search for those depicted, and if they found him, how would he explain it? He was a witness, a witness who had failed to come forward with evidence of a murder, who had refused to provide evidence that the Mayor could not have bombed the Charlotte arena. Why?

If found, the FBI would interrogate him, suspicious of his motives, suspicious of his recalcitrance to come forward, probing his story, his history, his financial records, his whereabouts for months on end. He would not be a hero, but a suspect, for undoubtedly the targets of his blackmail had concocted an explanation for the photographs, solid alibis that they were somewhere else, that the photographs had been doctored. And because four of the five were loyal servants of the system of justice, with no blemishes on their records, their credibility would not be questioned. He could not pin on them the murder of the Mayor or the bombing of the arena with the same perfection with which he had framed Alnoor for the country-club shooting.

And if the FBI did not trace the anonymous tip to him, Volkov would know nothing of the investigation, or whether the Bureau had taken the information seriously, or treated it as a prank. Perhaps they would conduct informal interviews of Judge Westlake and the others, polite conversations preceded by disclaimers that this was likely just a cruel joke, followed by denials issued with a stern countenance, and Volkov's evidence would be discarded as a hoax.

But if Volkov released the photographs now, the cabal would know. They would know that he had received the video revealing Alnoor was alive, and Volkov had responded by sending the photographs to law enforcement. Releasing the photographs would identify him to the cabal as the blackmailer and the bomber who killed 2,147 people. However he looked at it, he would become their target.

Volkov climbed into bed with an uncomfortable pressure in his chest. He clicked off the bedside lamp and lay there, staring at the ceiling. A vague notion of enlisting his Russian colleagues to search for Alnoor came to him, but it passed like a moth heading back into darkness from an extinguished porch light. His Russian handler thought Alnoor was dead, a loose end handled, information passed to the hierarchy, and were Volkov to reveal otherwise, the repercussions for him would not be favorable. His promised return to Russia, though perhaps an illusion, would evaporate, and he suspected the reprisal for his failure would be a cold grave next to Alnoor's. His body beading with sweat, Volkov threw off the bed covers. A minute later, his skin chilled, he pulled the blanket and spread back over himself. He laid there for an interminable time, his eyes fixed on something in the distance, working on a different plan.

33

Caroline Bannister gazed out at the traffic rolling past her office in Washington, D.C. Even though the bulletproof glass was state of the art, the view still held a certain murkiness, a slight distortion, the cars and delivery trucks misshapen on the edges, as if drawn there with a charcoal pencil. She had been Attorney General for less than a week, and already she felt the claustrophobia of D.C. The clutch of it made her heart feel closer to the surface, her skin tighter as it stretched across her forehead and cheeks.

Her confirmation hearing had gone as predicted, though the grilling at the hands of certain members of the Senate Judiciary Committee had been unpleasant, placing Caroline on the opposite side of the interrogation table for the first time in her life. It had become clear to her then, as Senators peppered her with inane questions, that she was not a natural politician. She answered the questions as best she could. No, she could not predict how she might view a hypothetical incident in the future without knowing all the details after conducting a thorough investigation. Yes, she was committed to upholding the laws and Constitution of the United States, as well as the civil rights of all citizens, regardless of race, gender or national origin. And no, she did not have a perfect plan to end gun violence in the United States, or have a blueprint for stopping terrorism, or know how to stem the tide of illegal immigrants entering the country's sieve-like border. Ascending to the top law enforcement post in the nation, she had expected these questions, but that did not ease her frustration that Senators used the occasion to grandstand and make political points. To Caroline, the televised confirmation hearing merely proved that the United States Congress had little idea of how justice truly operated. Justice was not attained in front of cameras, but in halls and offices and streets through the methodical work of thousands of agents, investigators and attorneys. And, sometimes, in a dark and secret courtroom.

She was asked by one Senator, in a sympathetic tone, whether the murder of her sister decades earlier had ever been solved. Knowing the cameras were pointed at her, focused on her every blink, grimace, and gesture, Caroline's mouth had said "no," while her brain wrestled with the knowledge that her father was responsible and that she had with her own hand executed an

139

innocent man for the crime. When asked about injustices she had remedied in her tenure as United States Attorney, she did not mention she had wiped Judge Hal Manning, who had taken bribes in return for light sentences, from our midst.

"Do you think the victims of the massacre at the Charlotte golf club were deprived of justice when the terrorist died in prison?" one Senator asked her.

"Absolutely." She paused, momentarily considering correcting the Senator's use of the word 'terrorist' to describe the perpetrator, for his murders didn't fit the legal description. She thought better of it. "One of those victims was a friend of mine. Another was a federal judge I frequently appeared in front of. They didn't get justice. They all deserved better."

"And do you think the victims of the bombing in Charlotte were deprived of justice because the bomber blew himself up?"

Caroline glanced at her notes and steeled her eyes, knowing the bomber was still at large. "In my opinion, suicide shows a lack of courage. It shows the bomber was himself terrified, terrified of getting caught, terrified of facing the consequences of his actions. The victims can rest assured he died a coward. There's some justice in that outcome." She had rehearsed these words, intending to send a message if *he* was watching, something to challenge him to emerge from hiding so a quintet of vigilantes could kill him in the dark. She lost her focus as the Mayor's visage passed through her mind. "I . . . I can't put myself in their shoes. Not really. I've talked to some of the survivors, and I've been to ground zero, and I can't adequately describe it for you. I don't think anyone can." She reached for a glass of water. "But that's what motivates me to keep going, to try and find ways to prevent these catastrophic events from happening in the first place."

Watching taped coverage of the hearing later, with lines of consternation creasing her forehead, she saw how good a liar she had become. Even her pauses seemed genuine, her silence the product of deep empathy rather than hesitation.

As she sipped from a mug of coffee in her office, behind a giant wooden desk covered with papers stacked neatly in rows, she already missed her job as United States Attorney where, for the most part, she had operated with little oversight and beyond the media's glare. She had given up the courtroom for policy meetings and press conferences and scrutiny by newspapers and television journalists watching her every move. Here, in D.C., eyes were upon her at all times. She couldn't fathom how anyone could endure the job for very long.

Caroline's assistant buzzed to let her know the driver was downstairs, ready to take her the short distance to the White House. Caroline preferred to walk, for the morning was sunny and crisp, but that was no longer an option for the Attorney General of the United States. She slipped into her briefcase a folder marked "**SECRET**", which had been delivered to her that morning, along with her daily briefing. Caroline snapped the clasps on her briefcase, its leather worn smooth by years of handling. The case had been given to her by the District Attorney for whom she had worked at her first job as a lawyer, prosecuting perpetrators of domestic violence. The briefcase had no handle and was small enough to fit under her arm.

"You have a big briefcase for Court," DA Sizemore had told her. "This is for personal stuff, or more discreet material."

She entered the private elevator that served her suite of offices and rode it to the underground garage. Her driver, who also had driven the previous Attorney General, was standing beside the armored SUV. He opened the rear door without prompting. His name was Robert and he was part of her Secret Service detail, but she knew little else about the man.

"I need to go to the White House," she said after buckling up.

"Yes, ma'am," Robert said.

They drove the 1.2 miles to the White House in the snarl of D.C. traffic, her black and bulky armored coach like a larger bug in a stream of ants, arriving fourteen minutes later, pulling in through the gate beneath the searching eyes of two guards who scanned their ID badges and ran mirrors along every inch of the undercarriage.

"I could have walked faster," she said to no one in particular.

She waited in an anteroom under the watch of the President's Executive Secretary until a desk phone buzzed and she was shown into the Oval Office. President Danny Roberts stood from the Resolution Desk and walked forward to greet her. His face was tan, and his thick hair was styled away from his face, the blond only recently tinged with gray.

"Good morning, Caroline," he said with a Texas drawl that had not been altered by three years in D.C.

"Good morning, Mr. President."

They sat on dove gray sofas that faced each other. Chief of Staff Carly Newman hovered about. The President had maintained the typical decorum of the Oval Office, except for two trophies on bold display. A large, stuffed polar bear occupied the curved wall opposite the Resolute Desk. Standing on its hind legs, with its paws raised as if on attack, the polar bear stretched above eleven feet high. A large fish was mounted above the entry door to the

Oval, a long snout of jagged teeth making it look like a remnant from a prehistoric world.

"Mr. President. I have to ask—the polar bear—is that real?"

"That's a fact. Shot him in Siberia. Weighed one thousand four hundred and eighty-three pounds. Killed him with one shot from a .30-06 rifle. If you look real close at the fur just behind his right ear, you might be able to see the bullet hole. Dead before he hit the ground." He said this without compunction, an enthusiasm infusing his voice, as if describing a key play he'd made in a football playoff game.

Caroline glanced at the polar bear and its gigantic head. It seemed poised to pounce on visitors. "I see. And when were you in Siberia?"

"Oh, I've been several times," the President said. "That bear was shot in 2008. I was still Governor then."

"And the fish above the door? It looks like some deep-sea creature."

"That's an alligator gar. Shot him with a bow and arrow. He's 71 inches long and weighs 157 pounds. And his teeth are razor sharp. It was quite a fight getting him into the boat."

"You shot him with a bow and arrow?"

"I did. On the Trinity River near Dallas, back in the late 90s."

"I knew you were an avid hunter and fisherman, but I had no idea." The trophies reminded her that this man craved power like no other man she had met, and he had an insatiable need to wield it. She felt it in his handshake, a grip that encircled her hand, not bone-crushing, but signaling that if he had no intention of letting go, she would become his prisoner. And she saw it in his domination of the bear and the fish, two apex predators in their own right. That he brandished these trophies in the Oval Office said he would conquer everything and everyone. It was both alluring and dangerous, all at once.

"When you're the head of an oil company, you do a lot of traveling. Gave me an opportunity to hunt and fish in some exotic places. So, Caroline, do you hunt or fish?"

"No hunting, but I do like to fish. Lake fishing, mostly. I fished Fontana Lake in western North Carolina in early spring. Do you know it?"

"I do know it. Fished it twice in fact, for steelhead."

"I see."

"With those beautiful mountains just outside your door, Caroline, I was a little surprised I was able to entice you to come to Washington."

"Once in a lifetime opportunity, Mr. President. I couldn't pass it up, even though D.C. is a bit claustrophobic for my tastes."

"I agree. D.C.'s a cesspool. Not like the wide-open spaces in West Texas."

"Or Alaska. How was the summit?"

The President waved his hand dismissively. "I'll give you a full report at the Cabinet meeting next week. In summary, Sokolov and I are more alike than we are different. We both want jobs, prosperity and peace for our citizens. It was a good start to warming things up. Now, as much as I've enjoyed talking about outdoor adventures, you didn't come here to discuss bears and fish."

"No, sir."

The President moved behind his desk and reclined in his chair, putting his feet on the desk.

"Tell me what you've got."

Caroline pulled the red file from her case and flipped to the first page. "ATF doesn't think the Charlotte bomber acted alone."

"ATF? I thought the FBI concluded otherwise and closed the case."

"Yes, sir. But ATF says there's a missing link that doesn't account for the Tovex, the bomb catalyst."

"I read the FBI report, Caroline. They suspect the bomber brought it back from Africa, by boat."

"Yes, sir. That's what it says. But ATF can't confirm it."

The President leaned forward and put his feet on the floor, rubbed his chin with fingers long and creased. "This isn't the first time these agencies have disagreed. I wish they'd get together on this before they announce a conclusion. What do you think, Caroline?"

"There are always holes in an investigation, sir. We go at things from a hundred different directions. The Mayor was in areas of Africa controlled by Boko Haram and other groups known to use explosives, so that's his opportunity to acquire Tovex. I personally reviewed financial records from his election campaign, and there were cash withdrawals in amounts sufficient for him to buy the Tovex and the van." She kept her eyes focused on the American flag, just behind the President's right ear, while she laid this lie. "There are lots of places domestically where you can get it. Loggers use it, for example."

"Does ATF have any theories as to where this phantom accomplice might be, what he might be doing?"

"No, sir. That's not their jurisdiction. They're only pointing out that they can't confirm the source."

"But ATF *is* your jurisdiction, Caroline. You need to fix this. You can't let this go any further. If something like this leaks, the public will panic, and our people will lose faith in our law enforcement capabilities."

"Yes, sir."

"Anything else?"

"The NSA reports unusual activity at the Russian Consulates in D.C. and New York, and there's been heightened activity on message boards on the dark web."

"What kind of activity?"

"Extra trips to safehouses in Maryland and Virginia, and upstate New York. Internet chatter about something big happening in D.C. on Black Friday."

"That's this Friday," the President said.

"Yes, sir."

The President's eyes narrowed. "Why am I hearing this from you, and not from the Pentagon or FBI?"

"I don't know, Mr. President. It was part of my briefing this morning, and I was asked to pass it on. Did I overstep?"

The President swiveled his chair and eyed her, his arms folded across his chest. "Sacrificial lamb."

Caroline looked at him with her lips parted. "Sacrificial lamb, sir?"

"You're here because there's nothing to it. Might even be a prank. This isn't protocol. I talk to the NSA and FBI directors every day, sometimes multiple times a day. You're the newest member of my cabinet. This is probably your initiation." The President laughed, shook his head. "Welcome to D.C."

"You think this is a prank, sir?" Caroline stood. "I mean, when I was briefed this morning, the agent seemed serious. I have summaries of the activity, both internet and otherwise. We can't just ignore it, can we?"

"No, we won't ignore it, Caroline. Of course not. But if there's actually something going on with the Russians, you won't be the one sitting here telling me about it."

34

Raleigh Westlake ran past the Lincoln Memorial, glancing only briefly at the giant sculpture of Abe gazing out upon the National Mall like the overseer of freedom. Raleigh wound his way around Constitution Gardens, then down the trails and sidewalks that paralleled Constitution Avenue. He passed the National Gallery of Art, the US Capitol, and stopped in front of the United States Supreme Court. He walked back and forth at the base of the marble steps, taking deep breaths, and finally ascended the steps.

This was not how he had envisioned his first visit to the Supreme Court. As a trial attorney in Atlanta, he had filed several petitions requesting the Court to review lower-court decisions rendered against his clients, but all his petitions had been rejected. And, although many of his decisions as a federal judge had been appealed, none of those appeals had reached the highest court in the land.

In running shorts and a sweat-darkened shirt he approached the statue on his left, a larger than life rendering entitled "Contemplation of Justice." The statue depicted a sitting Lady Justice, who appeared to be slumping in her stone throne. In her right hand she held a figurine of blind justice, almost doll-sized. The blindfolded figure grasped scales tightly against her torso, as if protecting them from attack.

Westlake traversed the steps to the statue on the right side of the entrance to the Court, a ready figure named Authority of Law. Resembling a warrior, his large sword rested at his side, poised for combat. He noted the two symbolic stalwarts of the law did not face each other, but stared ahead with fixed gazes, as if to challenge those who entered the building.

His eyes wandered over the statues and the building, the big Corinthian columns, the white marble facade. He supposed the intent was to portray a stalwart institution, with justice protected by law in all instances, but from his own experience on the lower rung, he knew it wasn't so. He had vaguely hoped he would feel something as he stood there at the temple, but all he felt was a twisting in his gut. The two wolves, probably.

He descended the steps and jogged back to his room at the Willard Intercontinental. He showered, donned a suit and a tie, and dabbed cologne on his wrists. He walked down the stairs, avoiding the elevator, a habit he had maintained for several decades. At some point he had approximated the number of calories he expended each year by shunning elevators and taking the stairs, but he could no longer remember the sum.

Caroline was sitting in a comfortable arm chair next to a live ficus tree, facing the reception desk, reading the Post.

He paused for a moment, leaning against a column, gazing at her legs, a good bit of them revealed below a navy skirt that almost reached her knees. It had been a month since he'd seen her, a month in which communication had been sparse. He was busy. She was busy. But it was more than that.

As he approached, she rose from the chair, as if she'd been peering around the newspaper at his approach, and offered her right hand. He shook her hand as he did the hands of attorneys who appeared before him, a greeting without familiarity. In her face there was no hint of the intimacy he and Caroline had once shared. During her confirmation hearing, his name had not come up, and the Senators had been wise in not asking the prospective Attorney General about boyfriends, for she would have chastised the questioner as boorish and then refused to answer.

They exited a brass-framed glass door manned by a doorman in an ornate uniform complete with epaulettes. They stepped onto the sidewalk and walked with purpose, she leading him though they were side-by-side, her eyes searching dark doorways and the faces of other pedestrians. They ate dinner in a restaurant in the next block, sitting in a booth in a back corner but not entirely concealed. Although it was Thanksgiving, they both ordered steak; his medium, hers rare. Their conversation was thin, frequently interrupted by people he didn't know, but perhaps she did know or should, who stopped by the table to congratulate her on her confirmation as AG. He saw the looks on their faces, the need to curry favor, to be invited into her realm of influence. She was polite, piling the proffered business cards in a stack next to the salt and pepper shakers.

In a lull in the activity, with entrees partially consumed, she leaned forward across the table. "This is my first time out in public since I was sworn in. I wasn't prepared for this."

"We don't have to stay," Raleigh said.

She lifted a wine glass half-filled with burgundy and took a sip, her eyes alive with the cat gleam of her irises. "Let's finish our dinner."

They ate in silence for a time, as he cast glances that gradually became less furtive, eventually drawing a smile from her. He dabbed his mouth with the cloth napkin and sputtered a laugh.

"What is it?" she asked.

"You know—this formality. Since when were we merely colleagues?"

"A while back," she said over the glass.

"What have you been working on?" he said. "Boy, that was an inane question. You probably can't tell me."

"I think I got pranked this week."

"Pranked? What do you mean?"

She thought about it a moment, about the "SECRET" designation on the file she had been given. She decided it was okay if she redacted all identifying information. "Three days ago, I briefed the President on a phony terrorist plot. I was set up."

"What do you mean set up?"

"I was given a fake scenario, complete with manufactured evidence, to present to the President in my weekly briefing. I feel like a fool."

"How do you know it was fake?"

"Because if it was real, I wouldn't have been the one briefing the President. It doesn't work that way. I'm not part of the intelligence community, not like NSA, DHS, CIA. There are seventeen agencies or organizations, some of which I didn't know existed a year ago. To think that I would be the one to brief the President on a terrorism issue . . . I was a victim of my own ego. This was my initiation into the club."

He took this in, tossing it about in his head, realizing he didn't know her anymore. She had merged into a different world, a new realm, one into which he wasn't invited. They resumed eating, the steaks becoming smaller, the chewing taking longer by intention. When the silence became uncomfortable, Westlake asked, "What's he like?"

"Who?"

"The President."

Caroline continued chewing, then swallowed. She wiped a dribble of juice from the corner of her mouth. "He's very engaging. He gives you his full attention. You two have something in common."

Raleigh looked up. "Oh, what's that?"

"Fishing. He's actually fished Lake Fontana."

"Fontana Lake," he corrected her. "When?"

"I don't remember. But he said he's fished it a couple of times. For steelhead, I think. He's quite the outdoorsman. In the Oval is a polar bear he shot in Siberia, and some prehistoric looking fish he shot with a bow and arrow."

Raleigh had never been in the Oval Office, never been inside the White House. "How often do you meet with him?" he asked without looking at her.

She emitted a brief laugh, then covered her mouth with the napkin. "I told you. We have a regular weekly meeting. Other meetings as necessary. It's all work." Was Raleigh jealous? It was almost comical, this conversation with a man she had seduced, a man with whom she had committed innumerable crimes. She gazed across the table at him, a faint smile on her lips. "You have nothing to worry about."

"Who says I'm worried?"

She wanted to reach across the table and touch his hand, but they were in public, so she restrained herself. She didn't want to be the subject of a gossip column in the morning newspapers. As the newest member of the President's cabinet and someone who gave frequent press briefings, the media wanted to know about her. She wouldn't let them intrude on this. She refused to give them anything to gossip about.

They left the restaurant and walked back to his hotel. A black SUV with tinted windows followed along behind them at an indiscreet distance. Caroline tossed her head in the direction of the SUV. "That's my security," she said.

Raleigh looked back at the vehicle. "I didn't realize … do they follow you everywhere?"

"So far," she said. "Except to the bathroom. And maybe even then. Who knows?"

They entered the lobby and anchored themselves beside a sitting area with four chairs and a stone table, but they did not sit.

"Do you want to come up, have an after-dinner drink?" he said, his right eyebrow arched.

She hesitated. "No. Yes. Both." She smiled at him in that way she had when they had first hiked together on the Cherokee Reservation—knowing, expectant and anxious all at once. Unguarded.

"I want you to," he said.

"My driver is waiting," she said with a nod of her head toward the entrance.

Westlake studied the people in the lobby, trying to identify others who might be protecting her, analyzing him and his movements, looking for a concealed intention. Then he realized how foolish he looked.

She took his right hand and leaned in, both feet on the ground, her other hand on his shoulder. She whispered into his cheek. "I'll be back later. Without them."

He went up to his room and waited. After an hour, his cell phone buzzed with a text and, less than a minute later, he heard a soft knock on his hotel room door. Caroline stood there in jeans and a yellow sweater, a ball cap covering her head, tendrils of auburn hair peeking from beneath. He pulled her into the room without saying a word and kissed her, nibbling her upper lip and then her left earlobe. They fell to the bed, and he ravaged her as one might a lover soon to be gone, savoring a final taste. There was no softness, no tenderness, only a message of urgency and something amiss.

Caroline didn't mind. This was the one thing that could pierce the facade she'd pasted on the moment she'd been nominated, and hadn't taken off since. This was normal. Since stepping into the spotlight, nothing else had been. She pulled him in tighter until she felt an almost forgotten shudder, and then he raised his head in guttural release.

"You're a little wound up," Caroline said after her breath returned.

"I'm sorry."

"You're angry with me."

"No. I just haven't figured this out yet."

"By 'this,' you mean did I take the job and move to D.C. to run away?"

He propped himself on one elbow and gazed at her. "Yes, that's what I mean."

She rubbed Catherine's locket between thumb and forefinger, then let it settle at the hollow of her neck. "I started with all of this, joining you, because I wanted to avenge my sister's death. Even though I was wrong about the Mayor, my quest is over. That's all this is—the next step. But I can see how you might take it another way."

"Yes."

They came to that moment, each knowing that the next words said, or not said, would dictate a direction. Their paths could remain united, or could diverge into mist.

"Can we talk about something else?" she said. His look told her he was not ready to accept a change in the conversation, that there were still questions to which he wanted—and perhaps deserved—an answer. "We can't go back, Raleigh. Not now."

"I don't want to go back. I want to know what lies ahead."

"You want me to predict the future. I can barely see into tomorrow. Everything moves so fast here. I feel like I'm standing on one leg, being buffeted by everything and everyone. What do you want me to say?"

"I don't know. I don't like change."

"And this is a big change."

He nodded, then plopped onto his back.

"You are always so sure," she said. "Sure of what you want, sure of how to get it, certain of the path that leads you there."

"And you're not?" he said this with a tone bordering on harshness, the rawness of her departure coming through.

"Not right now. I'm a little off balance. Have been for a while."

"Of course." He realized he had been analyzing every word, as if preparing to interrogate her. "None of this has been easy. I want you to know that I care. I care deeply about you. I care about us." He stared at the tray ceiling and an oily smudge on the upper plaster.

"I know all that, Raleigh." She turned her head toward him and entwined her fingers with his. "It will be all right. We'll be okay. If we let it."

"I don't know how you can be so sure." He stood up, donned a plush bath robe, and paced the room. He finally stopped in front of the bed, his hands intertwined behind his head. "Where do we stand, Caroline?"

"In what sense?"

"Us, the group, whatever."

Caroline stacked two pillows against the headboard and leaned against them, pulling the bed covers up to her neck. "Those are two different questions. I'm out of the group. I can't participate from here. You guys don't need me anymore. You and I are fine. Let's give us time to get adjusted to the fact that I live in D.C. now."

He turned to the refrigerator, pulled out a minibottle of bourbon, and unscrewed the cap. He poured it into a glass, then took a long swig. "We may never get adjusted to this."

From the bed she said, "That's a possibility. That's not what I want, but a lot of this is out of my control."

"You like it here, your new job."

"I like the job. It's exciting. I have a chance to make big policy changes, get ahead of things for a change. I don't feel like I'm always trying to catch up."

"It's easier for you."

"Why do you say that?"

He turned away, went to the window and parted the curtains, looking without focus at the glow of streetlights, the absence of trees. "I thought it might wind up like this. You here, me there. Our paths not likely to cross again. I'm going to release Alnoor. Soon," he said.

"That's not your call, Raleigh. That decision gets made at Justice, by me."

He turned back to her. "You said you were out of the group. This isn't your problem any longer."

She thought about it for a moment. "You could be releasing a terrorist. Are you willing to take that risk?"

Westlake dipped his head and curled his toes in the thick carpet. "I can't punish another innocent man," he said.

"You're never going to forgive me for the Mayor, are you?"

"Probably not." He thrust his hands deep in the pockets of the robe. "Better to let the guilty go than execute an innocent man."

"Now you're quoting Blackstone to me, Raleigh?"

"Paraphrasing. There's a reason that axiom has stood the test of time. It's one of the things that keeps us on this side of barbarism."

Caroline ran both hands through her disheveled hair, then locked her fingers on the back of her head. "After six secret trials, you're worried about barbarism? It's a little late for that, don't you think?" She hopped out of bed and wrapped herself in the other robe. "I can't do this with you."

They left it there, each of them entrenched, the argument unwinnable by either side. After showering, they left his room and boarded the elevator. Letting her leave the hotel alone didn't seem right, and it might constitute a finale. He wanted to spend these next few minutes with her.

At precisely 12:01 a.m. on Black Friday, the power went out. Raleigh and Caroline, descending to the hotel lobby, felt the elevator come to a jolting stop. They stood in total darkness, the elevator in a slight sway, listening to each other's breathing. Raleigh dipped into his jacket pocket and removed his cell phone. The screen lit up, casting a dim blue light. He dialed 911 and was greeted with this message: "All circuits are busy. Please try your call again later."

"Raleigh, I'm getting claustrophobic," Caroline said. Her breathing had become quick and shallow.

"It's okay, I'm right here." He gripped her right hand with his left. With his other hand he swiped across the screen of his phone, looking for the flashlight app.

"Maybe you have to swipe top to bottom. Don't you know how to use your phone?" Caroline said, her voice rising.

"No, I don't know how to use every feature. We're okay, calm down."

"You calm down. I got trapped in an elevator once for several hours. This is not good."

Forty-one seconds after the power went out, the hotel's backup generator came on, and the emergency light in the elevator glowed yellow.

"See, we'll be fine. The power is back on," Westlake said.

Caroline, breathing in short bursts, nodded her head.

The elevator began to descend again, and they came to the lobby. They stepped out onto the marble tile, the lobby lit only by emergency lighting. They exited through the revolving door and stood under the portico.

"I wonder what's going on. It looks like all of D.C. is out," Caroline said. "Let me call my assistant." Caroline pulled her phone from her purse. "Nothing. All circuits are busy." She tapped the icon for the web browser on her phone and was greeted with a message that indicated she was not connected to the internet. "Looks like cell service is out, and internet too."

"Let's see if we can get back into my room," Westlake said.

"Raleigh, I need to get to my office. I've got a satellite phone there."

A black SUV pulled to the curb, and an agent in a dark suit threw open the front passenger door, stepped onto the sidewalk, and gripped Caroline by the right elbow. "Ms. Bannister, we need to get you to the White House. Now." He ushered her into the back seat, her hair flying from beneath the ball cap, then slammed the door. The SUV drove off. Through the tinted windows, Raleigh couldn't tell if Caroline even looked back at him.

35

As the city plunged into darkness, Viktor Volkov stood across the street from the White House, leaning against the spiked metal fence of Lafayette Square. He was dressed as a woman. A self-made wig rested upon his head, and a muslin cloak draped his torso. A loose hood was pulled close around his face.

Washington, D.C. was in a blackout. The streetlights were out, as were the traffic signals. The White House was lit dimly, and he could hear the distinctive hum of generators across the street. He knew how it worked. He had a diesel generator in his underground bunker.

Even in the darkness, a darkness that he created, tourists milled about, snapping photographs of the White House at night while simultaneously exclaiming they had no cell service. Protestors in tents on the edge of the park held signs demanding that Tibet be freed. The air in the nation's capital was fetid and dense, breathless, as if in pause.

From behind a statue of Andrew Jackson on a horse, Volkov pulled a pair of binoculars to his eyes. The binoculars used thermal imaging for vision enhancement, and as he scanned the roof of the White House he saw a number of agents who had not been there before the blackout. Some of the agents were using similar binoculars to scan the grounds; others crouched behind the parapet on the roof, long guns pressed against their shoulders. It appeared to Volkov the White House was assuming the hits to the electrical and telecommunications grids were precursors to a possible attack. On the murky grounds of the White House, agents with semi-automatic weapons took up positions beneath the trees, their eyes on the perimeter fence.

The outages would be temporary, for even with the aid of Russia's best hackers, and cell phone jammers placed strategically throughout the city, cell service would likely be restored within twenty-four hours. Nonetheless, the outages might disrupt America's busiest shopping day, shut down credit card processing in wide swaths, paralyze the government, and interrupt electronic banking transactions. He would know only in hindsight, perhaps through a cryptic phone call, or a coded message delivered with medical supplies, how successful the blackout had been.

He wondered if Russia would take responsibility. If so, it would be a private admission entangled with a subtle threat, delivered by a diplomat far removed from the man who made the decision to rattle the US infrastructure. Russia would want the interruption to be seen as an example of its cyber-skills, an indiscreet message that it could unlock and climb through the bedroom window at any time, day or night. But to what end? On that point, he felt as much in the dark as the residents of D.C.

As a cadre of agents moved from the White House grounds to Pennsylvania Avenue, Volkov plucked a few strands from the wig containing hair from various patients and dropped them strategically along his escape route. Hunched over as if from a bad back, he trudged away from the Square, keeping his face hidden from cameras he knew must be there even if he couldn't detect them in the dark. He crossed H Street, glancing at the Episcopal church where an old woman might go to pray and light a candle on a night such as this, but he suspected the church would be closed at this hour.

He turned right onto I Street, using the maneuver to check the side-view mirror of a van parked at the curb to determine if he was being followed. He couldn't be sure. There were two men in dark suits walking in the same direction, perhaps fifty yards behind, but they were talking to each other and seemed not to focus on him. Of course, if they were government agents good at surveillance, they would be watching him without appearing to be.

A block later, Volkov stopped in front of a store with large columns supporting the cantilevered floor above, and leaned against one of the columns as if in need of rest. The store was closed, but its dark windows gave him a panoramic reflection of the street and the way he had come. The two men in dark suits had disappeared.

The chop of a helicopter overwhelmed the minor din of traffic noise, and he glanced up as the copter sped by overhead, aimed in the general direction of the White House, searchlights sweeping over the street and sidewalks. Every squealing tire, glaring headlight and excited voice raised the hair on the back of his neck. He had to assume they were looking for the party responsible for the blackout, keen to the possibility of manual as well as electronic interruption. Every pedestrian he encountered became his potential pursuer.

He reached inside his cloak and felt the familiar bulge of the Makarov, tucked beneath his arm in a leather holster. He had to remember to count any shots he might fire and to save at least one bullet, if it came to that. When he heard sirens screaming down K Street, one block over, he resumed his journey. It took all of his will not to run, to maintain the laboring gait of the old-woman disguise he'd adopted for this mission. He found the McPherson metro station, opened the flashlight icon on his phone and descended the stairs, then entered a dark bathroom, where he stuffed the cloak and the wig into a trash bin, revealing a zippered jacket with the Washington Capitals logo on the front. He emerged from the metro station as a somewhat inebriated patron of a sports bar, his evening cut short by the loss of power. He walked three blocks in a slightly stumbling gait, his arms jutting out on occasion for balance. He passed two policemen on bicycles and a policeman standing in the middle of an intersection, directing traffic. Volkov turned a corner and righted himself, thrusting his hands in his pockets, and walked with careful eyes the rest of the way to the parking garage. No one bothered him, and no one stared at him to compare his face to a photograph that might be circulating.

He retrieved the rental car and sped under the raised gate of the garage. Once on the Beltway, he felt relieved. It was no longer necessary to pretend, though he wondered whether the risk of capture had been worth it. Somebody much higher up thought so. Volkov had studied the actions of his homeland's leaders only after leaving Russia, and perhaps through the detachment of distance and time had gained some insight. He understood that even if he happened to land on the precise reason for his mission, something that made sense as a tiny piece of a larger plan, the motive might be more simplistic, or illogical, or explained as the thrusting fist of a bully exercising his might without thought of repercussions. So often decisions that alter the world and jeopardize people's lives are made on emotion, or misunderstanding, the response disproportionate to the catalyst, like the man in a bar who meets a perceived insult with a loaded revolver, his finger twitching on the trigger.

Volkov settled into the deep leather of the SUV. The faint odor of wet dog still emanated from the rear of the vehicle, even though he'd had it washed and sanitized twice since Danya had waded into his pond, bounded into the back of the car unbidden, and then shaken his burly body, flinging wetness and muck from the bottom of the pond across the upholstery. Volkov cracked the driver's window and turned his mind to another problem.

The disappearing video of Alnoor resurfaced in front of him, as if projected onto the inside of the windshield, and he watched it, some of the images clear and crisp, others murky. The video was no doubt real, although Alnoor may have been following a script. In fact, Volkov was almost certain of it. But whether Alnoor was the willing participant in an elaborate scheme perpetrated by a federal judge and a federal prosecutor, or simply a pawn—a pawn who

155

would be sacrificed in the same way Volkov would be sacrificed when the time came—Volkov knew he had to do something. As the glare of headlights confronted and then left him on his drive south, he set about concocting his plan.

36

Raleigh Westlake had become ill. Not a temporary illness that could be shaken in a few days, but a pervasive sickness grown from bad deeds that worm their way into the unconscious mind and your stomach and your heart. It had started with a tick in his left eye, the muscles in the outside corner flinching as if dodging a thrown punch. Now, as he walked along the sidewalk two blocks from the courthouse, his lungs labored in the frigid air.

He paused to look up. Low-slung clouds the color of iron filled the sky, covering the mountains to the west. The wind blew down the slopes from snow-capped peaks. He pulled his wool overcoat closed at the neck, clutching it with an ungloved hand. He had lost the top button of his coat somewhere.

He knew when his malady had manifested. As he'd watched the video on Robert's cell phone of his interview with Caroline's father, in which Herb Bannister had admitted accidentally shooting his own daughter, Raleigh felt the lurch within, a seismic shift of a tectonic plate in his life. He was responsible for Robert's death and the death of the innocent Mayor. Though Caroline had orchestrated the trial with a blind vengeance, Raleigh felt as if he had pressed the bolt gun to the Mayor's forehead and pulled the trigger himself. He didn't know where that left him.

He passed a few pedestrians huddled against the wind, their heads down, furtive eyes glancing to the sky. He approached the Basilica with his fingers clutching his right side. The pain emanated from deep within, as if he had been struck repeatedly with a sharp weapon that left no visible mark. He ran through the organs on that side, thinking cancer, the hidden menace that had taken his wife. He made a mental note to schedule a consult with his doctor.

As the first flakes of snow fluttered, he stood for a moment on the sidewalk, looking up at the replica of the patron, an arch deacon from the third century, burned on a gridiron for defending the Christian faith. It reminded him that men had been killing men for eons, usually for reasons that seemed in the moment justified, but whose validity paled in the sun of time. Westlake entered the church through the heavy wooden doors, dipped his fingers in a bowl of Holy Water, and genuflected before the tabernacle. In judgment, crucified Christ stared down at him from three sides with dark, unblinking eyes.

He entered a back pew, sliding onto wood with a worn finish, the grain of the oak visible. He sighed and took a deep breath, then closed his eyes. He did not see a way out. He prayed to a God he couldn't be sure was still there, maybe never had been, seeking some guidance and intervention. The empowering anger generated from the miscarriage of justice visited upon Hannah Sullivan, resulting in her killer going free, had devolved into an interminable fear, an almost-paralyzing terror. He started to ask how it had gone so wrong, but he knew the answer before his internal voice even uttered the question. Was there any point in debating it?

He rose and entered the confessional with his eyes turned down and his hands cupped. He gently closed the wooden door and knelt on the sinners' rail, a slat of wood with no padding. The metal screen between him and the priest was thick, the perforations sparse, and Westlake could make out only the outline of the priest's graying head as he bowed his own.

"Bless me Father, for I have sinned. My last confession was more than one year ago." Westlake closed his eyes.

"Bless you," said a raspy voice on the other side.

"I have committed terrible sins."

"What are your sins? They are probably not as terrible as you imagine."

Westlake hesitated and swallowed. In a part of his mind he tried to quell, a voice told him to stop. He was about to make a grave mistake. He ignored the voice and said, "I have killed."

There was no immediate response from the priest. A moment turned into ten. The bustle of other sinners sitting and rising in the chapel pews was the only sign the world had not stopped.

"Was this an accident?" the priest said finally.

"No, Father." Though this admission was covered by the clergy-communicant privilege, Westlake knew he had crossed a threshold. But he had to go deeper.

"Thou shall not kill. Commandment number seven."

"I know I have committed a mortal sin."

"Your soul is in imminent peril."

"I want to repent."

"Then repent, my son. You must rebuild your relationship with God."

"I am here for that purpose, Father. I am sorry for what I have done, but I felt I had no choice."

"You always have a choice, but we all are prone to temptation."

"I seek absolution."

Again a pause, a pause during which Westlake could hear the thump of his heart in his ears.

"If you are truly repentant, I must absolve you. Are you truly repentant?" the Priest's face turned toward him.

"I am," Westlake said, his eyes closed for fear they would betray him. "What must I do, Father?"

"You must pray. You must pray for forgiveness, you must pray for the soul of your victim, you must pray for the souls of all of those who have been murdered."

Westlake shifted on the sinner's rail. "I apologize, but I must ask—how will praying help? It hasn't so far."

"God has not heard you. Not yet. You must have faith. You must pray, every day, or more often, until you return for your next confession. I urge you to come again as soon as possible. Do you understand?"

"Yes, I understand. But is that all there is to it?"

Ignoring the question, the priest recited the Lord's Prayer, "Our Father, Who art in Heaven, hallowed be Thy name . . ." The intonation was flat, his words barely discernible in the vestibule.

Westlake recited the words by memory, his lips barely moving. They said it three times. Each time the pain in his right side heightened. At the final Amen, he rose from the rail with difficulty, his knees stiff and sore, his breath coming in short bursts. He left the confessional with his head bowed, his hands together in supplication.

He hurried from the church into snowfall that had begun to accumulate. The sidewalks were powdered and slippery. He could not see his building two blocks ahead. The leather soles of his black wingtips left an indistinct impression of his presence, the marks filling with powder almost the moment he took another step. He looked up in a gesture he knew was idiotic, hoping to be noticed. It could not be that simple. He no longer trusted he could receive redemption in that way, that confessing his crimes would relieve him from the repercussions of what he had done. As he walked in a slow trudge, each step treacherous and unsure, he felt a sharp pain in his lower back. It doubled him over. He stayed there, unable to breathe, the snow pelting him, his eyes squeezed shut.

37

Raleigh knocked softly on the wooden door. He had a key but refrained from using it, because he was embarrassed that he had visited so infrequently and felt he had no right to barge in. His mother answered the door. She waved him in and knelt to hug Shiloh. She then turned to her son and embraced him, the top of her head barely reaching his shoulders.

"To what do I owe this pleasure?" she said, eyes gleaming.

"You act as if I never come to see you," he said, though he knew she was right.

"It's been ninety-four days, but who's counting? I forgive you." She held him by the forearms and leaned back, appraising her son in the way only mothers can. "How's Caroline?"

"She's fine."

"Fine like she's doing well, or fine like you don't want to talk about it?"

"She's in D.C. She's incredibly busy."

"Well, tell her congratulations and that I'd love to see her when she comes back this way. But that's not why you're here, is it son?"

"I wanted to . . ." He stopped, unsure if the reason he had come was wise. He was never at a loss for words, rarely off-balance, but his mother's eyes peered into him, not criticizing, but searching, making him feel he was being inspected, even if she was motivated by genuine concern.

She pulled him to a worn sofa and they sat side-by-side. Shiloh curled at her feet, resting her head upon Joyce Westlake's tennis shoes. "Tell me," she said without judgment.

"I'm still running," he deflected. "Quite a lot. Four or five times a week."

"Are you training for another race?" his mother asked.

"Nothing on the horizon. Just, you know, trying to stay in shape."

She twisted her mouth to the right. "You're too thin. Have you been eating?"

"I eat. I just burn it off."

"You're pale."

"It's winter, mother."

"Not that kind of pale." She laid her hand over the back of his. "You're sick. Maybe heartsick. I can't tell."

"I'm not heartsick," he said without conviction. "It's just . . . I don't know."

"What is it Raleigh? I haven't seen you like this since Heather died."

He took in a deep breath and closed his eyes. He opened his eyes without speaking.

"So what is it Raleigh?"

"Do you remember that story you used to tell me, the Tale of the Two Wolves?"

"Of course. The Wolves Within," she said. "I told you that story too many times to count."

"Well, I've never forgotten it. And some things have happened recently, and . . . I feel like I'm living it."

She brushed the hair back from his forehead and laid her head against his shoulder. "I know."

"So what should I do? I've been praying, and I've been to church, to confession even, and that's not helping."

She sat upright. "That was your father's religion. It never made much sense to me. Maybe you should go see the medicine man." His mother retreated to her bedroom and began talking on a phone on her bedside table. She spoke in the old language, which Raleigh had never bothered to learn. Her cadence rose and fell like a series of waves, at times seeming to verge on anger, at other moments placid and almost peaceful.

After a few minutes, she returned to the living room, sat beside him again. Shiloh, who had followed her into the bedroom and returned at her heels, stood as if awaiting an announcement. "He'll see you at 2:30. Here's the address." She handed her son a scrap of paper.

Raleigh did not protest. He had come too far to protest. As he'd approached her house, he felt some of the tension ebb out of him. Somewhere in deep folds of his mind he understood he would return to the Reservation, to the land of his mother's birth. Not on a permanent basis, no, but for a respite, a recharge, whatever you wanted to call it.

He drove along the road that wound along the Oconaluftee River, and after passing through the village, Raleigh turned uphill until he came to a modern cabin. The cabin, made of symmetrical logs with gray mortar between, had a green metal roof dulled by time. There was no mailbox, no street number, no sign out front. When Raleigh opened the door, a bell on the rim of a dream-catcher announced his presence. He gently shut the door. A man who could have been fifty or seventy rose from a leather armchair and clicked off the television. They walked without pretense to another room, lined with shelves containing clear glass jars filled with specimens and powders and amber liquids. He could have been in a college biology lab. There was no examination table—just a wooden chair with a caned seat and back, into which Raleigh settled himself.

The medicine man began his examination without questions, perhaps having learned enough from the brief conversation with his mother. He peered into Raleigh's eyes using an ophthalmoscope, then placed his right ear abutting Raleigh's ear, listening. The medicine man palpated Raleigh's neck, then his shoulders and chest, working his way down, listening. Raleigh winced when the medicine man pressed his lower back and walked his fingers along his side. He asked Raleigh to slip off his shoes and then ran his index finger along the tops, sides and soles of Raleigh's socked feet, employing diagnosis, stimulus and massage all at once.

Next came a tincture dressed in blue-green, the color of water near certain islands in the Caribbean, administered with a dropper, two drops on the tongue. The tincture tasted better than it looked, something between metallic and lemony. They talked, a long, languorous discussion with frequent pauses, covering topics of which he would remember little. At some point, with two of the medicine man's fingers firmly against the pulse at his left wrist, they talked about his wolves. No, he did not remember the first time his wolves appeared. Yes, they howled loudly most of the time, as if forlorn or starving. Yes, one of the wolves had recently become quiet. He gave these answers to questions he wasn't sure were asked, speaking in a monotone that was neither his courtroom voice nor the one he used to pray.

"One of your wolves is dying," the medicine man concluded.

This declaration appeared to Raleigh as a half-moon behind windswept clouds, and when the clouds thickened, he was left with the impression that he might not have heard anything at all.

Afterward, as he rose from the chair, he noticed the sun had dipped and a few hours had passed, though it felt more like minutes. He was sore in ligaments and joints and lymph nodes, as if from a bout of fever. The twitch at the corner of his left eye had gone quiet.

"Which wolf is dying?" Raleigh said in a voice emerging from sleep.

"That's for you to decide."

"Decide?"

He received only a warm smile in return.

"And how do I decide?"

"You know how," the medicine man said. "You've always known."

162

38

David Johnstone navigated the twisting road up the mountain. When he neared the outside rim of the road, he avoided looking down the slope. He had been recently afflicted with acrophobia. Looking down made him disoriented and dizzy. The road was unpaved, the surface wash-boarded in places where braking tires had dug into the dirt. He gripped the steering wheel so tight that his knuckles turned white. Sweat beaded his face as he climbed the last switchback.

He finally pulled into the gravel driveway of the house, parking behind a dark sedan, and tried to slow his breathing, which came in quick, short gasps. With shaking hands he lit a cigarette, inhaled the smoke. He wiped a sleeve across his brow and eventually calmed. He picked up his phone and scrolled through his texts, finding nothing new since he last checked. He tried to log onto his JWSmythe email account but couldn't access the internet from deep within the mountains.

He exited his car and ascended two concrete steps, then rapped on the metal door. A US Marshal in plain clothes pulled the steel door open and asked to see his identification. Johnstone had never seen him before, but showed the marshal his driver's license. He was allowed into the kitchen.

The marshal leaned from the doorway, surveyed the parking area, closed the kitchen door, and engaged two deadbolts.

"You're his attorney?" the marshal asked.

"That's right. I need to consult with my client."

"Fine," the marshal said, standing against the counter with his arms crossed, his service revolver in a holster at his right hip.

"Where's Marcus, or Iggy?" Johnstone said. "I expected them to be here."

"You mean Marshal Cunningham and Marshal Perez?"

"Yes, I apologize for the informality."

"Marshal Cunningham takes over the watch in about four hours."

Abdul Alnoor came through the living room into the kitchen, slid back one of the two wooden chairs at the pine table, and sat down.

Johnstone looked over at the marshal. "Do you mind if we have a little privacy?"

The marshal walked into the living area and sat in an overstuffed chair in front of the television.

Johnstone pulled out a wooden chair, sat down, and propped his elbows on the kitchen table. "I have good news," Johnstone said. "You're going to be released soon, given a new identity and re-settled." Johnstone paused, thinking of the negotiations he'd had with Judge Westlake about Abdul's release. He'd made an impassioned argument that Abdul was innocent, and in the end the Judge had acquiesced. The timing wasn't settled, but the Judge had given his word that Alnoor would soon be free. "What do you think, Abdul?"

"I think I am ready to leave this place," Alnoor said. "To leave this country. Have you been in contact with my uncle in Baghdad?"

"Not yet," Johnstone replied. "But I will."

Alnoor nodded, and his eyes gazed at something on a cabinet door. Even though he had been in the United States for most of his life, he still thought of Iraq as home. "How long," Abdul said, "before I leave?"

"I don't have an exact date," Johnstone said, "but it looks like you'll be out of here in a few weeks."

"A few weeks is a long time," Abdul said.

"I agree, but it will be the start of your new life, Abdul. Given where you were only about six months ago, locked up in a federal prison and about to be tried for murder, it's amazing that you're finally going to be free."

39

Viktor Volkov stood among the trees, peering through binoculars at the house. He wore camouflage pants and coat, and his face was streaked with green, gray and brown paint that allowed him to merge into the underbrush. Using an electronic tracker tucked behind the bumper of David Johnstone's car, he had followed the attorney to this house in the woods. From his vantage point, Volkov could see only one door and two windows. As the sun set, he strapped on night-vision goggles and crept out of the woods. Cold rain began to fall.

Staying in the woods, at least fifty meters away, Volkov surveilled the rest of the house. He noted only one other window, on the side opposite the carport, and no other doors. *A house with only one door.* As he worked his way around the building, he saw that all of the windows were covered with thick curtains, and only a dim corona of light emerged around the fabric. The house sat upon a concrete block foundation, with no vents and no access doors, so he could not sneak beneath the house to listen.

Volkov pulled the Makarov from his shoulder holster and screwed on the silencer. He emerged from the woods with small steps and walked slowly toward the carport, settling in behind the car closest to the lone entrance. He slipped off the goggles and tucked them into the back pocket of his jacket.

Duck walking to remain low, he made his way around the car and crouched beside two concrete steps. The door appeared to be metal, probably ¼-inch steel panels on each side. With the rain pelting the aluminum roof of the carport, he could make out muffled voices inside, but few words. It sounded like three people inside the house, near the door, but he could not be certain.

He retreated to the side of a dark sedan and sat down on the gravel, his back against a front tire, and waited. Water dripped off the brim of his hat, pooling in the gravel. He rolled up the cap and put it in his jacket. He replaced it with a dark ski mask, adjusting the fabric so his eyes and mouth aligned with the cutouts. He strapped the night goggles back on and kept his eyes on the nearby woods and the road that ended just past the house. He listened for noises inside and out, but the rain was making it difficult. His breathing remained steady, his mind clear.

When the carport light flashed on, a burst like sunlight lit up the goggles, making Volkov nearly blind. He pulled the goggles off and tossed them on the ground. He heard the deadbolts being disengaged, and the metal door swung open. He rose and saw two men. David Johnstone was descending the concrete steps, a US Marshal behind him in the doorway. Volkov braced his forearms on the car's hood and aimed the pistol at the marshal's torso. The gun spit out its first bullet, the sound no louder than a whisper, and the marshal fell backward into the house. Before Johnstone knew what was happening, a bullet hit him in the chest. He toppled down the steps. Volkov stepped around the front of the car and fired an additional bullet into Johnstone's forehead.

Volkov crouched by the steps and eased his head into the doorway. The marshal was lying prone on his back on the linoleum floor, his breath wheezing from him, blood leaking from the chest wound.

"Who's there?" said a voice from around the corner.

"How many more people are inside the house?" Volkov said, making no attempt to disguise his voice.

"Just me."

"Are you sure?"

"Dr. Volkov, is that you?"

Volkov went through the door, staying close to the wall, his eyes scanning the kitchen and watching the downed marshal for movement. He aimed at the marshal's head and fired again.

Abdul was still in the chair at the table, his hands gripping his thighs, a terrified look on his face.

With his gloved right hand, Volkov kept the Makarov aimed toward the only other room he could see. With his left he pulled the ski mask up onto his forehead, but did not remove it completely. "Hello, Abdul."

"Dr. Volkov, it is you. Have you come to rescue me?"

Volkov nodded, put a finger to his lips. "Is there anyone else here?"

"No," Alnoor whispered back.

Volkov stood up, took two steps toward the table, and wrapped his left arm around Alnoor's shoulders.

Abdul wrapped both arms around Volkov's waist. "Praise be to Allah."

Volkov went through the kitchen into the living area, looking behind the couch and the chairs. He eased open the bathroom door and pulled back the shower curtain, finding nothing. He went into the last room, a bedroom, and searched it as well.

He came back into the kitchen. "We need to get moving, Abdul. Do you have a backpack, or a bag of some sort?"

"No, sir."

Volkov rummaged through the cabinets and found a box of garbage bags. He pulled out a white plastic bag and handed it to Abdul. "Here, pack everything you have in this. Hurry."

While Alnoor stuffed his clothes and toothbrush into the trash bag, Volkov dragged the dead marshal further into the kitchen, smearing his blood across a swath of the linoleum floor. He pulled the marshal's Glock from its holster, turned it over in his gloved hands. Then he closed the kitchen door.

Alnoor came back into the kitchen, breathing hard, the white bag dangling from his hand. He noticed the gun in Volkov's hand. "What's that for?"

"Let's go," Volkov said. "Wait. I need to remove your ankle monitor." Volkov laid the Glock on the counter, within reach of both of them, pulled a tool from the pocket of his camouflage pants, and worked the screwdriver into the strap of the ankle monitor until it came loose. He handed the monitor to Abdul. "Take this and leave it on the bed."

Volkov crouched in the open doorway and fired the Glock once, the bullet whizzing off into the tree line, and then placed it in the marshal's right hand. In the carport, Volkov crouched over Johnstone's body, feeling in his pockets for car keys. "Stay right here," he said to Abdul.

"Is he dead?" Abdul asked, his eyes wide, staring at two bullet holes and a pool of blood that was thickening and turning dark.

"Yes. Stay here." He stealthily moved to Johnstone's car, watching the unpaved road and the surrounding woods for movement. He pressed the key fob, and the trunk lid popped open. He spread garbage bags over the trunk carpet, then returned to the carport. He removed Johnstone's shoes and set them on the concrete steps. "Help me carry him."

Volkov reached beneath Johnstone's arms and lifted. Abdul hesitated, then grabbed his feet. They backed out of the carport with Johnstone's dead weight between them, stopping at the open trunk, then laid Johnstone's body on the plastic bags. Volkov closed the trunk lid.

"Get your bag of clothes and get in the front seat."

Volkov went back to the house, careful not to step in the marshal's blood, and filled a large bowl with water. Onto Johnstone's pooled blood he poured the water, hoping to dilute the blood enough that it would be hard to see. He repeated the procedure and watched the rose-colored water leach through the gravel. Volkov slipped his hands inside Johnstone's shoes, leaned into the house, and placed the shoes in the marshal's blood. Volkov left bloody shoe prints on the threshold and steps, trying to mimic the steps of a man making a fast exit. He closed the door to the house.

Kneeling next to the driver's door, Volkov rubbed the soles of Johnstone's shoes on the floor mat of the car, then on the accelerator and brake pedal. He pulled the mat and laid it across the back seat, Johnstone's bloody shoes on top. They drove away from the house, gravel crunching beneath the tires, the rain now nothing more than mist. Vapor hovered in the trees, reducing visibility. Fog swallowed the headlight beams. To see better, Volkov turned on the windshield defroster and lowered his side window.

Near the bottom of the gravel road, Volkov's SUV appeared out of the gloom. Volkov pulled Johnstone's car behind it and cut the engine. He didn't move for the better part of a minute, listening for the growl of another vehicle climbing the mountain road. He pulled the Makarov from the shoulder holster. "Stay in the car," he said to Abdul. "Not a sound."

Volkov moved toward his SUV, walked around it. Danya barked at the hooded figure of his owner, his jaws snapping near the glass. Volkov opened the front door, leaned in, and issued a command in Russian that quieted the dog. Volkov crouched and tapped the flashlight icon on his phone, then went down on his hands and knees, looking at the undercarriage for signs of a tracker or a bomb or something else suspicious. In this moment he let his heart slow, took a respite from the melee of shooting two people and watching them expire with little puffs of bubbly breath and the coppery stench of blood. He gnawed on his lower lip. He had another decision to make. His stomach lurched and he tasted bile in his mouth. He took a deep breath and pushed off the ground, wiped the road remnants sticking to his camouflage pants.

Volkov pulled open the passenger door of Johnstone's car. Alnoor was still strapped in, his eyes wide with fright. Volkov saw it then—this boy was not a killer—his breath was coming in short bursts, the sight of two dead men still frozen in his eyes. Alnoor's hands trembled in his lap.

"Sorry for this," Volkov said. He unfolded a knife from his multitool. The steel glinted in the dome light. He covered Alnoor's mouth with his left hand and thrust the blade into Alnoor's right calf.

Volkov's palm muffled Alnoor's scream. Volkov leaned in close. "Calm down, Abdul. Breathe slowly ... that's right, breathe." When Alnoor's breathing returned to some semblance of normal, Volkov removed his hand from the boy's mouth, then unbuckled his seat belt.

Volkov handed him the SUV keys. "You drive my car." Volkov eased him from the sedan, helped him settle his weight on his injured right leg. "I'll bandage your leg later."

"Why did you do that?" Abdul said, the first words he had been able to utter since seeing David Johnstone's body lying in the carport.

"Because this has to look like an abduction. You were kidnapped, and you were injured in the struggle."

Abdul nodded. "Okay. I understand. Where are we going?"

"Where you'll be safe. Follow me. It's not far. You have to drive carefully and stay close, because there might be people out looking for you."

Alnoor nodded.

"It won't be long."

Alnoor slid behind the steering wheel of Volkov's SUV. Volkov pointed out the windshield wiper switch and the gear shift. He waited while Alnoor started the engine. Through his mind passed the thought that Alnoor might try to flee, but he had to take that risk. If Alnoor tried to escape, Volkov would chase him down, dispose of him, and frame him for the murder of a US Marshal. "Don't worry about my dog. He'll stay quiet." He looked at Alnoor's face, at his trembling lips, and closed the driver's door.

They drove east to a small motel, threading a valley road that connected two towns, not much but trees and looming mountains in between. Volkov drove with both windows down, the mist seeping into the vehicle in swirling eddies, Johnstone's stiffening body in the trunk. Alnoor stayed on his tail at a speed a few miles below the limit.

The motel had two floors, the top floor with an outside breeze way and an old iron railing in need of paint. While Alnoor stayed out of sight in the SUV, Volkov paid in cash for a room for two nights, a vague mention of deer hunting tossed into the conversation to explain his garb and camouflage paint.

They parked in the back lot, only part of it paved, a dark dumpster anchoring one side. The lot angled toward a stream they could hear rushing as they walked toward the room.

In the hotel room, Abdul sprawled on the far bed, rubbing his right calf through the cut fabric of his jeans.

Volkov rolled up the pant leg, cleaned the wound, then taped butterfly bandages over the slice on Abdul's calf. He smeared lidocaine around the wound.

"It hurts."

"The lidocaine will help," Volkov said. Volkov left the room and came back with a bucket of ice. "Put some ice on it if it starts to throb."

In the parking lot, Volkov strapped a chain leash on Danya and walked him along the creek bank, not allowing the dog to stray into the undergrowth. His black fur almost made him invisible in the darkness. He walked Danya across the parking lot and up the stairs to the room, watching for the curious, for the hesitant swing of a curtain's edge in an adjoining room.

Volkov slept more deeply than he had in years, despite the hum and tick of the wall heater and the presence in the other double bed of a young man who tossed and murmured until grey streaks of dawn breached the curtains.

In the morning, Volkov put on fresh clothes, stuffing the clothes of murder into the white plastic bag that lined the bathroom trash can, checking the deer rifle that he had brought along as part of his disguise, though he knew he might have to use it for another purpose. As he slept, he had made a decision. It was not a conscious thing, but something that had worked itself out, and the conclusion appeared to him in the morning as he stared out the window at a thick mist hanging in the trees

"I'm going into town, to get you some clothes, and get us some breakfast," he said.

Alnoor lay on the bed, barely awake, eyelids opening and then closing against his new reality. "Did you have to shoot my lawyer?" he said.

"Yes," Volkov said without equivocation. "He was a witness."

"He told me last night he had arranged for me to be released, that I might be able to go back to Iraq."

"And you believed him? Did he give you any details, Abdul?"

"No details, but I believe him."

Volkov sat at the end of the bed and turned to face Abdul. "Your attorney and these other people are murderers. I have proof of that. I don't know if they truly were going to release you, or do something else to you."

Abdul sat up and backed against the faux wood headboard. "There were many times they could have killed me, Dr. Volkov. Especially when I escaped into the woods."

"So you did escape?"

"Yes, but I didn't know where I was. I fell into a hole and they found me the next day. My point is they could have left me there, or done something worse, if they wanted." Alnoor rubbed his hand along his injured calf. "How did you know I escaped?"

"It doesn't matter. I have sources in law enforcement." Volkov told this lie without compunction, then changed the subject to thwart further questions. "Do you want to go back to Iraq?" Volkov understood the draw that a birthplace could have on a man, even if for him it was an unlikely scenario.

170

"If I can live with my uncle. But if not, I would like to stay here, perhaps in California, near the desert."

Volkov placed his hand on Abdul's ankle and shook it in an awkward way, the way that people without children do when they have no sense of how to convey sentiment into touch. Before he left, he pulled a handful of granola bars from a backpack and tossed them on the bed. "I'll be back soon. They'll be searching for us. Don't open the door for anyone." Danya will stand guard. Then Volkov took the cord from the telephone on the table by the bed.

On the highway, driving David Johnstone's car, Volkov kept a wary eye on the traffic, looking for signs of a police presence, a surge in activity that might alert him the chase had begun. Though he was an hour east of the safehouse, undoubtedly they were searching for Johnstone's car. He pulled onto a highway that paralleled the Little Tennessee River, took a dirt road that climbed into the naked trees. He parked the car at a washout marked by reddish sand. He walked a hundred feet into the woods and began to dig a shallow hole, cutting through roots, removing shards of granite. The mist was still thick, hanging on the trees like wisps of cotton. He returned to the closed trunk, listening to the swish and rumble of tires on the highway below. He popped the lid open and wrestled Johnstone's stiff body from the well. The stench of pooled blood and fluids made him retch. With some effort, he gripped Johnstone beneath the arms and dragged him down the slope that ran toward the highway. Volkov dumped the body into the grave and, with his feet, raked dirt and leaves and broken branches over the dead lawyer.

Volkov drove to the Cherokee casino and parked Johnstone's car in the large deck. From the trunk he removed the white plastic bags, which had mostly caught the blood leaking from Johnstone, though there were dark, oily patches on the trunk mat that would leave enough evidence to make a match. He stuffed the plastic bags in a parking deck trash can. He removed the electronic tracker from under the front bumper of Johnstone's car and stuffed it in his pants pocket. He put Johnstone's cell phone in the front console.

The cab dropped him at a fast-food restaurant less than a mile from the motel, and he bought biscuits stuffed with scrambled eggs and bacon and four cartons of orange juice. He walked back to the motel along the highway. To drivers who might have noticed him, he was a man in camouflage pants and a flannel shirt, with a coat not thick enough for the weather, shaggy hair leaking from beneath a grungy cap, a backpack slung over one shoulder— just another vagabond trying to escape the crush of human existence.

40

The trail was damp. Decaying leaves made a spongy, quiet bed. Judge Westlake padded along, a season-long malaise punishing his lungs and his legs. He wound along the path on which he'd run hundreds of miles, a serpentine track following the contours of Fontana Lake, herself not fully awake this morning. Clouds the color of thin milk hovered over the lake. Shiloh cantered at his side in an easy stride, her mouth open, eyes focused on the trail. Around her middle was an elastic belt holding two water bottles, one for each of them.

Raleigh thought of Caroline and their weekend together in D.C. It had ended in trauma, some of it self-induced, some of it the product of outside forces. As she was whisked away in the armored SUV with opaque windows, he understood it might have been a curt farewell.

He feared the loss of her. Not since Heather died had he built a relationship with a woman. In his position, opportunities were limited. And though he missed the physical part of his relationship with Caroline, a different void troubled him. They had both been enmeshed in the law for decades, seemingly fighting for the same things, but their paths had recently diverged, as if she had decided to turn around and return to the beginning. The gap between them seemed wider with each passing day.

He glanced through the trees at the lake, at the opaque mist, feeling the cool, damp air on his skin. This was his solace. He had always understood that he came out here to heal.

The animal came from the woods at his left, emerging from the brush with not so much as a snort. It was on Westlake in a few seconds, and all he had time to do was to turn toward the charging beast and brace himself. The black blur leapt at him, hitting him in the chest and knocking him onto his back. He held his arms in front of his face and chest, and the animal ripped into his bare forearms with teeth sharper than he could imagine.

Shiloh growled and tore at the animal from behind, grabbing a hind leg and snarling with abandon. The attacker was more than twice her size, but the tactic worked, creating a momentary distraction that allowed Raleigh to roll out from underneath the animal and stand up. He found a rock and hurled it into the beast's ribs, but it made no difference. The animal had Shiloh pinned, its bulk concealing his dog as if she were being devoured. Raleigh reached for a broken limb the thickness of a bat and began beating the attacker on its back and head, the blows landing with a thudding sound. And then it ran off. As quickly as it had sprung from the woods, it galloped into the underbrush, leaving him heaving and spent, his right arm a mangled wreck, blood trickling down his face and his legs.

Shiloh lay in a heap, whimpering. He knelt and assessed the damage: a clearly broken forepaw; a gash in her side through which he could see white bone; at least two teeth twisted at horrid angles; and torn flesh at her neck. She was bleeding from multiple wounds, the blood soaking into the earth. He caressed Shiloh's forehead and removed one water bottle from the harness. He dribbled water into his palm and cupped his hand beneath her mouth. She was too injured to take it. Her eyes darted in their sockets but her head and body remained still. Raleigh presumed her neck was broken.

He gathered Shiloh up, holding her weight with his knee. When he lifted her, her eyes were placid and dull. She emitted a grunt of pain but did not resist his carry. He had come two miles from the parking lot, perhaps a little farther, and with his dog cradled in his arms he began the long retreat.

Once at the car, he stowed Shiloh in the back seat on her pallet of blankets. She made no noise. At the sound of her name she did not respond, did not even whimper. He ran his hand over the top of her head. He put the back of his hand to her nose. She was still breathing, but barely. He looked down at his hands and his shirt, splotched and stained with Shiloh's blood and some of his own.

At the emergency pet hospital they took Shiloh immediately into surgery without promises, then made him leave and go to the ER so he could take care of his own wounds. He drove himself and staggered in through the sliding glass doors, looking like a victim of combat. They took him quickly to a cubicle and attended his wounds. He had a long scratch across his right cheek, bite marks on his scalp above the hairline, and multiple gashes across his right arm, where the skin was split open like a red river. He refused a painkiller but allowed them to shoot lidocaine into the affected areas.

When the nurse appeared with a hair trimmer, he raised his hand to stop her. "What's that for?"

"I need to shave your scalp."

"Why?"

"You've been scratched and bitten on your head, multiple times. We can't stitch the wounds until we shave the wound sites."

He had not noticed the wounds on his head, and now his hand wandered there, feeling the lacerations and dried blood with fingertips that were almost numb. He nodded. "All of it, then."

"You sure?" the nurse said.

Afterward, she gave him a mirror.

He surveyed the damage, noting his scalp was bone-white, a mole or two in places he didn't know he had them. He almost didn't recognize himself, this visage without the dark hair, some punctures and narrow scratches on his scalp, the long wound across his right cheek.

The doctor came in and threaded a needle that looked like a fishhook, then went to work. "What attacked you?"

"A bear. Out on a trail at Tsali. Do you have any updates on my dog?"

The nurse poked her head into his vision. "No sir. I'll call over to the animal hospital when I have a minute."

The doctor asked him to stay still and began to suture the gashes on his head. "This wound on your cheek, it's not very deep, but any wound on the face produces a lot of blood. It's worse than it looks. I'm just going to close it with butterfly bandages."

"Okay," he said, his lips barely moving.

"You'll need a rabies shot. A series of them, in fact."

The doctor worked on Westlake's forearms, swiping up blood with alcohol wipes, bending his head to the work. When he finished, the doctor handed the needle to the nurse and stood up, placed his hands on his lower back. "Fifty-four stitches," he proclaimed. "Most of the wounds are superficial. You were lucky."

41

Westlake left the hospital and stood for a minute on the sidewalk outside, looking off into the distance, trying to regain his equilibrium. His wounds throbbed with every heartbeat. His lower back was sore from carrying Shiloh two miles through the woods. He re-lived the attack, feeling the pressure of the bear's weight on his chest, the claws and teeth slicing into his skin, hearing Shiloh's whimper as the animal turned on her. There was something odd about the bear's rush from the undergrowth, the approach silent and without warning. But he knew wild animals, especially wild animals starving in winter, did unpredictable things.

He slid behind the wheel of his car and checked his phone, hoping for a message from the vet. He had two messages. The first was from Marcus Cunningham and ended with the word urgent. The second voicemail was from a nurse at the animal hospital, her voice solemn, asking him to call. He returned Cunningham's call first.

"Are you where you can talk, Judge?"

"Yes, I'm in my car. Alone."

"Someone penetrated the safehouse last night. Marshal Reynolds is dead. We found him at the shift change last night. Two gunshots, one to the head. Alnoor is gone. We're still trying to piece it together."

"My God," Westlake said. "What can I do?"

"Not a thing right now. We've got a dozen people out here, marshals and forensics. They're going over every inch of the place. The most troubling thing is that Johnstone was scheduled to meet with Alnoor here last night. We don't know if he showed. There's nothing in the log to indicate he did or he didn't. But Alnoor is gone."

"You think David did this?"

"We don't know right now, Judge. I'll call when I have more."

Westlake put the phone down, the weight of the news not fully absorbed, hovering around him like thick smoke that wouldn't dissipate. He was only an hour from the safehouse. He could get cleaned up and drive over. He thought about it and, in a moment of clarity, decided that would be a mistake, that in the normal course of a murder investigation the presence of a federal judge would be hard to explain.

He called the animal hospital and endured a long hold before the surgical vet came on the line. "I'm sorry, Judge. She lost too much blood. We couldn't save her."

It was a longer conversation, but that's what he remembered of it. He sat in his car in the parking lot and stared through the windshield at nothing, finally crossing his arms over the steering wheel and lowering his head onto his forearms. His body shuddered, tears leaking from his eyes, tears that traced the wound down his face, the salt stinging his cheek. While he'd sat on a gurney in the emergency room, having his own injuries mended, Shiloh was taking her last breath. He should have been with her, but he knew if he had stayed he would have been relegated to the waiting room, his presence of no consequence to the outcome. He looked into the backseat at Shiloh's pallet of bloodstained blankets. He backed the car up and pulled out of the lot with no firm intention as to his destination. Just somewhere safe.

The safe haven turned out to be his mother's house on the Rez. He knocked on the door. She did not come to the door immediately. Her car was in the gravel drive. He peered through the window on the porch and saw that the television was on. She was lying in the recliner, her head tilted to the side, her mouth slack. He rapped on the window again. She didn't move. He tapped twice more. Finally, she stirred.

When she opened the door, his appearance startled her. Sleepiness changed to concern. "Oh . . ." Her hands immediately rose to his head, touching the stitched wounds and then the butterfly bandages taped across the gash on his cheek. Her trembling hands retreated to her own mouth. "What happened, son?"

"Bear attack. While I was running on the trails at Fontana. With Shiloh. Shiloh is dead." Even to him his tone sounded perfunctory and staid, as if he was reading from a police report about an event he had not been part of.

"Oh my God. Why didn't you call me?"

"What could you have done, mother?" This came with a harshness he did not intend. A harshness borne of near panic. He placed his hands on her shoulders, more to steady himself than to console her. "I'm sorry." He took a deep breath to slow his mind. "I should have called you. It's just . . . I spent most of the afternoon in the ER, getting stitched up, and then I found out about Shiloh."

"I could have come and sat with you. I really liked her."

"I know you did. I should have thought of that. I'm not myself right now." He walked into her living room and sat down on the leather couch, stared at the carpet for a few moments. Then he looked up. "She's still there, if you'd like to go over with me later to pay your respects." His voice had softened.

His mother nodded, tears welling up in her old eyes. "But I'm more concerned about you, Raleigh. You look terrible. Does it hurt?"

"Yes, now that the lidocaine has worn off. And where they gave me a rabies shot." He rubbed the injection site on his right bicep, a slightly swollen and rose-colored patch of muscle between two bite marks.

"Did they give you something?"

"I have a prescription for Percocet, but I haven't filled it yet. You know I don't like to take pills."

"Yes, but this is different. You've been attacked by a wild animal. I'm surprised they released you."

"They said I was lucky. Shiloh obviously wasn't." He fought for a moment against the tears building in his eyes, silently chastising himself for the weakness. He dipped his head and sobbed. His mother's arm curled around his neck. He knew his emotional state was not just about Shiloh, that it was produced by a culmination of events, loss and things stolen from him that he almost refused to recognize. He turned to his mother and cried into her shoulder.

She patted the back of his head and pulled him in closer. When he stopped, part of her blouse was damp, the fabric clinging to her skin. A sympathetic smile spread across her face. "I'll make us some tea," she said.

He nestled into the sofa and tried to fix his attention on a news channel that his mother seemed to have on 24 hours a day. He hoped the low babble might distract him, might take his mind off what had happened, but the chatter only annoyed him. After a few minutes, he grabbed the remote and turned the television off.

The tea kettle screamed, and his mother came back into the room shortly after, holding a tray with two steaming mugs, a bowl of sugar, and a crock of cream. She paused for a minute, sensing something was amiss, that things were not as they should be. It was too quiet. "You turned off the television."

"It was annoying me. I'll turn it back on, if you want."

She shrugged. "No, it's okay. You're here. I just like a little noise when I'm here by myself."

She set the tray on the table and spooned two teaspoons of sugar into her tea, followed by some cream. She twirled the spoon in her cup. "Want any sugar?"

"No, thanks. I've been off sugar for a while now. It's bad for you." He poured some cream into his tea, and circled the cup vigorously with a spoon, sloshing tea down the sides, then took a small sip.

"Chamomile. It's good for you." She smiled over the edge of her cup.

He held the cup chin high and inhaled the fumes, hoping to clear out the smell of death lurking in his nose. He wondered how long it would take.

"I'm sorry about Shiloh," she said, as if nothing else came to mind. Then, after a pause, "Is there something else on your mind?"

The tea and the quiet settled him. His breathing had returned almost to normal. "How have you been, mother? What have you been up to?"

"Son, I'm an old woman. I'm not up to much other than visits to the grocery store and the doctor."

"So tell me what's going on on the Rez. I haven't been keeping up with the news."

She sighed and decided to play along. She gave him the headlines from the past week, nothing that seemed to interest him, but she understood she would have to ease toward the things he wanted to say. "How's Caroline? I saw her giving a press conference about the blackout in Washington. She did very well. Not that I expected anything less."

"We're … we're taking a break. Nothing concrete or planned. It's just that the duties of being Attorney General take all of her time, all of her attention."

She saw it now, uncovered. "It won't always be that way, Raleigh. She'll settle in and figure it out. She has a very important job to do. I think you'll always be an important person in her life."

He looked up from his tea. "What makes you say that?"

"I've seen the way you are together. Not like you and Heather, but going down that road, in my observation."

"I do miss her, but I'm not sure she feels the same. I don't know. I'm just . . . I'm just extremely tired."

"Of course you are. With everything you've been through." Joyce held her cup of tea between two palms. "I know you won't do this, because it's not in your nature, but maybe you should take some time off and just rest. I don't think you've taken a vacation since Heather passed."

Raleigh shook his head, then drew the back of his hand across his eyes.

They drove to the animal hospital, both of them in a disheveled state. He introduced himself to the receptionist even though it was unnecessary. They were escorted down a hallway that took several turns before arriving at a closed steel door with no sign. The receptionist opened the door and flicked on the fluorescent lights. She led them to a large cooler, not unlike those in the bowels of restaurants.

Shiloh was lying on a shelf, her body shaved in various places where the surgeon had worked to save her life. Her cinnamon hair was matted, the whiskers on her nose flat. Her eyes were closed. Raleigh ran his hands over her fur, which had lost its gloss but not its softness. "Thank you," he muttered through swollen lips.

"She was a good dog," Joyce said, running her fingers behind Shiloh's ears.

The receptionist departed with the announcement that she was going to find the doctor.

"She loved to run in the woods with me," Raleigh said. "I couldn't always take her because, frankly, she was a bit out of shape. At home, she loved to lay at my feet in front of the fireplace. I let her sleep in the bed with me."

The veterinary surgeon appeared then and explained what he had done to save her, the lifesaving measures unsuccessfully employed. Westlake didn't hear him, not really, having heard similar words from an oncologist years earlier when Heather had passed, and thinking them as worthless then as they were now.

"Thank you," he said in a voice meant to conclude the doctor's monologue, without looking at him. "Can you cremate her for me?"

"We can arrange that," the veterinarian said. "We have a nice selection of urns and wooden boxes."

He said it in the quiet, pleasant voice of one accustomed to dealing with the bereaved, as if he were a funeral director as well, and Westlake thought for a moment how odd it was that vets served in both capacities. Well, maybe not so odd. He judged men, occasionally watched them die, and then sent them to the earth, didn't he?

Joyce stepped back from her time with Shiloh and gripped his hand.

"She saved me from a bear attack," Westlake said, absently rubbing the wounds on his arms.

The doctor, one arm folded across his chest, rubbed his chin with long fingers. "I don't mean to disagree with you," the vet said, "but I've treated a lot of animals attacked by bears. I don't think this was a bear."

42

Viktor Volkov moved the scalpel in precise lines around Abdul Alnoor's face. Normally, changing a patient's appearance to this degree would require multiple surgeries, but Volkov wasn't sure they had time for a lengthy recovery process, so he combined the procedures. He had snuck Alnoor into the surgical suite in his office after hours, and he was working solo, without his nurse.

While Alnoor slept beneath a haze of anesthesia, Volkov trimmed Abdul's nose, reducing the profile on the bridge and tip. He stitched in a chin implant to give Abdul a broader jaw line, and added cheek implants to raise and widen his cheek bones.

When he finished, Volkov applied anti-bacterial ointment across Abdul's skin and inserted splints in Alnoor's nose to help him breathe. Abdul would be sore and bruised for a week or more, but Volkov hoped the changes would be sufficient to allow Abdul to pass through life undetected as the teenager who had been accused of terrorism and died in a jail cell.

Volkov stopped the flow of anesthesia and stepped back, studying Abdul's face, the twitch at the corner of his mouth, as the Propofol began to wear off. Volkov could not pinpoint the moment he decided to save Alnoor, and even as they fled the safehouse, stray thoughts of killing Alnoor and disposing of his body in the woods flitted across his mind. Murder had become routine, the steps laid before him like a well-lit highway, the absence of compunction making it a smooth journey. But something had changed. He sensed it more than he knew it, a subtle shift, like the first gray hair that appears overnight, marking something inexorable. Volkov supposed that all assassins stopped killing at some point, either voluntarily or not, and if the former it must be from some reckoning, the resolution of a long-simmering debate.

He stepped outside his office and stood just beyond the halo of the security light covering the parking lot, one foot propped on the brick wall of a shrub bed. From his jacket pocket he withdrew a small can, pinched snuff between his fingers, and wedged it behind his lower lip. This too was new for him. He found himself seeking this ephemeral form of energy, nicotine here and, in weaker moments, caffeine from zero calorie soft drinks he once disdained. He spat a stream of juice into the shrub bed. The night was cool, mist hovering in the air. He heard a noise out by the trash bins at the back of the lot, and his right hand moved reflexively across his chest, gripping the butt of the pistol in the holster beneath his left arm. He waited for what seemed an interminable time for a repeat of the sound, and as the security light backlit the fog, the muted scraping sound of a foraging animal came to him in the night. He did not take his hand from the pistol butt until he was back in his building, the three-inch deadbolt slotted in the steel door frame.

Abdul stirred in the reclined medical bed, and his lips opened. Volkov brought the water bottle and inserted the hard, plastic straw between Abdul's dry lips. Abdul's eyes blinked open, leaving the vacant space of non-dreams, and winced at the pain. He brought both hands toward his face before Volkov nabbed his wrists.

"Abdul, you are in the surgical suite at my office. Everything is okay. But you must not touch your face." Volkov slid a vinyl mitten on each of Alnoor's hands.

Abdul's eyes acknowledged the admonition, but he did not speak. His throat was dry and irritated.

"Do you want more water?"

Abdul nodded, and when Volkov released his wrists the boy lowered his arms.

"I will give you some pain medication, and you will need ice packs to help keep the swelling down. As we discussed, you will be sore for a week or more."

"I feel like I've been punched in the face," Abdul said in a raspy whisper.

"Yes, that's what it looks like." The bruising will come later.

They drove from the medical office in Volkov's SUV, Alnoor lying prone on the backseat, covered with a warming blanket. He was still groggy. Volkov stopped at a light on the edge of the bombing site, now just a large, rectangular hole, its pit dark and unseeable. He noted the memorial across the street, a series of curved marble walls like half-ripples of water, on which the names of the dead were chiseled. Volkov could have taken a different route to his farm but tonight, for some reason, he chose this one.

That night, Alnoor slept fitfully in the spare bedroom at the back of the farmhouse. Because of the cheek implants, he could not sleep on his side, and he rolled back and forth, seeking comfort that would not come. Volkov stayed with him throughout the night, slumped in a non-reclining upholstered chair, rising periodically to give Abdul a drink of water or to hold a frozen gel-pack against his cheeks and nose.

181

In the morning Volkov made fruit smoothies, and Alnoor sat up, with his back against the headboard, sipping breakfast through a straw.

"If you can keep your face above your heart," Volkov said, "it will help reduce the swelling."

Abdul set the smoothie cup on the bedside table and climbed out of bed, flicked on the light in the small bathroom adjoining his room. He stood before the sink mirror, staring at himself. "It does look like I was in a bad fight, and I lost." He tried to smile, but the swollen tissue prevented it. "Why are my lips puffy?"

"I gave you an injection to make them fuller. All of these enhancements will make it easier for you to go back into society, unrecognized. I suggest you grow a beard."

"When my face has recovered, what then? Can I live with you?"

Volkov hesitated, then smiled like a man about to deliver bad news.

43

Raleigh Westlake sat on his dock, watching the last vestiges of orange sunlight fade from the water. He heard tentative footsteps on the wooden planks. Normally, Shiloh would have been serving as sentry and alerted him to the presence. Westlake did not turn around, instead making himself appear as a vulnerable target. He slowly slipped his hand to the butt of his pistol and unsnapped the keep on the clip-on holster.

"Raleigh?"

He turned to the sound of her voice, watched her hand cover an escaping gasp when she saw his face. Caroline came toward him. He rose from the deck chair, his legs responding with dull pain, another casualty of the attack. He said nothing, just looked at her, unsure of her intentions or purpose.

She came closer, stopping short. "What happened?"

"I was attacked," he said.

"Who?"

"Not who. What. A bear, I think."

She looked around for something to fix on besides his damaged visage. "I'm sorry, Raleigh. Your mother called and told me Shiloh died, but she didn't mention an attack."

"Shiloh saved me, Caroline. The bear was all over me. Trying to tear my face off." He stepped back and ran a finger down the red wound on his cheek, feeling the crusty ridge of it. "It will all heal, in time."

After another moment or two of examination, they sat down at the end of the dock, dangling their feet above the dark water. Their hips settled a few inches apart.

"Why is the water so low?" Caroline asked.

"The TVA lowers it in winter to help with flooding in the valley."

There was another period of silence, both of them uncomfortable over the new status of their relationship, different and undefined.

"I just got a briefing on the situation at the safehouse," she said.

He stared at the water. "Is that why you came?"

"No. I could have taken the briefing in D.C. by video conference, but I came here for you. I didn't want you to be alone."

"I appreciate it."

"You're carrying a gun now?"

His hand brushed the outside of the holster. "Yes. I think it's wise. Whoever shot the marshal at the safehouse, whether it was Johnstone or not, is probably not finished."

"Johnstone is missing," she said. "He hasn't been seen in his office in two days. Local police found his car in the parking garage at the Cherokee casino. No sign of him."

Westlake nodded. "He hasn't been answering his phone."

"His phone was in his car. You called him, Raleigh? There will be records of that."

"It's not a crime for me to call an attorney I happen to know."

"No, it's not a crime, but calls from you right after he goes missing might look suspicious. When the investigators come to question you, how will you explain those calls? You didn't leave messages, did you?"

"No messages, I'm not that daft. And I was calling him to talk about federal bar business. We're both on a rules committee. Anyway, David didn't do this."

"How can you be so sure?"

"He didn't have a motive. I told him three days ago we were going to release Alnoor from custody, as long as we could get him out of the country."

"You did what? I didn't authorize . . ."

"You would have. You know it's the only choice."

She huffed out a breath, stopped swinging her legs. "It was still my decision to make."

"Any news on Alnoor?" he asked.

"They found some of his blood in David's car, in the front passenger seat. And more blood in the driver's seat and the trunk, source not yet identified, but not Alnoor's."

He stared off into a space beyond the water line. It seemed to him the earth had tilted to a precarious angle, and all of the malevolence penned below had burst through the gates and spread its evil. He was caught in the thick of it, unsure whom to trust. He cleared his throat. "Did you do it, Caroline?"

Her mouth dropped open as if he'd slapped her. "No, Raleigh. You can't be serious, to think I would . . ." Her voice trailed off. "You think I'm capable of something like this, because of the Mayor?"

"I know you didn't want Alnoor to be released. You've always thought he's guilty."

"It wasn't me. You have to believe me." He refused to return her gaze, so she looked down at the dark water, feeling the cool air surround her feet. "It wasn't me."

He picked at a peeling piece of deck board, flung a long splinter into the water. They sat for a time on the dock, the chill creeping over them as the sun's heat receded.

"Whoever did it was professional," she said. "The marshal was shot in the chest, and in the head. Marcus says the head shot came last. I wonder if the shooter was the same guy who shot at Alnoor at the courthouse."

"How would anyone even know Alnoor was alive?" Westlake said.

"Did you send out the video?"

"No. It was too risky. Too many variables we couldn't contain."

Caroline nodded. "That was the right call." She stared at the fog rolling across the lake. "So unless we have a leak, how does anyone know Alnoor is alive?" She bit her lip, working her jaw muscles around a thought. "It has to be David."

Raleigh didn't want to believe it, couldn't yet accept that another member of their team had turned on them, murdered a US Marshal, and brought considerable scrutiny upon them. He felt the darkness tightening around him and stood up, scanning the lake and the yard and the twilight, as if preparing to defend against an invisible enemy. "How long are you here, Caroline?"

"I have to get back to Charlotte tonight, visit my parents, and fly back to D.C. tomorrow."

"Did you bring security?"

"Do I need it?"

"We probably all do."

"I left them in D.C. At least I expressed my wishes that they not follow me to North Carolina."

"Did they honor those wishes?"

"I think so. I didn't see anyone following me on the drive out. But you never know."

"Can you stay for dinner?"

She inclined her head toward him. "No, I'm afraid not, Raleigh. I'm really sorry."

"Well, then you should probably head out before it gets too dark. You know how bad visibility can get on these mountain roads when the fog rolls in."

They left the dock and walked up to the house on a brick path cluttered with moss, past unkempt gardens and the shriveled stalks of flowers and shrubs that had perished in winter's grip.

44

The lawsuits filed by the Charlotte bombing victims under the federal SAFETY Act were assigned to Judge Westlake. In the complaints, the plaintiffs alleged the Charlotte arena's security plans and the security service protecting the arena were not state of the art and, as a consequence, a bomber had been able to drive unchecked into the underground loading dock and detonate a bomb that killed and maimed thousands of people.

Westlake drew the assignment because he was the only federal judge in the Western District who did not know or have some attachment to the victims or any of the parties. On a day marked by cold drizzle, the lawyers and representative plaintiffs convened at the federal courthouse in Charlotte.

Judge Westlake drove down that morning and settled into temporary chambers behind the courtroom. He put on his usual robe and zipped it up. For him this was the start of the proceedings—the donning of the uniform, the quick look in the mirror in the private bathroom, the adjustment of the set of his jaw. A thin layer of stubble covered the punctures and gashes on his scalp. A thin layer of base makeup covered the healing cut on his cheek, but the pink line was still visible close up.

He entered the courtroom at the usual announcement and scanned the counsel tables and a gallery filled with attorneys. Though dozens of cases had been filed, including seven class actions, the cases had been consolidated for purposes of pre-trial proceedings. He had set aside three days to hear early motions. As he scanned the participants, he was not sure it would be enough. If every attorney in the courtroom wanted a mere fifteen minutes of argument time, they would be there for weeks. There were potentially billions of dollars and tens of thousands of billable hours at stake, and every lawyer in the room wanted a share.

A row of chairs behind the counsel tables had been reserved for parties. On the plaintiffs' side, all eight chairs were filled. The chairs on the defendants' side were empty. Westlake's gaze rested upon a woman who sat on the end of the plaintiffs' row in a sleeveless dress. Her arms were missing. Her face was marked by pale patches—skin grafts not fully healed—and her hair was swept back. Her eyes were wide, as if she could not fully comprehend all of the events that had led her to his federal courtroom. No doubt the plaintiffs' attorneys had placed her in that strategic seat to provide a poignant display of the horrors of death and disfigurement visited upon the bombing victims.

The lead lawyer for the plaintiffs, a South Carolina attorney Westlake knew only by reputation, began the presentation. After introducing himself and his team of lawyers, he introduced each of the plaintiffs behind him. Westlake wrote down the plaintiffs' names on his yellow legal pad. Then the defense team stood, one by one, and stated their names and the parties they represented.

Judge Westlake came down from the bench, something he rarely did while court was in session, and pulled over a chair from the clerk's station. He unzipped his robe and draped it over the chair back, then settled into the well of the courtroom. "Look, this is a preliminary conference, something I would ordinarily hold in chambers, but there are too many of you. I want you all to know, and I'm not judging anyone, not the defendants or their insurance companies or any of the lawyers in this room, that I am only now beginning to truly understand the magnitude of this catastrophe. I know the numbers of deceased and wounded, but this is an atrocity almost unparalleled in our country, and a magnitude of human devastation and suffering I'm not sure I can fully comprehend. So I want to hear about it, all of it, from every victim who wants to tell it."

The lead attorney for the plaintiffs began to speak, but the Judge cut him off. "Not from counsel. I hear from lawyers all day long. I need to hear it from the victims, and not through some affidavit carefully crafted by an attorney." He focused on the woman in the first chair, the woman who had no arms. "I'm not putting you on the spot, Ms. Winslow, but if you're willing to tell me anything, then please. I'm listening."

She composed herself and began to speak in a voice that would not have reached the bench, even though the courtroom was cemetery quiet. "My name is Ella Winslow. I don't remember the explosion. I don't remember anything until I woke up in the hospital about a month later." She paused, a pause during which most people would have fidgeted with their hands. Instead, she looked at her lap.

Judge Westlake leaned forward, his hands clasped between his knees, making himself appear smaller and unthreatening. "And your injuries, Ms. Winslow. Can you tell me about those?"

She looked up with damp eyes. "I lost both of my arms. I was told a wall fell on me and crushed my arms. My arms were amputated at the hospital because they were infected. My legs got cut up from flying debris. I had burns and cuts on my neck and face, and the top of my head. I will always have some scars."

Judge Westlake smiled in a way he hoped was a consoling gesture, unable to find suitable words. He remembered when the nurse had given him a mirror after the bear attack and he had stared at a person he didn't recognize, his internal image of himself and his actual visage nothing alike.

"It's hard, Judge. Until you lose your hands, it's hard to understand everything you can't do."

"Yes, ma'am. Do you have help?"

"Yes, sir. My mother helps. I live with her and my sister now. They both help."

There are conversations that commence with high emotion, and in which the sound of voices and evoked images soothe the rawness and lead to some type of solace. This was not one of those conversations. Judge Westlake could only imagine what this woman was going through. He did not dare ask her to describe her daily life, not in front of dozens of people. He did not fear that she would be embarrassed or unable to describe her plight in intimate detail. No, he feared that he would not hold up. He feared that the stored but fresh memories of all of the victims whom he had intended to vindicate with the secret trials of Henry Lawter and Tyler Becksdale and the others would emerge from behind his eyes and display themselves to everyone in the courtroom like a silent confession. "Thank you for telling me that," he said.

He heard from two other plaintiffs. A young boy with traumatic brain injury from falling debris struggled to utter words to describe his life after the bombing. Even so, he thanked God every day that he was alive and prayed for the soul of the man who had done this to them. A high school teacher who lost his wife in the bombing had endured seventeen surgeries and four transplants to replace organs that had been decimated by the concussive effects of the explosion. With other organs failing, he did not expect to live much longer.

Normally, the Judge had only a list of victims, sometimes accompanying photographs. But photographs usually were of shining smiles and faces, not of faces scarred by tragedy. These plaintiffs were . . . real, and poignant, a reminder of the reasons he had started down this road. It was for them he had hunted down and executed Henry Lawter and the others. He could award each of the bombing victims tens of millions of dollars, but it would never be enough. They still had to face themselves every day in a life that would likely be suffered through behind locked doors. He silently scoffed at the notion that the judicial system, or he as one of its thousands of judges, could even begin to rectify the tragedy that had been inflicted upon these people.

He returned to the bench and heard, in his shirt sleeves, position statements from counsel for the plaintiffs and defendants about the discovery plan and a schedule for expert designations and mediation and trial. He heard about the state court wrongful death claims against Mayor Carmelo Williams' Estate and the progress of the Special Master in marshaling modest Estate assets to be distributed to the victims. And though he listened enough to nod and make suggestions regarding deadlines, his mind retreated to that night, trying to put the scene together from news reports, these first-hand witness accounts, and pure imagination. He visualized the bomber—dressed in black he had to be—a face without contour or definition, standing a safe distance away on an elevated perch where he could see the coming devastation. He imagined an unmanicured index finger, perhaps dirty black with traces of explosive, tapping the screen of a cell phone. When the arena exploded, it sent plumes of smoke and dust into the air, masking the Charlotte skyline. It blew out windows in buildings many blocks away. It shook trees in distant parks. He tried to imagine the bomber's reaction to all of this. As the scream of sirens pierced the city, had the bomber shed a single tear over what he had done? Had he smiled?

45

After adjourning for the day, Judge Westlake drove the few blocks from the courthouse to the Dunhill Hotel, feeling the rush of traffic around his car. He parked in the garage and stepped out onto the sidewalk, looking up the street in the direction of the arena. He had seen the pictures and videos supplied by the attorneys, even listened to some of the frantic 911 calls from the victims, hearing the shock in their voices, an altered state that might never leave them.

From his spot on the sidewalk, he could not see the arena site, though it was only a few blocks away. He remembered Caroline recounting her first visit to the arena after the bombing. "Pictures and video don't give you the full impact," she had said. "To fully experience it, you have to breathe the dust that gets around your mask and hear the sounds of machinery and barking cadaver dogs, and experience the smell, especially the smell." If he went to the site now, he didn't know what he would see. He had been informed the site was a rectangular hole in the earth, shored up on the sides with wood battens, and it occurred to him that if he walked the few blocks to the arena site he might be disappointed. What did he expect from a crime scene where the devastation had been cleaned up and sanitized? He decided, instead, to check into the hotel and take a shower.

At a time in the not-so-distant past, he might have called Robert Crenshaw for dinner, or Caroline, or David Johnstone, whose disappearance remained a mystery. He decided to eat alone, as if doing penance, and then he thought of walking to a church for evening mass, or going for a run, and he realized, as he stood in the shower with water cascading over his head, evoking a sting here and there on his wounded scalp, that he was awash in self-pity and misery, much of it his own creation. He toweled off and scrolled the contacts list on his phone, tapping Cindy Crenshaw's number. He had not spoken to her since he'd returned Robert's lost cell phone to her several months earlier. He'd promised to keep in touch, and she seemed interested in that, as if he were a last, tenuous connection to her dead husband.

Judge Westlake sat across from her in her small apartment, the living room and dining room an undivided space that straddled the opening to the kitchen. He leaned forward in his chair.

Cindy held Elijah in her arms, a bottle to the baby's lips, as if it were normal to have an observer at feeding time.

"So you moved," the Judge said.

"I had to," Cindy said. "The house was too big, and too expensive, what with the insurance company delaying things."

"What do you mean delaying things?" he asked.

"There's been no death certificate issued because Robert's body hasn't been found. The life insurance company is stalling. They say I may have to wait seven years to get the money." She said this in the tone of someone who has endured much loss and doubts the tragedy will ever end.

The Judge furrowed his brow. "No death certificate has been issued? Robert passed almost a year ago."

Cindy shook her head. "I saw an estate lawyer about it, but he said that without a body, even a seven-year absence is only one fact a court would consider. I might not win, even then."

"This is ridiculous. Four people saw him fall into the lake and never come up. We all told the Sheriff that. Robert drowned. Pure and simple." In fact, Robert had been cremated in a funeral pyre after suffering a fatal head injury, and the Judge had scattered his ashes into the lake on Easter morning. But testifying that Robert had drowned would be an easy lie, a simple perpetuation, and he wondered when all of this deception had become a routine part of his life.

"Let me see what I can do to move the insurance company along. Can you email me a copy of his life insurance policy?"

"Sure. Anything you can do would be great, Judge. Much appreciated."

"I know this is delicate." He glanced around the room, trying to find the right words. "It appears you are financially strapped. I can help."

"My parents are helping, but they're retired, so they don't have much income. They offered to let us move in with them, but . . .."

Westlake nodded. "I can understand why you wouldn't want to do that; and I can understand why you would. I'm not offering you charity, Cindy. It's just that, you know, Robert and I were very close, and I'd like to help out his family."

"I've been looking for a job. I'll find something."

"But childcare costs would eat up most of your earnings."

"That's true. Look, I appreciate your kind offer, Judge …"

"Raleigh, please."

"I appreciate your offer, Raleigh. That sounds weird, calling you by your first name. But I . . . we'll manage. We'll be okay."

He, a widower with no children or grandchildren, had no clue about the challenges she faced. It occurred to him that, although he had learned a great deal in his career as a lawyer, and witnessed some tremendous human suffering as he gazed down from the bench, he knew next to nothing about family or parenting. His attempts to intervene in the custody battle with Maria Pitts and her three children so long ago had resulted in disaster. Four deaths. "I could pay the rent for you, at least until you find a job and childcare," he said, not knowing how this would land. "It's the least I can do."

Elijah took that moment to emit a muffled announcement that he was through with the bottle. Cindy set the bottle down and raised her son to her shoulder, patting his back.

"He looks so much like Robert. Maybe I can take him for a walk, or to the park?" the Judge offered.

Cindy's face registered surprise. "It's dark outside, and a little cold."

He glanced behind him, through the thin curtains covering the window, confirming his suggestion was inane. "Right. Is he walking at all?" He saw it as an ignorant question that he should have known the answer to. *When do children start to walk?*

"Just barely. I have to hold his hand. He doesn't have very good balance yet." She stood up from her chair and approached the door. "Judge, I don't mean to be rude, but I have to put Elijah down for the night. I appreciate you coming over and checking on me."

"Oh, of course," he said rising from the sofa, angling between her and the door. "Please email me that life insurance policy. I'll look into it for you and let you know."

46

The next morning, Judge Westlake sat behind his desk in his temporary chambers, re-reading the parties' separate motions for a scheduling order. The motions reflected a huge divide, one side requesting a lengthy period for discovery and the designation of experts and their depositions, the other side arguing that discovery was a waste of time and money, and the case should be disposed of through early motions to dismiss or summary judgment. He was disappointed at their jousting, if not surprised. Their motions were written in acerbic tones, accusing their opponents of ignorance and nefarious purpose. Both sides seemed to have lost the sense of the tragedy and suffering, relegating an act of terrorism to a debate about some ancient historical event.

He was interrupted by a knock on his chamber door. Nancy Framingham, his career law clerk, stuck her head in. "One of the plaintiffs is here to see you, Judge. I told her it's improper to discuss the case with the Judge without both sides present, but she says it's not about the case."

"Which plaintiff?"

Nancy looked at the post-it note in her hand. "Ella Winslow. She's the one with no . . ."

"I remember her, Nancy. How could anyone not? She says it's not about the case?"

"No, sir."

"Do you know what it is about?"

"No, sir. She wouldn't say. But she says it's urgent."

He checked his watch and noted Court was not scheduled to start for another forty minutes. "All right. I'll meet with her in the attorneys' conference room."

Ella Winslow was already seated on the far side of the table when he walked in. Her chair was back from the table because she couldn't pull herself closer. There was a moment when he started to offer his right hand to shake hers, but he rested it on the back of a chair instead, then pulled the chair out. He left the conference room door open. "Ms. Winslow, this is very unusual, to meet with a party in a case without all of the attorneys present."

194

"Yes, sir. Ms. Framingham told me, but this is not about the actual case, Your Honor."

"So, you don't want to talk to me about your injuries, or what happened that night?"

She hesitated, unsure how to answer.

He started to rise and leave the room, the nagging burden of judicial objectivity extant, but as he looked at her he realized she was confused, that this was not a situation in which she had gained his audience by subterfuge and, now that she had his attention, wanted to plead her case. "Ms. Winslow. I'm willing to listen, but this can't be about your claims in the lawsuit. If it starts to veer in that direction, we'll have to stop, and you'll have to return to the courtroom. Is that understood?"

"Yes sir," she said, her shoulders slumping.

"Nancy," he called out, but he received no response. He stood, checked the empty hallway, and closed the door. "All right Ms. Winslow, tell me what's weighing on your mind."

"I see you have some scars, too," she said. "May I ask . . ."

He saw it then, the connection, something he had been unconsciously hiding. "I was attacked by a bear." It slipped from his lips.

"I'm sorry. I know how much that must hurt."

"But that's not what you wanted to talk to me about, right?"

"No, sir. Yesterday, in court, you seemed like you really wanted to know if any of us had anything to say. Not many people are willing to listen to me ... you know ... in my condition."

"In your condition?"

"I had a traumatic brain injury, and lost some of my memory ..." She saw the concern cross his face, his right cheek pull that side of his mouth upward as she neared an off-limits topic. "That's just a fact, Judge, but you need to know it, because last night, when I was at the victims' memorial, a little piece of my memory came back."

Judge Westlake sat back in the chair, his hands gripping the leather arms.

"I saw something that night. The night of the bombing. Something that doesn't fit."

"What do you mean something that doesn't fit?"

"I was on my way to a park, with my fiancé . . ." Her voice caught, the memory swelling in her throat. "I saw a van drive down into the loading dock at the arena."

Westlake leaned forward, clenching his hands together on the table, fixing his eyes on her. "What kind of van?"

"A beer distributor van, just like the one the FBI says carried the bomb."

He glanced down at the table, unable to unclench his hands, his fingers turning red from the squeeze. Thoughts bombarded him, the knowledge of what they had done, the certainty that the Mayor had not been the bomber, that the terrorist was still on the loose. For a fleeting moment he wished Caroline was here with him.

"I saw the driver, or at least the profile of the driver, when he slowed down before going down to the loading dock."

"You saw Carmelo Williams driving the van?" he said, perpetuating a lie he had almost forgotten was impossible.

"It wasn't Carmelo Williams," Ella Winslow said. "The driver's skin was too light. I know this is going to sound crazy, sir, but before this . . . this . . . happened to me, I was a painter. I study faces so I can paint them from memory. Well, I did once. I can't paint anymore, not this way. But the Mayor wasn't driving that van."

The Judge realized he had been holding his breath, that his face was probably flushed. He exhaled and took in a slow breath through his nose. "Have you told anyone else about this?" he said, re-gaining control of himself.

"No, sir."

"How did you get here, by the way, to the courthouse?"

"My mother drove me."

By instinct he had given her this opportunity, through innocuous questions, to reconsider if she were going to lie to him, making her hold it in her mouth like a piece of spoiled fruit. "And you haven't told your mother?"

"No sir."

"Or your fiancé?"

"He's dead. He died in the explosion."

"I'm sorry," he said, looking over her head at a lithograph of the United States Supreme Court building. "You understand, Ms. Winslow, that if you lie to me, even though this is an off-the-record discussion, I can't just erase that knowledge. I'm human. It will likely affect how I view your credibility as your case moves forward."

"I understand that. I've been up all night, replaying it in my mind. Last night at the victims' memorial, standing there looking across the street at the driveway, it came back to me. I saw what I saw."

"Why are you telling me this? Why not go to the FBI, or the Charlotte police?"

196

"Because they won't believe me. They've already concluded the Mayor did it. By himself. If I tell them someone else was driving that van, they'll think I'm a crackpot. They might even lock me up for being mentally unstable."

He pursed his lips. "I don't think you're a crackpot, Ms. Winslow. I can see you're a sincere woman. Are you 100 percent sure you want to tell me this, and 100 percent sure of what you saw?"

"Yes, sir."

"All right," he said, girding himself. "If it wasn't Mayor Williams who drove the van into the loading dock that night, who was it?"

"My doctor," she said.

"And who is your doctor, Ms. Winslow?"

"His name is Dr. Volkov. Viktor Volkov." Her lower lip trembled, and her eyes were wide and unbelieving.

47

Viktor Volkov did not know about the legal proceedings in the civil suits filed by his victims. Had he known, he would not have cared. He had more important things on his mind. Last night, Alexei Perchenko, his KGB handler, had come to his farm with another man, driving a refrigerated truck. Volkov had not known they were coming until he received a coded message on one of his burner phones.

This morning, Volkov walked from his house to the metal barn, punching in the security codes on two separate electronic locks, codes which he changed every two weeks. The locks slid back with a snap. Before entering the barn, he looked back at the house, scanning the windows to see if Abdul was watching. Volkov saw nothing to put him on alert.

The truck's refrigeration motor was running, powered by a long extension cord plugged into a 230-volt outlet on the barn wall. Through the trap door, Volkov descended into the bunker and donned a biohazard suit, complete with filtration and respiration system. As he climbed back up the metal ladder and emerged next to the refrigerated truck, he looked not unlike the first astronauts to land on the moon. With gloved hands he opened one of the back doors of the refrigerated truck. A cool burst of air greeted him, momentarily fogging the outside of his face shield. He stepped up into the storage bay, flicked a light switch, and closed the door behind him.

At the front of the compartment, two men lay on the metal floor, frost on their hair, eyebrows and nostrils. Their faces were pale, tinged with blue, the holes in their foreheads dark and bruised. Volkov did not regret killing them. He speculated that once he had armed the flu vaccine vials with the biological agent, Perchenko would have taken him out, his usefulness expired. He imagined they would have killed Abdul next. In fact, he knew it to be true. And they would make it look like intruders had broken into an isolated farmhouse in the middle of the night.

From a plastic cabinet with drawers he removed a tray of tubes, and from the tray he pulled two test tubes with bright red stoppers. At this temperature, the solutions were still liquid, the biological agents not likely to infect him, though he knew there was some risk. He slipped the two vials into a soft-sided cooler and zipped it closed.

Volkov went back down the ladder into the concrete bunker beneath the barn, settling into a corner where he had a small desk and a microscope. Still garbed in the biohazard suit, he removed one of the test tubes and set it in a metal rack. He did not have all of the necessary equipment to examine the contents of the test tubes safely, lacking a negative air chamber or ventilator. The bunker was designed to keep out airborne toxins, not to disperse them. But he had no other choice. He turned on a portable fan, directing the air flow away from his table. He picked up a test tube, twisting it under the light, the contents clear but viscous, almost a gel.

Perchenko had divulged little about the contents of his shipment, except that they were to add one milliliter of the bio-agent to each vial of flu vaccine before delivering the tainted vaccine to clinics and dispensaries in the northwest. Perchenko refused to identify the toxin, even when Volkov had pressed the nose of the silencer against Perchenko's forehead. Perchenko had managed a sly smile. Perchenko knew something. Perhaps it was that they all would die, the manner irrelevant, but a bullet might be preferable to more gruesome alternatives. At the end, Perchenko's breaths had become ragged and irregular, and when he coughed in a sputtering way, a bubble of blood on his lips, the smile faded from his eyes.

Volkov replaced the solid stopper of the glass vial with a stopper with a hole in it and slipped in a glass pipette. Releasing the plunger, he sucked a few drops of the solution into the pipette, then released the vacuum and dribbled the solution onto a glass slide, adding a cover slide. A bit of the gel solution spilled over the edge onto the base of the microscope.

He put his face mask to the lens and adjusted it, finally bringing to focus the living organisms squirming about in the viscous fluid. What he saw was not readily identifiable as any single virus type. Some of the organisms were nearly spherical, and others had an envelope, a section of cell membrane, and were helical. He scanned his memory for the depictions of recent viruses and could find no matches. He ultimately concluded these viruses had been created in a lab, which meant there was no vaccine, which was irrelevant because vaccines were ineffective on viruses that already had infected organisms. Without further testing, on mice or monkeys, Volkov had no way of knowing the lethality of these viruses, but he had to assume the engineered viruses were deadly.

He plucked the slide from the microscope mount and slipped it into a plastic bag, then poured enough ethanol into the bag to cover the slide. He zippered the bag shut. With a cloth infused with bleach, he wiped the base of the microscope where the liquid sample had spilled over. He took both over to a plastic barrel, lifted the lid, and dropped the cleanup into the vat of acid. He added the unopened vial.

He sprayed a disinfectant on his suit, spent a good deal of time wiping down his gloves and face mask. After he had stowed the suit and scrubbed his hands and face with an alcohol-based gel, he emerged from the bunker, the metal door landing against the concrete with a loud rattle.

Abdul was standing there, the garage door open, backlit by a bright sun.

"Whose truck is this?" he said, approaching the back door of the refrigerated van.

"Abdul, don't touch that door. It's not safe. Back away, please." Volkov took slow steps toward the boy, his hands out, as if to keep him from tumbling over a cliff.

"Who drove it here?" Abdul said, a modicum of insistence in his voice. He stopped a few feet from the door.

"Some people I know. They dropped it off last night, then headed back out of town. It's a shipment of medicine for my clinics. Well, you don't know about those, but I have a foundation that operates clinics in various cities, mostly for poor people. This medicine is for them." The tale was partially true. Volkov did operate inner-city clinics through his foundation, and this truthful part allowed him to say it convincingly.

He ushered Abdul from the barn and into the sunlit yard. Volkov pushed a button, and the large garage door closed. Volkov secured the deadbolts. "Tomorrow I will have to deliver the medicine," Volkov said.

Back in the house, Abdul settled at one of the bar stools in the kitchen. Volkov switched on a chandelier over the island and turned to Abdul, examining the suture lines on his face.

"These are healing nicely," Volkov said. "In another week you won't be able to see the incisions. How are you feeling?"

"Most of the soreness is gone. My face still feels a little tight, especially on my cheeks." Abdul squinted, drawing his cheek bones higher.

"Those are the implants. Your skin is having to stretch itself a little to accommodate them. Make sure to stay hydrated. That's the best way for your face to adapt."

Volkov went to the kitchen window and gazed out at the barn. He drew his index finger beneath his nose and sniffled. That barn held two dead bodies and a lot of secrets. When Perchenko did not return to D.C., someone would come looking for him. Disposing of the bodies would not be difficult.

Disposing of the refrigerated truck would probably require a trip out of state. And Volkov had no idea what to do with the one million vials of a lethal virus.

48

Westlake sat at the desk in his office at the lake house, gazing at the small urn, cast in a paisley pattern of red and tan clay. Next to it on his desk rested a photograph of Shiloh with a blue ball in her mouth.

He had been sitting like this for the better part of an hour, his eyes shifting from the urn to the photograph. In his hands, he turned the metal dog tag over, feeling the imprinted letters of her name, date of birth, and his phone number.

He looked up to the corner shelf and Heather's blue urn. He had lost them both. One taken by an incomprehensible disease for which no one would accept responsibility; the other killed by a wild animal. He marked the distinction, that one had a perpetrator and the other did not, though the resulting loss from both deaths left an empty pit inside him. A pit that had begun to fill with anger.

He placed the red urn and the photograph on a shelf below Heather, for any other place would have been inappropriate, and kissed the blue jar that held her ashes, his eyes closed, his lips pressing against the cold clay. He stepped back and stared at the rug for a moment, feeling adrift. It was his habit to shift into an analytical mode in situations like this, to banish the emotions to a distant corner so he could think without that weight. But he knew he was not ready for that. Anger and frustration, and perhaps a dollop of fear, swirled in a bitter concoction that left him unable to focus, his mouth a tight line, his eyes wandering.

Marcus Cunningham and Ignacio Perez showed up in the afternoon as the wind whipped through the trees. Their SUV's tires left imprints in the rain-sodden driveway. Westlake stood on the stone front porch, the wooden door open, his hands thrust in his pockets.

They sat in front of a fire he'd kept burning all day. Of the five rocking chairs arranged in a loose crescent, the chairs on either end remained empty. Westlake balanced a tumbler of bourbon on his thigh.

"Is there any update on the investigation?" he said, postponing his news out of respect for their investigation into the shooting death of a fellow US Marshal.

"It's a cluster," Cunningham said. "We believe Johnstone came to the safehouse early that evening. We found tire tracks behind Marshal Reynolds' car, one set. Marshal Reynolds was shot twice, once in the chest, and once in the forehead. He wasn't wearing a vest." Cunningham paused here, trying to re-create the scene, knowing that the vest would have done no good against a head shot at close range. "Marshal Reynolds fired one shot from his Glock. We don't know if he hit anything. We never found the bullet, but we're assuming he wounded Johnstone."

"Again, I'm sorry," the Judge said. "Two US Marshals killed in the line of duty, all related to the Alnoor case. In all my previous years on the bench, we never had any threats, and no attacks."

Cunningham, in the middle chair, nodded, then took a long swig from a beer bottle. "All of the blood in the house belonged to Marshal Reynolds. The shots came from a 9-millimeter pistol, make unknown. Alnoor's ankle monitor was on his bed. I doubt he could have detached it himself, but we can't be sure of that." Cunningham went quiet, staring into the fire, as if some explanation could be gleaned from the orange flames licking the brick.

"Outside," Perez filled in, "we found blood in the gravel of the carport. It didn't belong to Marshal Reynolds or Alnoor. We don't have a sample from Johnstone, so we don't know if it was his blood, or somebody else's. But the blood in the carport matches blood in the trunk of Johnstone's car, which as you know we found at the Cherokee Casino parking garage. The same blood was on the driver's floor mat of Johnstone's car. The theory is that Johnstone climbed into the trunk at some point so it would appear there was one driver and no passengers. We found Alnoor's blood on the floor mat of the passenger side. We assume he was wounded too."

"Any video of the attack?" the Judge asked.

"No, sir. WITSEC protocol precludes cameras in safehouses," Cunningham said. "That might be about to change."

"Any evidence that David is dead, or alive?"

"No, sir. Best we can tell, the unidentified blood was a fair quantity, so whoever's it is probably needed medical attention. But no clinics, hospitals or vet's office reported any patients fitting either of their descriptions."

Perez added, "we're monitoring Johnstone's credit cards. No activity since that night. The techs are trying to unlock his cell phone, but no luck so far."

"And Alnoor?" the Judge asked.

"No sign of him," Cunningham said. "If I had to guess, Johnstone took a gun with him to the safehouse, got in a gunfight with Marshal Reynolds, killed him, then drove off with Alnoor. No idea where they might have gone, but we've got BOLOs out at the airports."

"That doesn't make any sense," Westlake said. "Why would David do something like that?"

"The same reason he tried to help Alnoor escape from the cabin—to free Alnoor regardless of the risk," Cunningham said.

"But he knew I had agreed to release Alnoor and send him out of the country," Westlake said.

"Maybe he didn't trust you, Judge," Perez said. "Or maybe he knew the approval had to come from Justice, and Ms. Bannister wouldn't consent."

Westlake rolled the tumbler of bourbon between his hands. He stared at Astrophe, Caroline's cat, as it lay curled on the braided rug on the fireplace, distracted by the crazy thought that somehow Caroline had placed a listening device on the cat's collar. He got down on the floor and checked, but the collar was lean and tight, and the cat's tag was one he'd purchased from a pet depot and had engraved in a machine.

"What about video from the parking garage?" the Judge said from the floor. "I know they have cameras. I've seen them."

"It's self-park, no ticket needed," Perez said. "Whoever drove the car in there might have spotted the cameras and avoided them. We've got video of the car going in. That's it. No video of anyone leaving the vehicle."

"So where does that leave us?"

"Same place we are with the shooter at the courthouse, Judge. Not much to go on. We've either got one body or three, the likelihood of a professional, and no forensics tying anyone to the crime, unless Johnstone or Alnoor did it."

"I just don't see David carrying out something like this," Westlake said.

"I agree," Cunningham said. "But he's a criminal defense attorney. He might know somebody who's capable."

Westlake leaned forward in his chair and stopped rocking. "So there could be a fourth person."

Cunningham got up from his chair, tossed his empty bottle in the trash can, and retrieved another beer from the refrigerator. He returned to the fireplace, leaned a forearm against the warm stones of the chimney. "We didn't know Alnoor's release was official," Cunningham said. "Nobody at WITSEC was informed."

"It wasn't official," the Judge said. "David and I were discussing it, but it was going to happen. And when we decided where and when, I was going to let Caroline handle it through official channels. But I think that rules David out. There's no motive."

Cunningham stared down into the fireplace, then turned his bulk toward them. "Judge, permission to speak freely?"

"I'm not your CO Marcus, you can say anything you want to."

"Yes, sir. Look, there are only three of us now. I assume Ms. Bannister is out of the loop. Seems like she has been since she was nominated." He took a deep breath, then a long swallow of his beer. "We have to work together as a team. We all have our strengths. We follow your orders. You have to be the leader. But … with all due respect … you have to act like it. Working out side deals without our knowledge doesn't work."

"You're exactly right, Marcus. And I apologize. To both of you. I'm not saying this as an excuse, but only as a circumstance. The Mayor … what Caroline did … and then finding out he didn't kill Caroline's sister after all … that threw me because …"

"Wait," Cunningham said. "The Mayor didn't murder Ms. Bannister's sister? This is the first we're hearing about it."

The Judge bowed his head, closed his eyes, preparing to confess. "No, he was innocent. It's a long story, but ultimately Robert Crenshaw figured it out. Caroline's father accidentally shot and killed his own daughter more than 25 years ago."

"Holy shit," Perez said. "So this whole thing, the blackmail, us being targeted, is all because Caroline went after the wrong guy?"

"Hold on," the Judge said, surprised at his own tone. "It's not that simple. It turns out the Mayor was innocent of homicide, but he was there when it happened. Carmelo Williams was Catherine Bannister's heroin dealer. Mr. Bannister was a cop. He went there to rescue his daughter, and Williams grabbed for his gun, and it went off, hitting his daughter."

This seemed to mollify the marshals—the explanation that Williams was not entirely innocent—but it didn't fully justify this being kept from them.

"Judge," Cunningham said, leaning his head on his forearm against the stone fireplace. "We've lost two of our own. Crenshaw is dead, and Johnstone probably is. I didn't have any great love for either one of them, but they're dead because they didn't play team ball. They thought they could go it alone. We saw it all the time in the desert. The lone ranger usually gets killed. In this case, we're dealing with at least one professional here, maybe three of them, or a whole group. Working alone, we don't stand a chance. We have to work together, make decisions together."

"I agree. I think I've been a Judge so long, making decisions on my own, that I've forgotten how to rely on other people. That's my fault. It won't happen again. I don't want to put you guys at risk. Not anymore."

Cunningham and Perez exchanged an inconclusive look, wanting to believe, wanting to trust him again.

"I've got something else," the Judge said. "Before now, I might have been sure how to handle this, but I think we need to discuss it. I don't know if this is a solution to our problems, or I'm just leading you both down another blind alley, but it might be important."

He told them about the civil suits over which he was presiding in Charlotte, plaintiff Ella Winslow, who lost her arms in the bombing, and her revelation that Carmelo Williams had not been the man who drove the van beneath the arena.

"Do you believe her?" Cunningham asked when the Judge finished.

"I don't know. The day before, she told me and a full courtroom she had no memory of that night. The next morning, she identifies Viktor Volkov as the driver. She sustained a traumatic brain injury from the explosion. There are a dozen reasons to believe she's mistaken, but can we take that chance?"

49

Judge Westlake drove to the trail-head and hiked to the spot where he and Shiloh had been attacked. The weather had turned warm, and glimpses of green had begun to emerge as buds on the hardwoods. He walked at a slow pace, hunting for something near the path, restraining his urge to run. When he came to the site of the attack, he stopped and examined the ground where he and Shiloh had battled the bear. Time had altered whatever evidence had been left. There were no rusty droplets of blood, no matted grass, no strands of hair lying in the leaves.

He gazed in the direction the bear had escaped and moved toward the tree line. He stopped on the edge, looked around for a den or a hollow, checked the trees for scratch marks. He saw nothing. He placed his left hand upon the bark of a poplar tree, tracing the pattern with his fingers. He took a few more steps into the woods, mottled brown leaves beneath his feet. He was looking for scat. Bear scat has a distinctive shape, a unique color. There were sporadic depressions in the leaves where an animal might have sat, observing, stalking. He turned, looking back toward the trail and, beyond it, the shimmering waters of the lake. A wind rustled the boughs of cedars and firs, created the tiniest white caps on the lake.

He continued deeper into the forest only because ending his search would seem like quitting. He headed up-mountain through thick underbrush, away from the lake and the trail and the parking lot and the highway. This area was designated on maps as wilderness, steep grades and large, granite boulders left by retreating glaciers. He followed what appeared to be a game trail that might have been his imagination, winding through bare trees, his breath coming in quick chugs as he climbed. It was in this place that he sought, and sometimes found, the best wisdom. Not in the law books or the religious tomes. Here he found clarity, basking in a purity that could not be replicated through man's manipulation. This was not a recent revelation. He had known for a long time that this was the place he came to heal, drawn here like steel filings to a magnet. The oxygen-rich haven of a deep forest, with its protective brambles and wild animals obliged to defend their turf.

He plunged higher, and when the trail seemed to end at a tumble of granite boulders, he climbed upon them, grabbing onto trees that clung to the crevices between hunks of rock. The back of his shirt was soaked with sweat. Near the top he spotted an opening in the cascade of boulders, a slim crevice where part of a rock had cleaved away. He stared at it for a time. The granite on the inside of the slim doorway still glistened and sparkled, not yet worn dull by the weather. It was possible, damn possible, that he was traversing ground that no man had stepped on before. Not his ancestors, or those who conquered them, or even a man fleeing humanity.

He slipped through the aperture, which opened into a canyon ringed on three sides by sheer granite walls. The horseshoe-shaped area was bisected by a stream that disappeared into a hole in the ground. The hole was surrounded by smooth river stone. He climbed the terrain beside the stream, which meandered in a lazy way, until he came to its source, a shallow pool fed by seeps that dripped from a series of mossy rocks. And there it stopped.

From above, he looked back at the structure, something that might have been created by God, or left by glaciers, and realized that in an ancient time the array of rocks might have served as a large cistern. He walked back down to the place where the stream disappeared. He scraped one foot across the ground, peeling back a layer of rich dirt, as dark as night. He knelt a few feet upstream of the hole and cupped his hands in the water, quenching a thirst that had been building for hours. The water tasted of minerals and was as clear as liquid glass. Edging closer to the hole, he looked in and could discern the point at which the water plunged over rock, disappearing and falling into a pool far below.

He sat back and marveled at this underground waterfall. He had not known such a thing existed, but his not knowing came in a moment to seem naive and ignorant. As he hugged his knees and his heart stopped pounding, the sounds emitted by himself, even his breath, became null, merging into the murmur of the stream and the sighing of the trees, the fluttering of pine needles from a high breeze he could not feel. He leaned back against a rock, angled in a way that accepted rather than rebuffed him. It held the warmth of the sun and transferred some of that warmth to him. In a few minutes, with his brain no longer swarming with emotions, he fell asleep.

He awoke, perhaps an hour later he judged by the altered shadows, to a slight pressure across his shins. It was not unpleasant, just there. He peered through a slim gap beneath his eyelids, drowsy but unconcerned, at a rattlesnake. Its girth was the size of his wrist. Its scales felt like a dried sponge dragged lightly across his skin. Its tongue darted out, tasting the air, and within a few seconds, the serpent had traversed the small impediment that his legs presented, heading for a higher perch where the sun still reached.

He found he had been holding his breath. When the snake was little more than its body length away, he rolled carefully in the other direction. He stood and rubbed his shins, searching for puncture wounds. He had not been bitten. He looked at the snake as it crawled away and said, "Let us not see each other again."

From his mother he'd learned the rattlesnake's Cherokee name, utsa'näti, and its position in Cherokee lore. He watched it slither between two stones, and on its entire journey it did not hesitate or hiss. It disappeared into a hole, perhaps a den, perhaps a portal of some sort. He wondered what message this snake had brought him. He pondered briefly Congressman Lyle Walker and the bin of rattlers at the roundup in Texas, and what Walker must have been thinking as he writhed among the serpents, in the throes of death.

Clouds drifted in from the southwest, announcing themselves with rumbles of thunder. Cold rain began to pound the rocks, producing a spattering sound that reminded him of frying bacon. Westlake huddled beneath a hemlock that spared him the worst of the downpour, but its branches soon became sodden and heavy, and the rain dripped upon him. He stayed there as the light waned. He knew the way he had come, but had no inclination to leave. The shining granite and the sound of dripping water pleased him, imbuing him with a sense of peace. And so he stayed as darkness fell. And he stayed as the insects began their sonata. And after he felt his way to the stream and drank again from it, he nestled against the inclined granite and closed his eyes.

Even in sleep, he heard the night sounds of owls and wind rattling leaves and trunks bending in the breeze. When the clouds broke and a three-quarter moon emerged, the canyon lit up like a cathedral. And still he stayed. He did not dream. Or, if he dreamed at all, he could not remember. Before the sun reappeared he knelt again by the stream and ladled water upon his shins and washed his face. He saw crudely chiseled ledges in the opposite wall, now weathered and worn from an epoch of wind and rain, and placed his left foot in the toe-hold and began to climb.

The ledges, wide enough for one foot but not two, wound upward to his left. He moved slowly, the handholds uncertain and shallow, and he once looked down and realized he had climbed almost three stories. He came to the top abruptly, to a surface that was flat but not wide, and he stood upon it with his hands on his hips, as if he had conquered something. He did not know what he expected to see at the summit. What he saw was a clearing surrounded by trees, almost discernible as a ragged circle, with a stone monolith in the middle.

The slope of the slab's opposite side was gentler, and he was able to descend with his feet in front and hands behind, his torso slung low over the surface of the stone for balance. At the bottom he waded through knee-high brush until something bit into his shin. He parted the underbrush to discover a smaller stone, in the shape of a crude arrowhead. A thin trickle of blood marred his leg. He knelt and examined the stone, running his fingers over the symbol carved upon its face. Bird clan. He walked in a semicircle, treading lightly this time, leading with the toe of his shoes, and found six other stones of similar size and shape, each carved with a clan symbol. He settled next to the stone marking the Wolf clan, *his* clan, facing inward toward the monolith. The surface of the granite had a red hue, as if painted or pocked with rust, and he rubbed his hand along its rough edges.

He sat there for the better part of the morning, watching each stone blaze as the sun found it, lighting each as a separate but connected candle in a ring of mythical fire. There was meaning here. He tried to remember what his mother had told him about such things. At times he had been attentive, but mostly he liked the sound of her voice, deep and resonant and lulling. He knew of the seven clans. He was a wolf. He remembered that most of the war chiefs had come from the wolf clan. Wolves were protectors. And that was the extent of what he remembered.

An overgrown path cluttered with limbs and debris led away from the circle of stones. This path led to another, which led to a trail, no wider than a footfall, and soon he was running in the direction of his car.

50

Westlake drove through downtown Charlotte, passing the pit that had once been the site of the arena and the memorial across the street. He passed the hospital where many of the bombing victims had been taken and navigated by office buildings that housed various medical practices. He turned onto a side street and parked at the curb. He changed clothes, repeatedly glancing in the mirrors and around him to ensure he wasn't being watched.

He walked two blocks, his silhouette preceding him in the late afternoon sunshine. Wearing long pants, a long-sleeved shirt, a ball cap, sunglasses, and three weeks of salt and pepper beard, he was hoping no one would recognize him. On a street corner, he waited for the traffic to pass, watching the orange numbers on the crossing signal tick down like grains of sand in an hourglass.

He entered the office and gave the fake name under which he had booked the appointment, noting there was no one else in the waiting area. The receptionist, in blue scrubs, was the only person behind the glass window.

"I'm the last patient of the day, right?" He said this in a voice that wasn't his, the tone intentionally nasal because of the cotton he'd tucked behind his molars.

"Yes, sir. Just as you requested."

"How long will this procedure last?"

"There's no way to know for certain, but most rhinoplasty takes two to two and a half hours."

"Okay."

Westlake sat in a leather chair as plush as any he'd ever seen and picked up a business magazine. The conversation with the nurse had been transmitted through the microphone embedded in the cross dangling from his neck, or so he hoped. Pretending to read an article he wasn't interested in, he wondered if he was being observed. Of course he was. He kept the brim of his hat low and his eyes fixed downward.

The nurse swung open the door to the treatment area and ushered him down a short hallway that led to a brightly lit space. Dr. Viktor Volkov stood by the patient chair, a reassuring smile on his face, wearing a long white coat with his name stitched in blue on the chest pocket.

Westlake had practiced having this conversation without saying much. Because Volkov might have been in his courtroom, he feared his voice, though altered, could give him away. He shook hands with the man who had killed thousands, a firm grasp, and nodded. "I'm nervous."

"That's natural," Volkov said. "I'm about to change your appearance. Everyone gets nervous." Volkov stepped to a porcelain sink and washed his hands, then donned surgical gloves. "Go ahead and sit in the chair," he said over his shoulder.

As the nurse reclined the chair and took his hat, Volkov approached from the side and adjusted the angle of the bright light on an articulating metal arm.

Westlake shut his eyes to the glare, trying to trust people he could not see.

Volkov leaned forward and ran his index finger along the scar on Westlake's cheek, its color faint, like a dried-up creek merging back into the desert. "How did you get this scar?"

It was the question he knew he would be asked. With the surgical light temporarily blocked by Volkov's head, Westlake opened his eyes. "I was attacked by your dog."

Volkov reacted as Westlake hoped, his brain connecting the dots, and Volkov's eyes widened as he stumbled backward. "Yes, well, I can't perform the rhinoplasty until the scar completely heals. Too much risk of infection."

And now Westlake knew. His strong suspicion had been confirmed. The eyes never lie. This was the confrontation he was not able to produce in a courtroom, with lawyers and the Fifth Amendment protecting the accused.

Volkov was doffing his gloves when Perez and Cunningham came through the unlocked door of the surgical suite. The nurse was quickly subdued by Perez who, with one hand over her mouth, injected her in the neck with Propofol solution. Within seconds, she slumped, and he laid her carefully on the tiled floor.

As Volkov reached inside his coat for the pistol in the holster beneath his left arm, Cunningham triggered a stun gun, which launched two probes at Volkov, striking him in the chest before he could dodge. Volkov went down, dragging a tray of surgical instruments to the floor with him. Cunningham rolled him over with his foot, pulled the Makarov from Volkov's right hand, then bound Volkov's hands with a zip tie. Cunningham and Perez hauled Volkov to the patient chair and secured him with cargo straps.

Westlake stood a few feet away, staring at the man who had murdered thousands of people and blackmailed a federal judge and US prosecutor. "Dr. Volkov," he said, "I am Judge Raleigh Westlake of the United States District

Court for the Western District of North Carolina. But you know that already, don't you?"

Volkov, whose heart still fluttered from the electric jolt, simply stared back at the Judge. He was trained to say nothing. At least for a while, he intended to adhere to that training.

"We know that you bombed the Charlotte arena and framed Mayor Williams for the crime."

Volkov ran his tongue over dry lips but remained silent.

"We know, sir, that you stole the Mayor's body and put it inside the van."

"You killed the Mayor, not me," Volkov said before he could stop himself. He gritted his teeth over the mistake. If he had not said it, perhaps he could argue reasonable doubt, but he then realized that there would be no arrest, no trial. These men were here for a different reason. This was the way things were done in Russia, guilt determined by men in dark, paneled offices, with trials only for show.

"You forgot to read me my rights, Judge." Volkov grinned then, the irony of it sweeping over him, followed by a laugh he could not control.

"You're Russian," the Judge said.

"I'm an American citizen. Just like you."

"Yes, emigrated from Russia for medical school, and you became an American citizen soon after graduation. But Russian."

"Is my nurse all right?" Volkov said, glancing at her prone body on the floor. "What did you give her?"

"Propofol," Perez said. "She's fine. Sleeping, but fine."

"It was your dog that attacked me in the woods a few months ago," Westlake said with anger rising red in his cheeks. "It killed my dog, Shiloh."

"I don't know what you're talking about, Judge. I don't have a dog."

Westlake knitted his hands together. "The Marshals saw him, Dr. Volkov. A Russian bear dog. At your farm on the outskirts of the city."

51

The rented van pulled out of the back parking lot after dark with a cargo of four. Westlake sat in the cargo bay on the steel floor, his back against the side panel, his eyes on Volkov. Perez drove. In the passenger seat, Cunningham kept turning around to make sure the prisoner remained subdued.

"This is similar to the van you used to blow up the arena, is it not?" Westlake asked.

Volkov shrugged. "What does it matter?"

"It all matters. It's all relevant. I want to understand why you did it."

"Don't be naive, Judge. Do you think that because you sit on a bench and pass judgment on people that somehow you have a right to understand what motivates people to do the things they do?"

"I hope to," Westlake said, adjusting a shoelace. "Perhaps you can help me."

Volkov laughed and looked away. "Help you? And if I help you, what do I get in return?"

"Nothing," Westlake said. "That's the truth."

They rode in silence for a while, the sounds of city traffic only a lane away. There was a moment, when they stopped at a light, when Westlake thought Volkov might yell for help, but he did not.

As they navigated the Interstate loop around Charlotte at 70 miles per hour, Volkov asked, "Where are you taking me?"

"It's dawned on you that you're not going to jail, hasn't it? That's not the way this will be handled," Westlake said.

"Like the Mayor then. No justice, just an execution."

Westlake stared at him in silence, not interested in reliving Mayor Williams' trial.

"You gave me the opportunity, Judge. You and your cabal."

"Are you saying you wouldn't have bombed the arena if you didn't have the Mayor to frame for it?"

Volkov thought about that, peering into a corner of the van, the light fading. "No. I still would have set off the bomb, but it might have been a suicide bomb."

"I doubt that. You're too vain to kill yourself. You had a chance to do that, just this afternoon."

Volkov's hands moved, rattling the chain binding his metal cuffs to the leg irons. "You know, I worked on many of the bombing victims, repairing their faces and their skin, bringing them back to normal."

"Like you did with Ella Winslow?"

At the mention of her name, Volkov's brows went up, an involuntary movement he could not mask. "You've met her?"

"Yes. She's a party in a case pending before me."

"Her arms were badly damaged in the explosion. I amputated them to stave off infection. Then I performed seven surgeries on her."

"She has a lot of courage."

"Was it her?" Volkov said.

Westlake knew what he meant. "You left a lot of clues, but it took a while to put them together. You're very good at deceiving people."

"So are you. The fake announcement about Abdul's death?"

"You were in the courtroom, I take it?"

Volkov nodded. "Dressed as an old woman. I gave myself a facial scar, but I can remove them almost as easily. I could do the same for you."

A wan smile emerged on Westlake's face. "I have a doctor, thank you. And if mine doesn't completely heal, maybe I deserve it." He ran a finger across the scar on his cheek.

"For the Mayor?"

"For the Mayor. And others."

"Is this a confession, Judge? Two men who have murdered, huddled together, expressing remorse?"

"You don't exhibit any remorse. Not that I can see."

"No, it is not within me," Volkov admitted.

"How did you lose it?"

"You are assuming that I was ever capable of remorse."

"Weren't you, even as a child? Don't tell me Russian children aren't capable of remorse."

"Perhaps. It is not as terrible a place as you might believe. My childhood was happy."

"But?"

215

Volkov shifted on the bench. "I had a sister. Older. She was born without arms. A birth defect. Her life was miserable."

Westlake pondered this, the difficulty of navigating daily life with that disability. "Like Ms. Winslow."

"No, not like Ella. My sister had it from the moment of her birth. She never knew what it was like to have her arms. She was quite adept at taking care of herself, could do amazing things with her feet. Ella, she . . . she was unlucky. Wrong place at the wrong time."

"Where is your sister now?"

"She's dead."

"How did she die?"

Volkov emitted a vague smile, remembering.

"Did you kill your sister?"

Volkov nodded. "My first. I smothered her with a pillow. It was best for her. Her life was miserable. I think she even welcomed it."

"My God. How old were you?"

"Thirteen." Volkov shuffled his feet, recalling a nightmare two nights ago when Anna had come to him, her face decayed and eaten away, and challenged him to fix her. "And what about your first, Judge? Surely the Mayor was not the first one?"

Westlake hugged his knees together. "No. He was not." His gaze fell somewhere outside of the van as he spoke. "There was a young woman. She was murdered by a maniac while she was riding her bike up Mt. Pisgah, just outside of Asheville. Murdered with an icepick. Her killer was caught, tried and convicted. By me. I gave him the death sentence. He deserved it."

"Some men cannot be restrained by laws."

The Judge looked at him then, a look of recognition, a tacit acknowledgment that they shared something.

As he'd been trained, Volkov tried to keep the conversation moving. "How did you kill him if he was in prison?"

" The court of appeals reversed his conviction, and I was forced to set him free."

"And how did you do it?"

"It doesn't matter."

"You said everything matters."

The Judge sighed. "Drug overdose. Heroin."

"And there were others?"

"Yes," Westlake said, looking at his feet. "Did you kill Alnoor, at the safehouse?"

"Kill Abdul? No, I rescued him. Rescued him from you."

"You tried to kill him once, at the courthouse."

Volkov glanced into the cab, at the backs of the heads of two US Marshals. "At some point I realized he did not deserve what was happening to him."

"Where is he now?"

Volkov wondered if there was some leverage to be gained from the information. He coughed, a cough filled with sputum, and wiped his mouth with the sleeve of his doctor's coat. "Abdul is safe."

"Safe where?"

"If I tell you, what do I get in return?"

"Only the knowledge that he'll survive and, hopefully, live a long and peaceful life. I can offer you nothing more."

"He wants to go back to Iraq."

Westlake thought about it for a moment, pondering his connections to the shipping industry, connections he'd made as the owner of a handful of shipping trailers and containers. "If that's what he wants, I can make that happen for him."

"I'll think about it."

The Judge tried a different tactic. "Did Abdul have anything to do with Marshal Reynolds' death, or does he know where Johnstone is?"

Volkov answered. "No on both counts. I was the one. I did both the marshal and Johnstone. It was the only way to free Abdul."

"But it wasn't," the Judge said. "We were planning to release him. We just needed to decide when and where."

"Yes, Abdul told me. After. I did not know that at the time."

"So you killed David?" Westlake asked.

"Yes. Two gunshots."

"Was that necessary? I doubt Johnstone even knows how to use a gun."

"Yes, it was necessary."

"How did you even know Abdul was alive, that he wasn't dead, as I announced in Court."

"I got a video from him. Asking for my help."

"A video? How . . ." the Judge trailed off, wondering who had sent Volkov the video. "And how did you find the safehouse?"

"A tracker on Johnstone's car."

"So you followed him there?"

Volkov shrugged.

Westlake challenged him. "Did you even feel anything when you shot Johnstone and Marshal Reynolds?"

Volkov contemplated this for a moment, thinking back to when he held the pillow over Anna's face on a Wednesday night, the moon slicing through the window glass, and all of the times since. "I felt nothing. You must know how this works. You convince the mind that these are targets, like the silhouette targets at the shooting range. The sole goal is to hit as many targets as possible in a given time. And what about you, what do you feel when …"

"Judge," came the voice from the front seat. "We'll be stopping up here in a few miles for gas and a pee break, and I'll make a call. We need to gag the prisoner."

Westlake looked at Volkov. "Will you sit still while I put a gag in your mouth?"

"Better let the big man do it," Volkov replied, angling his head toward the front seat.

Westlake took this as a warning, not an insult. For a few minutes he had forgotten that he was dealing with a man who killed without compunction, thousands of people, for reasons that were still unclear.

After the stop they rode in silence for a time, their progress visible only through the windshield. The way ahead was lit solely by their headlights. The tires hummed beneath the metal floor, changing pitch as they moved from asphalt to concrete and back again. The van began to climb the southern edge of the mountain range.

"Why did you decide to spare Alnoor?" Westlake asked.

"We all have a good side."

Westlake knew it was true, that there was some good inside this man. Maybe it was the ultimate truth, none of us completely good or completely evil, the lines of demarcation constantly shifting like unseen tides.

They remained silent for the rest of the journey, the van navigating the curving incline, winding along the edge of the lake. When they arrived at the trail head after midnight, the parking lot was empty. Cunningham re-installed a gag in Volkov's mouth and cinched a black hood over his head, then unlocked the cuffs and leg irons. He looped a zip tie around Volkov's wrists.

Westlake shouldered a pack provisioned for an overnight stay. Cunningham and Perez did the same. With a rifle pointed at Volkov's torso, they began their journey into the wilderness, the forest swallowing them. The trail was filled with roots and jutting rocks. Even so, they did not remove Volkov's hood. Westlake led the way, for only he knew precisely where they were going. His halogen headlamp lit the trail.

At a point where the rutted trail jogged left across the side of the mountain, Westlake plunged to the right, taking a game trail no one else could see. He pulled a machete from a scabbard at his waist and hacked at vines impeding their path. Thorns and jagged limbs tore at their clothes. Westlake's headlamp locked the eyes of several animals peering from the trees, but the animals remained still. They hiked in this way for an hour or more, until they came to the granite wall and the aperture between boulders.

They slid through. Cunningham and Perez settled their prisoner, looping a rope around his ankles and tying him to the trunk of a giant hemlock. They divided up the watch hours, then leaned back against the stone wall to rest.

"I'll be back before sunrise," Westlake said. He stopped and surveyed the scene, dimly lit by a clouded moon. "Please make sure he doesn't escape. We can't afford to chase him through the woods like we did with Alnoor."

Perez lifted the rifle from his lap. "No, sir. If he tries to escape, he won't make it out of this little canyon."

Westlake dipped a water bottle into the stream that split the canyon, then capped it. He began to climb the sheer rock face, finding the narrow toeholds carved into the rock eons ago, the headlamp gliding over the surface like a searchlight. When he came to the last ledge he pulled himself up and scrambled onto the ridge. He found a depression in the rock that was smoother and laid down in it, tucking the pack beneath his neck and head. He stared at a sky in which the half-moon emerged on rare occasion. After the sounds of humans in motion had abated, the sounds of night forest resumed. To his left an owl screeched, and he heard the flutter of wings as it dove from a tree. A wolf howled from a distant ridge, the forlorn call carrying over miles of wilderness. Somewhere, there would be others.

Before the false dawn broke the night's ink into gray, Westlake streaked black and green grease paint on his face and forehead, guessing at the symmetry of the markings, for he had no mirror. He switched his long-sleeved t-shirt for a traditional hunting shirt, and his pants for buckskin leggings, both of which he'd bought in the village.

He had come into the forest with a mass murderer, with a vague plan of a sentence without a trial. He did not need a prosecutor or a defense attorney, not this time. The protections of the Constitution no longer concerned him. As Volkov had said, some men can't be restrained by laws. As he stared at the place where the sun would emerge, he realized what he had become. The descent had begun some unmarked time ago, and he, a federal judge who sat upon a high bench in an ornate courtroom wearing a black robe, no longer respected the imprimatur of the office. Perhaps he no longer respected himself. But when dealing with men like Volkov, the law would never be good enough.

He swiveled his head to the sight of a doe rummaging in a stand of blueberry bushes in the clearing, her tawny head dipping to eat, her ears pointed and aware. Without making a sound, he detached the compound bow from his pack and loaded a razor-tipped arrow. The arrow covered thirty-five yards in a whisper, and the deer went down. From his pack he took a game knife and drew it through a ceramic sharpener until its edge gleamed. Then he began to pray.

He prayed for Heather and Hannah and Robert and David, and for the souls of victims he'd never met and whose deaths he could not avenge. He prayed for the souls of men he had condemned to death, knowing that, even though he had not executed them with his own hand, he was responsible just as if he had pushed the plunger or pulled the trigger. And he prayed for Caroline and Marcus and Ignacio, whom he had pulled along in his wake. He prayed for the deer lying in the clearing. He did not pray for himself. He did not pray for Volkov.

In the tribal archives he had researched the methods used by the war parties of his ancestors, reading accounts that caused him to grimace. Crude drawings depicted prisoners burned at the stake or flayed, anguish on their faces. And he suspected that, despite the advent of constitutions and laws written in lofty rooms, man had not changed much over the centuries. Men still committed barbarous acts, and the enabling of huge institutions to deal with these men, and occasionally women, had done little to alter that behavior. He wondered if other lawmen felt the same, if they questioned the viability of a system that processed the violent and depraved in an incessant circle, abiding rules written in stone capitols. Did they ever ponder the impact that such restraint had on their very beings? These were questions he could not ask of anyone, of course, but he had come to understand that vanquishing his desire for revenge, subduing the base urge to take an eye for an eye, had damaged him in ways he could not describe. And thus he had chosen this course. Or, it had chosen him.

His wolves represented the ultimate truth: within us all exist good and evil, each able to dominate in the right circumstances, with the proper feeding. Out of necessity he had made himself deaf to the howls of his wolves, as Henry Lawter had pierced his own eardrums to obliterate the screams of Hannah Sullivan. But was that really true? Did the screams come only from without?

Judge Westlake prepared himself this way, shunning the black robe for war paint and buckskin, and when the sun first spread peach-colored rays onto the mountain ridge, he rose and extended his arms to it, feeling its welcoming warmth upon his face. He descended the ledges, placing his feet carefully in the narrow toeholds, and knelt over the deer. He pulled his knife from the sheath.

The others were awake and alert when he descended into the canyon. Cunningham and Perez rose stiffly at the site of Westlake in native garb, recognition slow to come.

"Good morning," he said to them, shaking their hands. "Thank you for guarding the prisoner through the night." He prepared a breakfast of venison over an open campfire. Three of the men ate hungrily with aluminum utensils. The fourth, his hands still bound in plastic shackles, picked at his food.

When breakfast was finished and plates washed in the stream, Cunningham and Perez pulled Volkov to his feet and tied him to the stake of the hemlock, wrapping a hemp rope around his legs, torso and arms. Westlake stepped forward and tested the bindings. Finding them secure, he said, "Please head back to the van." He looked over at the marshals who had for many years stood by his side, protecting him from known and unknown threats. "Don't wait for me. I'll find my way back."

"Judge, are you sure?" Cunningham said. "We should stay."

"No." He said this more firmly than intended. "Thank you, though. There are some things a man has to do alone. Pick me up at the trail head at dawn tomorrow. Oh, and leave the rifle."

Only after he placed a hand on their backs and gave them a gentle press did his soldiers leave the canyon. Their gaits were slow and reluctant. He wondered if they might be questioning whether he would emerge from the woods at all, or if they would have to mount a clandestine search and rescue mission. Or simply come back to retrieve his body.

Westlake approached the prisoner and tipped a water bottle to Volkov's lips. He swallowed in big gulps. Though the stream's susurrus could be heard from this spot, Westlake guessed that Volkov had not been given any water since his capture, for that was not the way Cunningham and Perez treated men who had massacred innocent people.

"There are at least a dozen ways to do this," Westlake announced. "I could poison you with hemlock. It would be rather fitting, don't you think? I picked some from a big stand of it just last week."

Volkov said nothing.

"Perhaps I already have made a potion," Westlake said, shaking the bottle in his hand. "Or perhaps I could lure a bear over here. There is one foraging nearby. A Russian mauled by a bear would be rather poetic, wouldn't it?" Westlake stepped back, eyeing his prisoner. An orange and black Monarch butterfly drifted into the canyon, circled the hemlock tree, and lit in a high branch.

"Do you expect me to ask how you plan to kill me, Judge? Do you expect me to beg for mercy?"

"I don't expect any of those things." Westlake began pacing in a large circle, murmuring to himself, traversing most of the canyon floor. He passed the spot where the rattlesnake had slipped over his ankles and glanced at the crevice in the rock into which it had disappeared. It was likely still there, perhaps in a den with others.

Holding the rifle in his right hand, Westlake tossed it to his left, then held it in both hands and thrust his arms above his head. After four or five circuits he stopped in front of Volkov. He pulled the buck knife from its sheath. "You know what flaying is, I presume. The Russians used that method for centuries. My people used it also."

As recognition spread through Volkov, his chin began to quiver. It was the first sign of fear Westlake had seen in the man. He might not be capable of remorse, but fear could not be fully suppressed by anyone. Westlake stepped forward and pressed the knife against the skin behind Volkov's left ear. The starting point for stripping a man's skin would be recognized by a man who cut and tightened skin as a profession. And then with a swift arc he cut Volkov's clothes away.

"Imagine how those people in the ballroom felt that night, with you standing there with an automatic weapon, spraying bullets like you were flocking a Christmas tree."

Volkov's throat had become tight. "I have some valuable information for you," Volkov managed. "I also have the photographs."

Westlake hesitated for a moment, a second or two of indecision. "I don't care," Westlake said. "I'm not here to negotiate a deal. We're long past that." He stepped back a few yards.

"I know who disrupted your power grid, and cell phone network and internet. There's a deadly virus about to be unleashed on your country. I can help you stop it."

Westlake shoved the gag into Volkov's mouth. Then he pulled the hood over Volkov's head.

For hours he rested against the granite wall, its lean like the welcoming back of a wooden chair, and stared at a prisoner whose senses had all been muted. Volkov could see nothing through the hood, his view a murky blackness. Perhaps he could smell the remnants of the campfire, which Westlake had doused with water from the stream. Volkov's sense of hearing would help him little in a forest that had grown silent as the sun moved off its zenith. If Westlake moved with stealth, he might come within inches of the condemned man before Volkov detected his presence. And the silence of the unknown birthed the greatest fear.

As the afternoon descended, Westlake loaded his bow and aimed it at Volkov across the narrow space. "I could shoot you with this bow. It's aimed right at your throat."

To this Volkov responded with a contraction of muscles, bucking against ropes that refused to relinquish their hold. This is what Westlake wanted to see. A murderer facing death without hope of escape, without knowledge of the method or timing of the end. Naked, as at birth. If the terrorist could experience terror, this was it. The tremble produced by not knowing. The mind chaotic with possibilities and imagined scenarios, attempting to contemplate unfathomable pain, wondering when that final breath would come.

Shadows lengthened across the canyon like a shade drawn down. At sunset, Westlake dipped his hands in the deer's entrails and spread them upon Volkov's body, ladling blood upon the black hood and over his shoulders, smearing the man's neck and chest with it. At Volkov's feet he laid the deer's carcass.

Westlake retreated to the plateau on the rock, placing his bow nearby, the string not yet stretched in anticipation. He loaded the rifle with a single bullet. From this vantage point he could see that Volkov's head hung in submission, or sleep. It was the same. All hope had bled from his pores and escaped on his waning breath.

There were howls in the night. Westlake could not decipher the messages, yet they emitted from different voices, from the high ridges nearby. And as night progressed into its deepest darkness, the howls came closer. He felt involuntary stirring inside, the good wolf and the bad wolf moving together, a welcome shift, as if they were, for once, acting in concert.

They came into the canyon together, murky shapes whose numbers he could not discern, moving in a pack with one at the lead. They sniffed the air and perked their ears at perceived sounds Westlake could not detect. He peered over the ledge at them, as still as a downed log. While they might not be able to see him, they knew he was there. But they were undeterred. There was no command or bark, just a charge, stealthy at first, and then a run that finished in a leap.

At Westlake's sides lay the loaded rifle and a cocked compound bow, but he did not reach for either of them. In the dim light the pack looked like an undulating mass, no individual animal discernible. Their throats uttered a voraciousness that pierced him. In the din of the snarls and the snapping jaws, he might have heard a man scream.

When he moved before daybreak, the wolves remembered his presence as watcher and scattered, some carrying pieces of their meal in their jaws. He descended from the ledge, watching as his feet found purchase, surveying the canyon floor with every step to ensure they were gone. Inside of him, all was quiet. He set the empty rifle against the stone wall, then approached Volkov without looking at the fatal wounds. With his knife he cut away the ropes, from top to bottom, and Volkov's body toppled to the ground. Grabbing Volkov by ravaged feet, he dragged the naked carcass to the creek, where he washed the body in cursory fashion.

"Volkov—of the wolf," Westlake said in a whisper. It felt strange, after such a prolonged silence, to utter words. He wondered then if this man who had murdered so many, who inflicted pain and death and terror upon innocents, was much different from himself. Two wolves: one evil; one good. Both inside of all of us. He placed Volkov in the stream, feet first, his soles perched above the hole that led to the bottom of the earth. With a shove, Volkov left the surface, nature purging him from our midst.

EPILOGUE

Judge Westlake knocked on the door and waited. He turned to the street and, seeing nothing amiss, turned back to the door and knocked again. She eventually came, unlocking the deadbolt but not the security chain.

"Judge, what are you doing here?"

"I brought you something."

"Oh, come on in," Cindy Crenshaw said, unlatching the chain and pulling open the door.

He sidled into the apartment, and before they could get settled, he handed her an envelope. "I can't stay, but I wanted to deliver this in person."

Cindy took the envelope and slit it with a fingernail, removing a certified check for $500,000. "How did you . . . this is from Robert's life insurance company."

"It took awhile, but I finally prevailed on the insurance company to acknowledge that Robert has passed and to release the funds."

Without warning, she threw her arms around his neck. "Thank you. Thank you. This means so much. This means everything in the world to us."

"Can I see Elijah? Is that all right?"

"Sure. He's in his playpen, right around the corner."

Westlake knelt at the playpen and picked the boy up, cradling Elijah in his right arm, looking into the child's dark eyes. "You're the spitting image of your father. He was a great man. I just wanted you to know that. He did some great things in bringing people to justice, things I can't even tell you about. I hope you grow up to be just like him."

He left then, uncertain if anything he said would be remembered, but certain he needed to say it, he needed Cindy to hear it. He doubted he would be back, because it was too difficult to face the woman whose husband's death he had caused. But it was possible. He might once again need the sustenance they could provide.

He arrived at Volkov's farm in the afternoon, the thick smell of dogwood in the air, corners of the land littered with pink and white blossoms. A cadre of men in uniform, US Marshals Service and FBI stenciled on the backs of their windbreakers, milled about on the grounds. Yellow tape surrounded a metal barn, whose doors were open. Formless people in biohazard suits entered and left the back of the truck parked inside, carrying plastic coolers into the side yard, removing trays of test tubes and ampules and placing them on blue plastic tarps spread upon the ground.

Marcus Cunningham approached and put a hand on the Judge's shoulder. "Alnoor is inside."

The Judge nodded. "How close was Volkov to launching a biological attack?"

"Not sure," Cunningham said. "They won't tell us what's in the glass tubes, only that it's still virulent, and deadly."

"And the plan was to put this . . . into the flu vaccine itself and infect people that way?"

"That's the speculation. There are close to a million vials of vaccine in refrigerators in the bunker under the barn. As well as two dead bodies in a commercial freezer down there."

"How are they connected?"

Cunningham shrugged. "Above my paygrade. But there are some NSA and Homeland Security people wandering around. They don't wear name tags advertising their agencies."

Westlake surveyed the scene, the bustle of activity beneath a white tent lined with tables and electronic equipment. He didn't fully understand what he had averted, or the magnitude of suffering and death he had unwittingly prevented. He walked to Volkov's house, pausing at the back door. "Is it safe? The house isn't contaminated, is it?"

"All clear, Judge."

Westlake wandered through the house, past a couple of FBI agents standing guard. It was noteworthy for its lack of anything unusual, a house that a family or a farmer might have lived in for decades, three comfortable bedrooms and a brick fireplace and a formal living room and dining room, a kitchen with dated appliances and butcher-block counters. Westlake expected to see something else, a telltale sign that a mastermind terrorist had lived here. But there was nothing, and perhaps that was the primary asset of killers who lived in plain sight. They seemed perfectly ordinary.

When they entered Alnoor's bedroom, Alnoor was on his bed. In his hands was a book with a black leather cover. Westlake almost didn't recognize him. His face was broader and tan, his lips thicker, the nose less prominent. A full beard the color of coal covered his jaw.

Abdul stood from the bed and shook Westlake's hand with a firm grip. "It is good to see you, sir."

"You've been through a lot young man, but that's over now. You're off to a fresh start soon."

"Yes, sir."

"I want to apologize for what you've been through, Abdul. A lot of unfortunate circumstances colluded against you."

"Yes, I know. Dr. Volkov was both a friend and an enemy."

Westlake arched both eyebrows. "Oh?"

"He left me a letter." Abdul pulled folded pieces of white copy paper from the back pocket of his jeans, offering them to Westlake. "It explains a lot. Not everything, but a lot. He admits he is the one that shot up the country club, and he lays out how he framed me, how he left my blood and skin there."

Westlake studied Alnoor, looking for signs that he knew something more, perhaps something about how Volkov had disappeared. But there was no suspicion or accusation in Alnoor's eyes. "That has to make you feel better," the Judge said. "Does he mention anything else in the letter?"

"Only that if I received the letter, it was because he's disappeared and will never be found."

"When did he leave the letter for you?"

"Four days ago."

Westlake counted backward to the date they snatched Volkov from his medical office. Four days ago, on a Monday night. "Are you sure it was four days?"

"Yes, sir."

Westlake rubbed his chin, the skin raw where he had shaved his beard, uncovering his face to the sun for the first time in almost a month. Perhaps Volkov had planned to flee on the afternoon they captured him. Or perhaps Volkov had known his appointment with a new patient would be his last. Maybe an associate had dropped the letter off for Alnoor, which would mean Volkov had not acted alone.

"The letter also tells where he buried Mr. Johnstone," Abdul said.

Judge Westlake took the letter and read it, its flow pulling him in, the words written in a matter-of-fact style befitting a murderer who wants to confess, but without exhibiting any contrition. There were no words of apology, no hint of remorse. There was no mention of the bombing at the arena, or of the former Mayor of Charlotte. He re-read the portion detailing where David Johnstone was buried.

"Abdul, have you shown this letter to anyone else?" the Judge asked.

"No, sir."

"That's good. We'll keep this, Abdul, in a safe place," the Judge said. He handed the pages to Cunningham. "I have something for you. Several things, in fact." From his inside coat pocket Westlake produced a sheaf of papers in a plastic sleeve. "A passport, a one-way plane ticket to Baghdad, along with a cashier's check. And a letter from the Attorney General of the United States exonerating you for what happened at the country club." He handed the packet to Abdul.

Abdul shuffled through the documents, opening the passport. "How were you able to get a passport so quickly, and with a recent photograph?"

"Friends in high places. You can thank Ms. Bannister for that."

Abdul looked toward the closed bedroom door, his brow furrowed. "Is she coming?"

"No, she couldn't be here, but she sends her best wishes."

Abdul opened the envelope and looked at the check, his eyes growing wide. . "This is a very big check ."

"Yes. It's a small token of appreciation from the United States Government. You should definitely open a bank account when you get to Baghdad."

"Thank you, sir." Abdul said, extending his hand again.

"You're welcome. Keep in touch . . . well, you won't. Put this behind you and live a good life, an honorable life."

"I will do my best to do that."

Outside, a huddle of trailers encircled the barn. Cattle filled several trailers, and another held horses, whose stamping hooves rocked the tongue hitched to a pickup truck. Behind a wire panel in the back of an animal control van, a brindle-colored dog peered outward at the commotion.

"Is that Volkov's dog?" Westlake asked, pointing.

"Yes, sir," Cunningham said. "They're taking him to the animal shelter. He'll probably be euthanized."

"He doesn't look the same. In the woods he was a smoky black color." Westlake approached the van, whose white metal doors were open like wings. From a distance of several yards, he stared at the dog, at its honey-colored eyes, its abundant and matted fur, its bulk the size of a small bear. The dog sat on his haunches panting, a pink tongue lolling from the corner of his mouth. The Judge replayed the memory of the dog charging through the underbrush.

"There's something else, Judge." Cunningham handed him a manilla envelope, a red string holding the flap shut.

"What's in it?"

"Photographs. The three that were delivered to your house, plus a few more. Of you, me, Iggy, Johnstone, Ms. Bannister, the Mayor. All of us."

Turning the envelope over, the Judge could find no label, no handwriting, nothing revealing whether the photographs had been left for him or a third party. He began to slide the photographs from the envelope but stopped, realizing it would only reopen wounds that had almost healed. "Did you find the camera or cell phone he used to take them?"

"He used a digital camera. I have the SD memory card. He had lots of burner phones, most of them still in the packages. I still have the cell phone we took off him at his medical office. No photographs or videos on it. He may have scrubbed it."

"Or uploaded everything to the cloud," Westlake said.

"That's a possibility. We may never know. You want the memory card?"

Westlake shook his head. "Destroy it for me. For all of us."

On the pocked asphalt road out front, Westlake stopped his car for a school bus. As he waited for elementary kids to cross the road in front of the bus, he looked up at the sky, at clouds being pushed and buffeted by winds he could not see. For the first time in months, maybe for the first time since he'd signed the order releasing Henry Lawter from prison, he felt an internal calmness. The wolves were still there, but quiet, and as he watched the last of the children shoulder their backpacks and walk toward home, he allowed himself to think that perhaps he had figured out how to nurture his wolves in the proper proportions, how to keep them both alive and in harmony. He also had the sense that this peace would be temporary.

When the stop sign on the bus swung inward, Westlake sped ahead, making a detour from his planned route, heading toward the shelter where Volkov's dog had been taken. With Shiloh gone, he needed a dog. Perhaps adopting the bear dog would be a step toward atonement. And once the paperwork was completed, he and Danya would head west, toward Fontana Lake and the slope of a mountain where David Johnstone lay in a shallow grave.

Thank you for reading this book. This is the third and final book in the *Ultimate* series.

If you liked this story, which took hundreds of hours to complete, please take a minute or two and review the book at:

Good reviews are an author's best marketing tool, and are much appreciated. If you didn't like the book, please reach out to me at my website link on the next page and tell me why. Your critique might help me to become a better writer.

ABOUT THE AUTHOR

Michael Winstead, a thirty-three-year veteran of courtroom battles, has tried dozens of cases in our state and federal courts. He is intrigued by the judicial system and how it affects the human condition, frequently altering lives in unforeseen and irreversible ways.

The author of two other novels—Ultimate Verdict and Ultimate Tribunal—his stories examine the motives and purposes that drive people to commit horrible and evil crimes. His books also portray the devastating impact that violence has on victims, their families, and the judicial system at large.

Winstead lives and writes fiction in the mountains of North Carolina and on the first coast of Florida. He occasionally hunts and fishes on a farm ruled by a donkey named Hotee.

You can contact the author at **michaelwinstead.com**.